Bridle Path
Press

THE BLUE VIRGIN

M. K. Graff

Bridle Path Press, LLC
8419 Stevenson Road
Baltimore, MD 21208

www.bridlepathpress.com

Direct orders to the above address.

Printed in the United States of America.
First edition.
ISBN 978-0-615-35514-6

Library of Congress Control Number: 2010902389

Designed by Giordana Segneri.

Cover photographs © Maciej Laska/istockphoto.com and © Sara Kwong/istockphoto.com.

Bridle Path
Press

FOR ARTHUR

Vous êtes l'haleine de ma vie.

CAST OF CHARACTERS

in order of appearance

BRYN (BRONWYN) WALLACE — model turned photographer

MILES BELCHER — photographic studio owner and Bryn's boss

VAL ROGAN — textile artist; co-owner of The Artists' Co-operative; Bryn's partner

DETECTIVE INSPECTOR DECLAN BARNES — Senior Investigation Officer, Thames Valley Police Criminal Investigation Department

DETECTIVE SERGEANT WATKINS — Declan's right-hand man

CHARLIE BORDEN — Home Office pathologist; Declan's friend

NORA TIERNEY — American writer; Val Rogan's best friend

KATE RAMSEY — owner-operator, Ramsey Lodge, Bowness-on-Windermere, Cumbria

SIMON RAMSEY — artist; Kate's brother and partner at Ramsey Lodge

DETECTIVE SERGEANT DOUGLAS MCAFEE — newly minted member of Declan's team

DAVEY HASKITT — bakery worker; Bryn's basement neighbor on Magdalen Road

TOMMY CLAY — Magdalen Road resident

DR. TED WHEELER — Exeter College don in English literature

LOTTIE WEBER — potter; Val Rogan's business partner at The Artists' Co-operative

CAMERON WILSON — male model; Bryn's former boyfriend

JANET WALLACE — Bryn's mother

IAN TRAVERS — Cumbria Criminal Investigation Department; Kate Ramsey's fiance

ALTHEA ISSACS — lecturer at Trinity College; Bryn's next-door neighbor

MAY ROGAN — Val's stepmother

LOUISA ROGAN — Val's half-sister

JEFFERY NICHOLS — Val's solicitor

DR. EDWARD VANCE — Exeter College don; Dr. Ted Wheeler's colleague

WILSON — Exeter College warden

THE HONORABLE MR. GARDINER — Her Majesty's Coroner

THE BLUE VIRGIN

*"When we want to read of the deeds that are done for love,
whither do we turn? To the murder column;
and there are rarely disappointed."*
— George Bernard Shaw

CHAPTER ONE

"All around us everything was changing in the order of things we had fashioned for ourselves."
— Chaim Potok, *The Promise*

Oxford in August
Thursday
6:30 PM

The device that set The Blue Virgin apart from other clubs of similar taste was the flashes of pornographic films projected into the room. They flooded the large white-walled room at uneven intervals, competing with the pulsing music, shocking and suggestive and enticing all at once. The club was known in that haven of academia and tradition as the premiere alternative-lifestyle meeting place. The stone building formerly housed a video store, which had boasted the area's largest collection of blue movies in its back room. The current renters had pressed into service several cartons' worth, left carelessly behind by the previous tenant when he fulfilled a lifelong yearning to move to Amsterdam.

Bryn Wallace sank gratefully onto a padded stool at the bar, breathing in the scents of old wood and warm ale, nodding to two men she'd seen at Val's art co-operative. "A glass of Merlot, please," she ordered from the bartender, resisting the urge to stare at the woman's multiple nose piercings.

It had been a grueling day at the Miles Belcher Studio of Photographic Portraiture, and not for the first time, Bryn was questioning her decision to leave the runway and pursue photography on the other side of the camera. She loved the camera the way it loved her and had made a decent living from local magazine work. But she had quickly tired of people leering at her lithe body and sculpted features, her chocolate brown eyes and glossy brunette hair; tired, too, of fighting off the cocaine so easily obtained.

Bryn sipped her wine and reflected on the relationship most models had with the camera. She loved photography, capturing an idea, letting the walls down and acting for the lens trained on her, making love to it, in fact. Once she'd become intrigued with the idea of becoming the person who could cause that reaction, she'd resolved to learn the other side of the camera from a master: Miles Belcher.

Miles had the talent of portraying his subjects in their most flattering light. He had achieved a reputation in Oxford for making the most odious of families appear pleasing and harmonious; even the least comely face was softened with grace. As much as he annoyed her personally, Bryn knew she'd snagged a good apprenticeship. Her job was to get the client sorted for a sitting, then take digitals Miles would approve or change while he sipped his double mocha cappo in his office overlooking Clarendon Street.

"Move the boy in closer to his mother's arm and try again," he'd announced this morning, resuming his review of the latest month's issue of *Photography News*. Once he was satisfied she'd achieved the pose and lighting to show off the best bits of the Freeth family, he appeared. Sporting a huge smile, his long white hair dropping foppishly over his brow, Miles commenced the color shots. Wagging his left hand in the direction he wanted their eyes trained, Miles snapped away, eliciting giggles effortlessly from the children.

Bryn checked her watch and wondered how Val was doing

with the shopping list. She was cooking for Val tonight, as she did at least once a week. A warm sense of comfort filled her at the thought of Val Rogan. An extraordinary textile artist, Val had started The Artists' Co-operative to provide exposure to Oxford's new talent. Bryn's own photographs had been shown there just last month. There was just one small snag in their growing relationship, but Bryn would try to explain it to Val tonight and smooth it over, hoping Val's legendary temper stayed in check.

Bryn smiled and raised her glass to the light, enjoying the ruby color, thinking back to the spring art show. At the time, Bryn had considered herself heterosexual and had chosen her past lovers accordingly. When she'd been introduced to Val that night she had been acutely aware of a shift in the air. At first she admired the creative joy of Valentine Rogan, her odd golden eyes and artistic flair, the way she zipped through life with good humor and a snappy word for everyone. Because they traveled the same artistic circles, they kept meeting, and Bryn soon found herself looking forward to evenings when Val would be present. Bryn increasingly felt a kind of comfort in Val's presence she hadn't experienced before. She also found herself tingling whenever they touched and began to realize she was engineering such moments. To her credit, Val never came on to her sexually, sensing Bryn's lack of experience.

Bryn checked her watch, remembering the night Val had driven her home from a gallery show. She'd invited Val up to her flat, and over glasses of wine, confessed her attraction and her lack of experience with same-sex partners.

"How did you decide you were a lesbian?" she asked Val, coloring.

"I tried to like boys. Especially when I was twelve-ish. But I found myself admiring the girls more. It wasn't just those nubile breasts I saw in gym class, either," Val said with a laugh. "It had to do with the goodness women project—maybe I'm really looking for a mother, not having had mine for long." Val recounted her anguished fifteenth summer when she had confronted her feelings then hid them from her father and stepmother for another three years. Finally, on her way to art school on a full scholarship, her father bursting at the seams with pride, she'd confided her feelings to him. After a moment's shock and a few more of rational thought, he pragmatically had been quietly supportive of what he called her "exploration," as though it were a class she would be taking at The Glasgow School.

"I guess the biggest attraction for me is that women don't hide their emotions like men. I crave that accessibility and having it in return without pulling teeth to get it."

Bryn remembered nodding in understanding as Val elaborated.

"That all adds to the physical side when I'm with a partner. Besides, I know how to please her—sometimes it's almost like making love to me."

Not moving, Val had waited for Bryn to absorb it all. By the end of that evening two things had happened to Bryn Wallace: she experienced what it must feel like when a man made love to *her*—the soft skin, the velvet places—and she decided she had fallen in love with someone she respected and admired, a person who just happened to be a woman.

Twisting her watch, Bryn checked the time. She looked up at the entrance and there was Val, her pleased smile crinkling those golden eyes. Val gave her a hug and settled on the stool beside her. "I got everything on your list and then some," she pronounced, waving to the bartender, who brought Val her usual glass of Shiraz. "How was Belcher today?"

Bryn smirked and described today's family, including two boys who were hellions. "They'll probably look angelic when the prints are done," she admitted. "Miles does have that special touch."

Val drained her glass. "So do you, my dear. Let's see what you do with this list of ingredients I've got in my backseat."

Bryn had to admit the dinner was an enormous success. Her one-bedroom flat on the trendy Magdalen Road in Oxford's spiritual Mecca became a lavish home whenever Val visited. In Bryn's mind the photographs she used as decoration became museum art pieces; the noise of the busy outside road diminished, elevating the cheap ground-floor space to an elegant penthouse.

The two of them had taken their time cooking, Val acting as sous chef under Bryn's direction. Eating late gave Bryn the feeling she was in France or Italy. Val had eaten with gusto, enjoying the pork loin stuffed with prunes and rosemary, and an eggplant dish with pine nuts, feta cheese and cinnamon. Over coffee and fruit, Bryn looked over at Val, feeling a rush of exhilaration mixed with trepidation as they chatted. She thought of Cameron for a moment, but Val had none of his huge ego, nor his fondness for drugs. Definitely a better choice of partner.

"I know you've met Nora, but you'll love Simon, too, I promise." Val was talking about her best friend Nora Tierney, who was driving from the Lake District back to Oxford on the weekend to pack up her flat for a permanent move to Cumbria. "I can't believe we've been renting in the same Summertown building for six years, ever since Nora came to Oxford. I'm going to miss her."

Bryn sipped her coffee, happy to talk about Val's friend or anything to postpone the argument she predicted. "Simon's the artist who gave you the new design for the co-op. He's illustrating Nora's book, right?"

Val nodded. "He showed me how to rearrange the stalls for maximum traffic and exposure. And you should see the figures he's come up with for Nora's fairies. Kids will adore them. I hope Nora figures out soon what a prince she has in him. He's crazy about her."

"It can't be easy for Nora to be pregnant when the father's dead, much less make a commitment to someone else," Bryn pointed out. "What a sad situation to find herself in. Tough in the best of circumstances, but to take on a dead man's child? This Simon must be a jewel."

"Nora will be a great mom. And Simon would be a wonderful father if she'd give him the chance." Val ruffled her short hair. "I don't see how they can work on this collaboration and not let their chemistry interfere." She finished her coffee. "Simon will just have to be patient and let Mother Nature work her magic."

"I'm looking forward to seeing the draft of her children's book," Bryn said. "After work Saturday I'll come over and help with the packing, get to know them better."

"I'd like that." Val sat back with a contented sigh. "That was a stupendous meal. After we do the dishes, I'll show you the brochures I brought from the estate agents."

Bryn twisted the silver Luckenbooth pendant she wore, two intertwined hearts topped with a crown, a gift from Val. She traced the outline as she groped for the words she needed to say. Feeling distinct dread, she rose to clear the table.

"That is what is known as a pregnant silence," Val observed, bringing in a stack of plates. "We agreed we'd need a bigger place if we're going to move in together."

Bryn's eyes filled with tears as she ran the hot water and squirted soap on her sponge. The lobby buzzer sounded.

"Oh, Christ," Val said, going to the door and hitting the intercom. "Who is it?"

"It's Davey," a wavering male voice said. "I've left a box outside your door."

Opening the flat door, Val picked up the hot pink box on the door mat and brought it inside. Bryn applied herself to washing up, back straight, avoiding confrontation.

Val opened the box. "A delightful assortment of pastries from your downstairs admirer," she pronounced stiffly.

Just stay calm, Bryn repeated silently in a mantra. She was aware of Val studying her rigid back. Val changed the disc, which was playing melancholy strains of Erik Satie, to the soundtrack from a movie they'd enjoyed, *Notting Hill*. Skipping tracks, Val stopped at Elvis Costello singing "She." The song held special meaning for them; they'd seen the movie the same night they'd agreed to live together. Val had copied the lyrics in elegant calligraphy and framed it for Bryn only last month.

Bryn swallowed hard, trying to find words. Val picked up a dish towel and dried plates and pans, stacking them on the counter, putting utensils away in drawers. She's waiting for the sappy song to get to me, Bryn thought.

"Unfair, definitely unfair," Bryn said at last, turning off the taps as she finished the washing up, reaching to dry her hands on the end of the towel Val was using, finally meeting her tawny eyes.

"Do you want to tell me what's going on?" Val said in an even tone.

Bryn immediately dropped her gaze, turning to fuss with the dishes.

"Christ, this is one of those times I wish I still smoked," Val said, her patience starting to wear thin.

A thread of anxiety wound itself around Bryn's stomach, knotting tightly. Bryn abruptly turned to face her, summoning up her courage.

"Nothing's really wrong. It's just that moving in together has to be postponed a bit." She strove for casual, leaning back against the sink, wiping the harried expression off her face.

"I see," Val said. "Now that you've sucked the air out of me, mind telling me what's gone wrong?"

"You don't see—not at all. Look, I really want to move in together, it's just not economical for me right now. I don't have as much saved as I thought I would—my bonus was delayed." She gulped and scowled at her false tone.

"I think I've told you money is not an issue." Val's voice got louder. "I've the money from my father and can do the deposit and security without a problem."

"We've been through this before. I pay my own way," Bryn snapped back just as loudly. This was going all wrong.

Val's voice kept rising. "And what if I want to lay it out for you? Can't you allow me to do that? You can repay me if you insist, when you're a famous photographer." Bryn snorted and Val pressed her advantage. "Why postpone our lives together for a financial issue?"

Bryn's voice hardened in the face of Val's insistence. "Why can't you understand I'm not comfortable being taken care of like that? I need to feel this is a partnership on all fronts." She crossed her slender arms defiantly in front of her.

"And I don't like being put off like this." Val's hard tone matched Bryn's. "Unless there's some other reason you don't want to move in together? Is Cam pressuring you?"

"Don't think that, please," Bryn assured her in a rush. "That's over. I love *you*. You're the first person who's made me feel whole. I just need a little time to save money—it's important to me that things are equal." Val sucked in a breath of air and Bryn knew at last she was listening instead of reacting. "I don't ever want to take advantage of you and your goodness." Val let out her breath heavily and Bryn hurried on. "Does it help if I admit it's totally my hang-up?" Her brown eyes pleaded with Val for understanding. She didn't want to ruin this.

At last Val sighed. "As long as you really mean it's financial, not anything to do with us."

"It's nothing to do with us. Just give me time to save more, all right? Then I'll feel comfortable with the whole thing." She approached Val and gave her a warm hug. "Go on then, you look exhausted. You have co-op duty tomorrow, and you're helping Nora pack up this weekend. I'll finish up here, it's almost done."

Val nodded and left quietly, looking subdued and hurt.

Bryn rummaged through her medicine chest, swallowing two paracetamol tablets to stop the throbbing headache from her argument with Val. Although Val seemed reassured when she'd gone, Bryn hated any thread of tension between them. She couldn't bring herself to tell Val the real reason she didn't have quite the bank account she'd been hoping to produce.

As she left the bathroom, a tentative but insistent knock came at the door. Bryn waited a few moments before moving to answer it. Whoever was there had avoided the lobby buzzer. Crossing to the door, she reluctantly opened it, fearing another bout of arguing with Val—and certain it would not be productive. Things were changing rapidly and she was changing with them, but she felt drained on all fronts.

"What you are doing? . . . Oh, look, forgive me, I'm so confused. You'd better come in and help me sort things out."

CHAPTER TWO

"There are, fortunately, very few people who can say that they have actually attended a murder."

— Margery Allingham, *Death of a Ghost*

Friday

5:30 AM

Detective Inspector Declan Barnes of the Criminal Investigation Department pulled his sizable frame out of his classic MGB, admiring the way the flashing blue lights from the uniform's car reflected off the glossy British Racing Green repaint. The roadster had cost him far too much—no out-of-country vacation for him this year—but it looked superb, a perfect mate for the replaced saddle-tan convertible lid. He really ought to name her, he decided. Even though it occasionally took two slams for the door to catch, the motor turned over smoothly every time he fired her up, even at unconscionable pre-dawn hours such as this.

The first suggestion of dawn appeared, streaks of orange and pink light on the horizon piercing the darkness. The beginning of yet another ordinary day in Oxford for most of the town's inhabitants, Declan thought, locking the car and pocketing the key. He looked longingly at his car, postponing the roller coaster ride he knew awaited him.

His sergeant, waiting in the shadow of the entry on Magdalen Road, waved him over. The building was located just off the Cowley Road, across from The Inner Bookshop. The popular New Age haven boasted CDs, postcards, the inevitable self-help courses, and a huge collection of new and used books, ranging from the esoteric to the occult. Declan knew the area from questioning a comely actress waitressing at the spiritual Magic Cafe next door about her connection with a former boyfriend's death. That case had been determined a suicide, the actress cleared of any suspicion, but he had found himself returning for a cup of what he'd decided was the best French Roast in town, chatting up the pert lass with the ready smile and energetic air. Last month she suddenly disappeared, and the manager explained she was playing Titania in a modern Scottish production of *A Midsummer Night's Dream*—another dead end in his relentless search for a woman who could keep pace with him and his chosen profession.

Across the road, in stark contrast to the contemporary feel of this side of the block, the building Declan approached sat positioned firmly in the last century. Four floors of pale Cotswold golden stone were set in a neo-Georgian design with symmetrically placed windows. An elaborate black wrought-iron railing curled around the basement entry gate and above the entrance. Declan bounded up the steps with his energy coming on, adrenaline pumping as it always did at the start of a new case. He followed Sergeant Watkins into the lobby, bending down under the crime scene tape with ease.

"This better not be a suicide, Watkins. I might have left a delightful lady behind." Declan winked.

Watkins smirked and led him toward a ground-floor flat. It was a joke between them that the rumors of Declan's stable of women were more fiction than fact. A well-built man of thirty-six with light brown hair, a tanned face with a square jaw, and a brow that furrowed in concentration, Declan had a nose with a slight bump that kept him from appearing overtly handsome. His singleness since his divorce fueled the rumors. As if. The dependable sergeant answered: "Oh, I wouldn't worry about suicide, sir. Not too much of a chance of that. I think you'll agree once you pop inside."

They paused at the door and Declan nodded to the uniformed guard on duty.

"Duty detective notified the Senior Scenes of Crime Officer. Police surgeon on his way, guv," Watkins continued.

Declan knew the SOCO chief would inform Her Majesty's Coroner to schedule an inquest as he was finding his way to Magdalen Road. The wheels of a murder investigation were in place and turning.

"Do we have a positive ID?" he asked, opening the door.

Watkins consulted a notebook. "The neighbor who found the body identified her as Bryn Wallace."

Despite the adrenaline rush, Declan disliked viewing a body. He pulled on shoe covers and gloves then thrust his hands into his pockets. Early in his career, his fingerprints had been left on a piece of evidence he'd handled in the excitement of the find; it was a mistake he'd never repeat.

The stereo was on when he came in but he didn't recognize the song. He glanced at Watkins, raising one eyebrow in question.

"It was found on repeat, sir, the reason the neighbor came by, being on since just after midnight and finally driving him batty a few hours later. When he came up to ask her to turn it off, he found the door ajar and the music blaring away. That was about 4 AM. We merely turned the volume lower—with gloves on, of course. No sign of forced entry."

"And this neighbor?" Declan asked, pulling out his notebook, hating the way the gloves constricted his fingers. The hair on one knuckle pinched and he shifted the rubber to release it.

"One Davey Haskitt, twenty-three, lives in the basement directly under this flat. Works in the bakery at the Covered Market. We have a woman police constable sitting with him in his flat. He was pretty upset—knew the deceased fairly well from what I've gathered."

"All right, Watkins, thanks for the update. Get someone to turn the bloody thing off after it's been printed. I'll want a transcription of the song's lyrics."

The forensic people were already swarming through the flat, collecting evidence, their white coveralls evoking a mass of colossal assiduous moths. Cameras flashed, the fingerprint men dusted, a video camera recorded details. Declan entered the bright kitchen and was surprised to see the home office pathologist leaning over the body lying on the floor.

"Give me five, Dec," the pathologist said.

Charlie Borden. Declan was relieved the case had been assigned to someone he knew and got along with well. He averted his eyes in a semblance of allowing Charlie private space as he worked. While the stocky bearded man on his knees continued his inspection of the dead girl, Declan took in the rest of the room.

It was a small but well-equipped kitchen with a recently used cooker, as evidenced by the strong food odors that lingered. Two clean baking dishes and a sheet pan were stacked on the counter, waiting to be put away. The cooker stood at the end of a run of contemporary white cabinets, next to a small refrigerator. Stacked wire baskets held an assortment of colorful fresh fruits and vegetables. Next to the sink, one of the upper cupboard doors hung open. Declan imagined the victim had been in the process of stowing her clean dishes when she'd let the murderer into her home. The stark doors and butcher block countertop had a few moderate blood splatters sprayed across them, as did the tile floor, but it was not a huge amount of blood. His alert glance revolved around the room, taking in the magnetic strip mounted on the side of one upper end cabinet. It held a series of knives, already dusted for prints. An empty space at the near end stood out prominently.

Finally he let his glance fall to the floor, where the body took up one half of the floor space. A slender brunette on her back had one arm flung above her head, the other curved gracefully at her side. Both hands had cuts on them. One leg was straight, the other bent: a ballerina pose in death, in horrific contrast to the brutality of the murder.

Not a sexual attack, he decided, as her bloodied jeans and white shirt appeared intact except for the dark cuts around her torso. He wondered if there were any on her back, building up a mental picture of the victim turning away from her attacker to open the cupboard door, reeling from a slash to her back, turning back and holding up her hands to ward off more blows, the knife slicing into her hands before finding the abdomen. The pathologist stood, finishing his dictation into a small hand-held machine, and Declan heard him agree with his assumptions.

"No obvious signs of sexual interference, probably surprise attack. Autopsy and report to follow." Clicking the recorder off, Charlie stripped off his gloves. "When I heard this was just around the corner, I decided to stop by and see the body in situ. Not a nice thing to be gotten out of bed for, Dec." Both Oxford natives, they occasionally shared a pint of real ale at The Old Tom, the pub within walking distance of St. Aldate's Station, Declan's base. Charlie was fond of heckling the numerous Christ Church and Pembroke students laboring on the *Daily Express* crossword.

"I can think of other things I'd rather be doing at this hour," the detective replied, and before his friend could inquire about the status of his much-discussed private life, added firmly: "Sleeping."

Charlie grunted in agreement and scratched his ample belly, shirt buttons just beginning to strain against their burden, and launched into his professional recital.

"Dead approximately four to five hours, multiple stab wounds, but there's something unusual here—let me get her on the table and I'll be sure. Late twenties, well kept, well groomed. Several defensive cuts on the dorsum of her hands—one laceration on her wrist hit the radial artery. That one's made the high splatter, but it appears random. Anyway, I doubt that was the actual cause of her death. The other wounds are deep, and there was bound to be massive internal hemorrhaging. No sign of the weapon yet from what your boys can see."

"With forensics these days, only an idiot would leave the weapon behind," Declan commented.

Charlie agreed as he packed up his gear. "There's obviously anger here, but the killer quickly became rational, enough to take the weapon with him, which I'm assuming will turn out to be that missing knife." He pointed to the magnetic strip. "Very thorough, your team."

"Thanks, Charlie. When do you think you'll have more for me?"

Charlie rubbed his left ear while he considered this, yawning before answering. "Let's try for late afternoon today, after 4. I'll call your mobile. And afterward you can buy me a few pints for squeezing you in."

"I believe it's your shout," Declan said good-naturedly. "But I'll buy if you promise to leave the puzzlers alone."

"No promises—too much fun. We'll go dutch." Charlie grinned in compromise. "Let me get out of here so I can have a shower and nuzzle my lovely wife before heading into the lab."

"Some people have to stay and work," Declan called after him, and turned back to the scene of the girl's murder. After the multitude of homicide cases he had covered, he recognized the numbing curtain that fell in the face of violent death, a barrier he'd learned he sorely needed to distance himself so he could remain objective and solve the crime. Humor, often misunderstood by onlookers, provided an outlet.

He already knew something about this murderer. He had acted in anger but retained enough sense to take the weapon. He wasn't calm enough to close the door or turn the stereo off. Both actions would have delayed the body's discovery. Unless that was deliberate, of course, and the killer wanted the body found. Declan looked down at the corpse of Bryn Wallace.

He examined the slim body in impersonal segments. Her limbs were long and well formed, the nails on the bagged hands polished a soft pink. After noting the wrist laceration on her slender arm, he wondered if she were a dancer or a fitness trainer. By now Watkins probably knew from the team interviews of the neighbors.

Bryn Wallace's brunette hair fanned out artistically around her head, adding credence to his impression the body had been arranged. He made a note to ask Charlie if he had the same perception.

The woman's face was finely sculpted, her eyes closed, thick dark lashes splayed out against prominent cheekbones. The milky skin of her neck was circled with a silver chain that disappeared beneath her white cotton shirt and hung down over her right breast. Declan knelt down beside the body and leaned closer to find the pendant that weighed it down, using his pen to gently withdraw an ornate silver charm.

"Rodgers, get a snap of this thing, will you?" he asked the photographer, who appeared quickly and took several from different angles as Declan held it aloft. He dropped the pendant back inside the woman's shirt, pondering its significance. Was it a personal choice or had someone given it to her?

Nodding to the coroner's crew to remove the body, Declan quickly sketched a site plan of the kitchen in his notebook. Turning a page, he did another of the general layout of the flat. He scrawled notes from habit and experience, hoping something would jump out at him later—perhaps even a clue to this woman's murder.

The answer to who had killed her would lie in uncovering who Bryn Wallace was and how she had lived her life. No Morse-like ruminations for him—everyone and everything in her circle would be inspected with a magnifying glass in this investigation. He was thorough to a fault, a trait Declan considered the hallmark of a good detective. He would evaluate the information gleaned from various angles, knowing cases had been solved when the evidence had been viewed from a different direction. Murder was a giant puzzle, and he owed it to the victim to sort out the pieces until they fell into place.

After learning Bryn's background from Watkins, he started in the sitting room, where her interest in photography dominated the room. Raspberry walls and high white ceilings were bordered with thick white crown molding, setting off the black and white photos which, simply framed and labeled, circled the room in an eye-level arrangement. Worn, comfortable brown leather furniture and a vintage sideboard almost faded into the background as the framed images eclipsed everything else in the room.

Declan took his time with the images Bryn Wallace had captured, citizens of Oxford seemingly unaware they were being photographed, frozen in revealing moments of humanity. A white-haired man in a business suit checking his watch against Carfax Tower evoked a frenetic hummingbird caught in a rare instant of stillness. A stout woman in a heavy tweed coat, walking a Scottie dog sporting a tartan collar, cast a lingering look at a shop window filled with diaphanous lingerie. At the end of the row a group of insouciant teens satisfied late-night munchies, slouching against the front of a kebob van on the High, secure in their infallibility. Declan decided Bryn Wallace had been talented.

Declan moved into the bathroom, nodding to a SOCO who was leaving. He noted the absence of birth control pills or prescription drugs in her medicine cabinet, then entered the small bedroom with its neatly made double bed, the duvet white with lavender sprigs of lilac. The room was feminine but not fussy, the walls painted a pale, restful green. Sheer curtains hung over drawn shades, shutting out the world but not the rising traffic noise from the road as life went on outside the windows, and the street woke up.

His eye was drawn to a framed document that took pride of place over the upholstered green velvet headboard. Stepping around a fingerprinter working on the bedside table, he leaned over to inspect the hanging.

On a piece of thick, creamy parchment, two poems were inscribed in flowing calligraphy. The top portion was devoted to a set of lyrics, noted as the song "She" by Charles Aznavour and Herbert Kretzmer. Declan scanned the lyrics of loving devotion to a woman. A hand-drawn Celtic knot divided the sections. The more succinct bottom portion read:

From E. B. Browning, but pretend I've written them for you:

Love me sweet, with all thou art,
Feeling, thinking, seeing;
Love me in the lightest part,
Love me in full being.

Eternally, Val

"Rodgers," Declan called out, "Get me some close-up shots

of this, please." Someone loved Bryn Wallace, Declan mused, quickly dismissing the sting the thought gave him.

He opened the closet door and searched through the clothes that hung there or were stacked on two upper shelves, checking pockets and along hemlines. Everything was of decent quality; she'd been a sale shopper, from the discount stickers on several shoe boxes. Declan had found you could discern a person's traits by the way they kept their closets and decided Bryn Wallace had been neat, kept to a budget, and respected quality over quantity.

A used dresser against the far wall had already been finger-printed. When he got to the underwear drawer he grimaced at invading a stranger's privacy. As he opened it, the faint scent of verbena rushed out. Under the scented paper lining he discovered a memory card from a camera. He filled out a chain of evidence card and put it in an evidence bag, handing it over to a SOCO leaving the room. He would get prints done up to review later in his office. What was on that card that it deserved to be hidden under Bryn Wallace's underwear?

Declan moved back to the alcove in the sitting room, where more of Bryn Wallace's personality was on display. He had to notify the family and obtain a formal identification, he thought as he studied a picture of her standing in a garden with an older, shorter, white-haired woman. Standing before the bookshelf, he pulled a few books at random, flipping through the pages. A few novels, many more on the history and techniques of photography, and two entire rows of books of photographers' works. He paged through a show catalogue titled *Dear Friends: American Photographs of Men Together, 1840–1918* and stopped when he saw text underlined. It showed a 1915 studio picture of two men sitting together on the chin of a huge, curving half-moon, fabricated in wood and painted white. Wooden stars hung from the ceiling; the men's feet dangled off the floor. Unrelated in appearance, one man had his arm affectionately draped around the other's shoulders; accompanying text explained how men in that era were more physically affectionate than in modern times, the homosexual aspect uncertain in these public displays.

Had Bryn Wallace been investigating social climates regarding homosexuality? Or was it the photography aspect and setting that had interested her more?

His interest piqued, he continued to examine the books, coming across the titles *Our Right to Love* and *Our Bodies Our Selves* resting alongside a paperback edition of *Best UK Lesbian Erotica*. Had he been wrong to imagine the murderer a man? A lovers' quarrel gone badly would be a classic motive for murder.

Just as Declan put the book back on the shelf, Watkins came over to him, holding out a driving license. "There's a woman outside you might want to talk with."

Declan glanced at the photo. He wasn't the least bit surprised to hear Watkins add: "She says she's the victim's partner."

CHAPTER THREE

*"Can any thing, my good Sir, be more painful to a friendly mind
than a necessity of communicating disagreeable intelligence?"*
— Fanny Burney, *Evelina*

7:15 AM

The woman paced outside the building at the front of the cordon, whirling around as Declan opened the door. He felt his pulse pick up. This must be the Val of the framed calligraphy. The murderer returning to the scene of the crime seemed to be out of a Golden Age mystery, but he knew it happened routinely. He motioned to the uniform to let the slender woman inside the sawhorses and walked down the steps to meet her.

"Miss Rogan? Detective Inspector Declan Barnes, CID."

The woman's face flushed. "What's happened to Bryn?" she demanded. "Why can't I see her?"

A murmur rose from the watching crowd lining the police barrier.

"Let's talk, shall we? I'll clear everything up." He guided her away from the spectators, up the stairs and into the small entry hall, lined with post boxes on one side and a bench with an umbrella stand on the other. Watkins followed discreetly, notebook in hand.

Val Rogan stood in front of the bench, refusing to sit down. "What's happened to Bryn?" she asked, right in Declan's face. "Why can't I go to her flat?"

"Let's get a few preliminary questions out of the way first," he answered. "Have a seat and tell me how long you've known Miss Wallace."

Val clapped her arms at her side. "We met last year at an exhibit at the art co-operative I run with another artist. And I don't want to sit down. I want to know what's happened to Bryn."

Declan ignored her, and all three continued to stand. "How would you describe the nature of your relationship?"

Val bristled. "I already told your sergeant we're partners," she answered, sticking out her chin defiantly, adding, "We're going to move in together shortly."

Declan watched her jaw clench in tension when he asked: "Would you know of any relatives she might have?"

"No siblings." Fear clipped the woman's answers. "Only her mum in Chipping Norton."

"Do you have an address or phone number for her mother?"

She nodded. "At home in my address book." Her hands twisted in anxiety.

"When was the last time you saw Miss Wallace?" Declan continued smoothly.

"We had dinner here last night." The woman's voice had gone flat.

"What time did you leave?"

"I was home before midnight, so around 11:30." She met his eyes. "Please tell me what's happened to Bryn," she begged.

"Just a few more questions, Miss Rogan. Can you supply us with the names of her employer and any other close friends?"

She replied in robot-like fashion, dictating to Watkins the address and number of the Miles Belcher Studio. Val added her own co-op partner, Lottie, and paused in thought. "I don't know of any other close friends, except . . ."

"Yes," Declan prompted.

"Someone she dated before we met. He recently started calling her again, annoying her. He's a model named Cameron Wilson, lives in Oxford."

"Miss Wallace was a model, too, before she got into photography, correct?"

Val agreed sullenly, and he continued on. "Are you familiar with a tenant in this building, a young man called Davey Haskitt?"

Val's voice was husky when she answered, fighting back tears. "Bryn calls him the bakery boy in the basement. He brings her pies or tarts from the Covered Market—he brought us some last night."

"Anyone else?"

She shook her head. "Not that I can think of right now." Her patience ended, Val's voice rose along with her anxiety level. "Look, are you going to tell me what's happened here?" She glowered, her anger surging forth.

"Perhaps you should tell me what brings you back here so early, Miss Rogan." Declan stood his ground, regarding the woman looking up at him.

Val answered grudgingly. "I tried to call her this morning, but the phone just rang and rang. We had an argument before I left last night and I —" She clapped a hand over her mouth.

Declan raised an eyebrow; Watkins cleared his throat and made a note. "I'm afraid I have very bad news for you about Miss Wallace," the detective said. "She was murdered sometime very early this morning." Declan nodded to Watkins, who took the woman by the elbow as her tears spilled over and ran down her cheeks. "We'll continue this discussion later down at the station."

"If you'll come with me, Miss," Watkins said, guiding the woman toward a panda car.

Declan met the woman's gaze just as Watkins ducked her head into the back seat. The anger had vanished, replaced with anguish. But was that over the loss of her partner, or the realization she'd just made herself a suspect in the woman's murder?

CHAPTER FOUR

"Ill news hath wings, and with the wind doth go . . ."
— Michael Drayton, *The Barons' Wars*

7:50 AM

From the dining room of the large stone building called Ramsey Lodge in the town of Bowness-on-Windermere came the clang of silverware and the chink of china as the early-morning help set the tables for breakfast. In the long timbered hall, a damp coolness radiated from the original flagstone floor. Nora Tierney paused by the heavy oak door to scoop her wavy auburn hair off her face and tie it into a ponytail that hung to her shoulders. Pushing her glasses up her nose, she watched Simon Ramsey and his sister Kate at the far end of the hall, their heads bent together as they stood behind a worn Jacobean desk in deep discussion over orders for Ramsey Lodge for the next two weeks. A wave of fondness washed over Nora. How fortunate she was to have them as friends these last five months.

She hated interrupting them. They were intent on sorting business before she and Simon left tomorrow for ten days in Oxford, but they'd grown quite protective of her in the time she'd lived with them. The last thing she wanted was to cause her friends anxiety if they couldn't find her. Her hesitation over slipping out for a walk ended when Darby came prancing to her side. The Lakeland Terrier began barking and leaping in his eagerness to join her. Both Ramseys looked up, Kate's tall, slender frame a feminine version of her lanky brother's, her sandy hair curling against the nape of her neck.

"Darby, down," Kate chastised the small dog. "We really need to keep him from jumping up on you now, Nora," she said, smiling. Nora smiled back, and her hand instinctively went to the growing bump at her waist.

"He's my buddy," Nora crooned to the wheaten dog, bending down to rub his small V-shaped ears with affection. "Yes, you can come with me."

"Better take him on leash," Simon said. "Too many tourists this time of year to trust him without it, and I don't see you chasing him across the quay." His smile crinkled the corners of his deep blue eyes.

"Good idea," Nora answered, pulling a leash from the brass umbrella bin, clipping it to his collar as the dog sat obediently, short, stiff tail wagging. "Be back in a bit."

Darby sniffed with deep interest as they made their way through the rose arbor, past the terraced patio and down the path, lifting his leg at intervals. The tree at the corner of the Promenade was of particular interest, and Nora tugged him away to cross Rayrigg Road, heading toward the shore of England's largest lake. Pale ribbons of apricot and pink streaked the powder-blue sky as the sun warmed the shore. Puffs of clouds that hung without seeming to move in the warm haze were sharply reflected in Windermere's surface. Nora had never seen such a startlingly blue sky.

She walked the dog among the early bustling throngs of tourists touring the quay across from the lodge at the eastern edge of the lake. The travelers, who wore hiking shoes or trainers, searched among the ice cream stalls and trinket shops for the perfect postcard to send back home. Nora was convinced no card could capture the beauty of the Lake District.

Connecticut-born Nora Tierney had loved England ever since she'd spent a year at Oxford in Exeter College. She returned after graduate school in journalism to the place that had given her comfort after her father's tragic death. Now that she knew Oxford inside and out, she was learning about this section of the Lake District. On one of her exploring walks she had been amused to find that St. Martin's Church, consecrated in 1483, contained stained glass windows that included the coat of arms of John Washington, ancestor of George. It gave Nora a sense of connection to the area; perhaps some of her mother's ancestors had lived here. She would have to do a family tree search when she had the time.

Guiding Darby onto the pathway along the shore, Nora paused to sit on a bench opposite Ramsey Lodge. Nora looked back at the lodge, its solid dark-stone edifice and white, ornate trim a testament to its Victorian roots. It was difficult at times for her to absorb the changes that had occurred in the last six months. Her body was altering, her small breasts and thin face fuller, the growing mound at her belly patently obvious. She wistfully watched a young couple with matching backpacks walk past as the terrier jumped up next to her. Together they watched the steamboat *Swan* depart for Ambleside on the far side of the lake, nosing out varied sizes of motorboats and noisy Jet Skis in its path. It was a scene that had gotten remarkably familiar to her since last March. She had fallen irrevocably in love with the land of Wordsworth and Beatrix Potter.

Until March Nora had been working as an editor for the Oxford magazine *People and Places*. In her six years there, she'd moved up from reporting to editing, then found herself bored, missing the excitement of chasing a story. Her fiance Paul's work with the Ministry of Defence kept him frequently traveling, and Nora was often alone. When she'd decided to enter a writing contest sponsored by a Cumbrian travel agency, Paul had been unusually supportive. She suspected Paul thought her desire to write her own books would keep her occupied and stop her pestering him about his long work hours. The prize was three weeks in the Lake District at the historic Ramsey Lodge, working with artist Simon Ramsey on the book's illustrations. The time would allow her to start the collaboration process on *The Secret of Belle Isle*, her series about a group of fairies inhabiting the small island that split the center of Lake Windermere.

Nora's excitement over winning the contest had been short-lived when Paul was killed a few days later in a small plane crash. They'd been on the verge of breaking the engagement—Paul could be distant emotionally; Nora worried she didn't love him enough to be married to him—but nevertheless it was a shock, especially when she found out seven weeks later in the middle of her stay in Bowness that she was pregnant.

Stroking Darby's wiry coat, Nora caressed her growing belly, wondering at the sex of the child she carried. She'd thrown herself into the work with Simon when she'd found out she was pregnant, trying to work out her mixed feelings over the man who was the father of her unborn child.

Nora looked across the lake to the distant crags of the ancient fells surrounding the lake, tipped in a purplish haze. Green and yellow fields dotted with sheep rose along the uphill paths Simon had taught her were called "rakes."

"They remind me of a quilt my Grandma Tierney made," Nora had told him when she'd first arrived in March.

"The seams would be the dry stone walls then," he'd explained, and commenced educating her about the history of the enchanted place he called home. Now he was coming back with her to Oxford, to pack up her flat in a move to Ramsey Lodge, where they would continue their work as she awaited the birth of her child.

A gentle breeze brought fresh air and the susurration of the long grasses around the shingle at the water's edge, mingled with the noises of boat traffic on the lake. Please, she prayed solemnly, let me be making the right decision to move here. Too much for this child and our future depends on it.

Her reverie was broken when she heard her name being called. She turned and saw Simon frantically beckoning to her from the corner of the lodge, holding his hand up to his ear, mimicking a phone. It must be important for him to seek her out, she knew, hurriedly crossing the road back to the lodge. Who could be calling her at this early hour? Thoughts of her mother back in Connecticut made her increase her pace.

She was slightly out of breath when she reached the kerb. "Who is it?"

Simon took the leash from her. "It was Val. Something's happened to Bryn. She needs you to call her back right away." He stopped Nora by a touch on her shoulder. "Nora, be prepared. Val was crying so hard I could hardly understand her, but I could swear she said Bryn was dead."

Kate pushed the desk chair toward her and Nora gratefully plopped down. She was aware of Simon slipping away.

"Val, I'm so very sorry. What do you need me to do?" Nora listened intently, grabbing a pen. Kate pushed a pad toward her. Simon returned with a mug of hot tea and left it by Nora's elbow. "I'll meet you there." She replaced the phone and turned to Kate and Simon. "Bryn's been murdered. Val's being taken to the police station for questioning, and I need to be there. I'm leaving for Oxford right away." She stood up, ignoring her tea.

"I'm going with you," Simon said.

"Yes, Simon, you must. It's only a day earlier. I can easily manage here," Kate agreed.

"No," Nora said. "You've done so much already. I'll be fine."

Of course you will," Kate soothed. "But then Simon would have to take the train tomorrow. Besides, maybe he can be of help to you and Val."

"I'll go pack," Simon said, "and be ready to leave in half an hour." He left the room without a backward glance.

"Kate —" Nora started to protest again.

Kate stopped her with a hand up. "Nora, let him do this. He won't let you drive there, not when you're upset. It's the right thing to do. Now go get packed and I'll make you some sandwiches for the ride."

The Celica strained and groaned its way along the M40 toward the golden glow and magnificent spires of Oxford, a trip of more than four hours total if they didn't hit traffic. The engine was on its last gasp, and there was little absorption left in the car's shocks.

Simon Ramsey glanced over at Nora, strapped into the passenger seat beside him, seemingly unperturbed by the bouncing. Her auburn curls bobbed loosely around her small face, glasses slipping down her nose as the car lurched. Pale lashes, darker where the ends fanned out against her cheeks, gave her a look younger than her thirty years. Nora had been largely quiet, lost in her thoughts since leaving Ramsey Lodge. They'd eaten Kate's sandwiches after the first hour. Now the soothing strains of Beethoven's "Pastoral" accompanied their journey.

The engine whined again, and Simon hoped the old car would survive the trip to Oxford. Nora had arranged to trade it in for a slightly newer and definitely safer Volvo wagon next week.

Simon had met Val Rogan when she'd traveled last spring to

Ramsey Lodge, right after Nora had found out she was pregnant. Val had been full of enthusiasm, bubbling over with news of her new partner, Bryn Wallace. He'd liked Val immediately, responding to her artist's nature, and understood why she and Nora were friends. Kate had liked her too, and his sister always had good instincts about people.

Simon recalled his first meeting with Nora, his attraction to the petite redhead immediate. After learning Nora was recovering from her fiance's death, he had held himself in remarkable restraint; except for that one gratifying afternoon just before she found out she was pregnant. He wanted to repeat it, and soon, but more than that, he wanted to swoop down and protect her from the outside world. He'd lain awake several nights trying to figure out if the child could possibly be his.

He recalled her shock at finding out the antibiotics she'd taken for a chest cold just before Paul's death could destroy the efficacy of birth control pills. He hadn't envied her the tough situation she'd been in, trying to decide whether to raise the child alone, give it up for adoption, or abort it. Simon was certain she would move back to the States at that point, to her mother, Amelia, and her new stepfather. But once she'd decided firmly not to terminate the pregnancy, it was the combination of her old friend Val and her new friend Kate who had convinced Nora she should stay at the lodge for the next year.

"We have the room, and it would be so much easier to manage your collaboration with Simon if you were here." Kate was the voice of reason.

Val agreed. "You don't have family over here, and you shouldn't be alone during these months. As much as I'd do for you, I'm at the co-op all day. These guys are right here."

"Besides," Kate persisted, "it will do us all good to have a baby around here. And when you get on your feet and can see where the books are going, you can move on."

Simon felt he had held his breath for a week as Nora mulled their offer over, trying not to pressure her, something he'd been guilty of in his past relationships. Finally she had acquiesced.

"The last thing I want to do is flee home to be fussed over by my mother. I love her but only in small doses—her constant fussing makes me claustrophobic after a few days. She can fuss to her heart's content over Roger. He adores her every suggestion. Besides, they're enjoying traveling, and they've earned their retirement."

Once it was settled, Val returned to Oxford, and Simon spent the summer trying to ignore the chemistry that flew between them as they polished the book. At least Nora seemed capable of ignoring it, he reluctantly admitted. Why do bloody relationships have to be so difficult? Simon wondered, as Nora stretched, yawning noisily. He waited for her to push her glasses back up her nose, an endearing gesture she repeated hundreds of time a day.

Simon stretched his left leg and rotated each hand in turn to uncramp his muscles. He insisted on doing all the driving, much to Nora's chagrin, providing her with direct evidence of what she called his "Renaissance Man syndrome."

"Just because I'm pregnant doesn't mean I've ceased to function," she complained in clear Connecticut tones as they'd packed up the car.

"You can drive after we stop for our sandwiches," he'd said, but then slid behind the wheel before she could get in after a quick stop for fuel and a bathroom break.

Now she looked at the road sign they were passing. "Only about ten kilometers and we hit Banbury, then less than thirty to Oxford." She watched the verdant countryside for a moment, and then added: "I do appreciate you driving. I know you'd rather I stay mollycoddled and such —" She put up her hand as Simon started to protest. "I just wanted to say I know you drove out of concern, not control," she finished quickly, searching through her discs for another selection.

Simon nodded but remained silent, carefully keeping his eyes on the road. It was like walking a bloody tightrope, but maybe Nora was seeing he respected and cared about her.

"I wonder how Val is doing. I hate to call her if she's talking to the police." Nora frowned. "This is so unbelievable, Simon." She turned to face him. "I can't believe the police could think Val had anything to do with it."

It was Simon's turn to frown. "I'm sure it's a misunderstanding. She'll be able to explain herself."

"I certainly hope so," Nora said, ejecting Beethoven and putting in Jack Johnson.

Simon hid a sigh. These next days were going to be difficult, helping Val cope with Bryn's death, packing Nora's flat, and meeting with a publisher who had shown an interest in their book. The last thing any of them needed was for Nora to go about sticking her nose into a murder investigation. In the five months he'd known her, Nora had twice taken it upon herself to solve what she called "her little mysteries." One had involved a missing ledger at the lodge. Nora and her ever-present notebook had gone around asking the staff questions, serious in her snooping. It'd been humorous at the time, he admitted, and indeed, she'd located the ledger tucked up high on a kitchen shelf, where a grocer unloading supplies had moved it.

The second incident had been more critical and occasioned a rebuke from Kate's boyfriend, Detective Sergeant Ian Travers. A child in their neighborhood had gone missing, and Ian got the call as all four of them were having tea together. Nora immediately brought out her notebook and prepared to dog his tracks.

"Leave the policing to the professionals, Nora," he said firmly but kindly when he left.

Simon remembered Nora had nodded solemnly, but as soon as Ian had gone, she'd decided to walk around the corner to the mother's house and interview her. "I'm a reporter by training—questioning people is what I do," she'd said when Simon had tried to stop her. "I might get her to remember something she's forgotten to tell Ian in her distress."

Simon had snorted and given up, and yet again, Nora had prevailed. She'd calmed the hysterical mother down and asked her if anything was missing of the boy's. The minute the mother saw his favorite rabbit was gone, she knew where he was. He'd been found at The World of Beatrix Potter down on Crag Brow, showing his rabbit to Mrs. Tiggy-Winkle.

Simon regarded Nora. She liked to snoop and didn't hesitate to stretch the truth or prevaricate if it served her purpose. So far she'd managed to keep herself out of genuine trouble. But this was Oxford and a real murder. He added "protecting Nora from herself" to his mental list of chores on this trip.

CHAPTER FIVE

"In the study of criminal psychology, one is forced to the conclusion that the most dangerous of all types of mind is that of the inordinately selfish man."
— Sir Arthur Conan Doyle,
Strange Studies from Life and Other Narratives

8 AM

Declan watched as Watkins guided Val Rogan into the back of the panda car then returned to his side.

"What do you think?" Watkins asked.

"I think Miss Rogan will need to be vetted, Watkins, but with care. We can't afford to arrest her and blow our hours in custody without firm evidence. We'll let her make a preliminary statement we can throw back at her later."

Declan ran his hand through his crop of thick hair. "McAfee!"

An eager detective constable ran up the steps. "Sir."

Declan suppressed a smile as McAfee almost saluted. "Get the house-to-house started, please."

McAfee ran back down the steps to carry out his orders.

"Let's go see this lad of yours downstairs," Declan told Watkins, "and find out what he really knows."

His sergeant led the way back outside the entrance, opening a small gate in the railing on the side of the stairs and leading the way down four cement steps to a door. "Watkins," he boomed, knocking on the door.

It was opened almost immediately by a woman police constable who looked relieved to see them.

"He said he needs to call the bakery where he works, but you said not to let him use the phone." The constable stopped just short of whining as the men advanced into the bedsit.

There was a faint smell of marijuana, but that was not the purpose of this visit, Declan decided as he scanned the flat. It was one large room, with an alcove holding a two-burner hot plate, a microwave on top of a small fridge, and a tiny sink beside it. The one interior door stood ajar, revealing an equally compact bathroom with a shower stall, no tub. A poster of Rowan Atkinson as Mr. Bean was used as a dartboard. The bed had been made up as a daybed, with two long bolsters and several pillows to disguise it, and was covered in a dated brown-plaid Oxfam reject.

As Declan and Watkins entered, the pale young man who had been slumped against the pillows sat up straight, then slid to the edge of the bed and twisted his thin black ponytail around one finger, waiting to be noticed. Declan introduced himself and Watkins, complimenting the boy on his compact lodgings.

"Very neat and tidy," he smiled approvingly to Davey Haskitt, who smiled back. "I've just been in another flat that was clean and tidy, too. If you could overlook the body on the floor and the blood, that is." Declan gauged Davey's reaction carefully.

The boy flinched, his smile fading rapidly. "Gotta call work. They'd expected me at 5," he said quietly, looking down at the floor.

Declan nodded, listening as the boy put through the call. It was obvious Davey worked hard to pronounce his H's to soften his broad accent, dropping his G's instead.

"Peggy? It's me, Davey . . . yeah, I know, don't get barkin'. That's why I'm callin'. Tell the boss I'll not be in today. My neighbor's been killed and I'm the one found the body. The police are waitin' to talk to me."

Declan exchanged glances with Watkins at the undisguised

pride in Davey Haskitt's voice as he told his story to his boss.

"Let's sit right here and chat a bit," he told Davey, as the young man handed the phone to the constable to give his boss confirmation. "And then you can tell me everything you know about Miss Wallace."

Davey launched into his explanation of meeting Bryn Wallace the day he moved into his flat eighteen months ago after getting his job at the bakery at the Covered Market. "It's an early start, but that suits me. I like being up to see the sun rise and all that. Usually comes up just as I'm crossing Magdalen Bridge. This year I went to Magdalen Tower for the May Morning sing."

Declan nodded. "I've never done that myself, but I hear it's quite the spectacle."

"Too right," Davey said enthusiastically. "It's not just the singin', ya know, there's Morris dancin' and everythin'."

Declan felt the envy emanating from the boy. He intuited that Magdalen was where the boy wished he went to school, instead of working in a bakery down the road. "What's your job at the bakery?" he asked.

"In the mornin' I help make the batters. I taste it all, ya know. With a clean spoon each time," he assured Declan.

"Certainly."

The boy's narrow face lit up. "After lunch break I get to work on the fondant." He described the process of learning to roll out the sticky fondant to fashion elaborate figures and scenes that were used to decorate the occasion cakes that were the bakery's specialty. "It's white, ya see, until I add just a pinch of food colorin' and then I shape or mold it. Sometimes I even paint little details on it." He sat back, proud of his accomplishment.

"Sounds very meticulous," Declan said, wondering if this were the kind of trait a savvy killer needed in order to remember to take the murder weapon away. "I understand you liked to bring Miss Wallace goodies home from the bakery?"

The boy blushed. "Yeah, ya know, they let us take some here and there that don't sell. But they're still fresh. And Bryn was always happy to have them."

"I'm sure she was, Davey," Declan said, wondering just how much of a crush Davey Haskitt had on his neighbor. His cell rang, and he excused himself to take it.

Watkins took Davey over finding the body, receiving the same explanation Davey had given to the first uniform on the scene. The boy had listened to the same song playing over and over for hours, not getting any sleep before work, when it dawned on him Bryn might have fallen ill. The door had been on the latch, and when he'd seen her body, he'd backed out. His cries had brought Bryn's neighbor to her door.

Declan rang off and listened to Davey's story. There was something off here. "Did you enter the flat?"

Davey's face turned dark. "No."

"Then how did you know Miss Wallace wasn't alive? You told Miss Isaacs to call the police, not an ambulance," he pointed out.

Davey looked confused for a moment, then shrugged. "Don' know. She just looked dead, ya know?"

Declan chewed his lip and decided not to press the issue for now. "All right, Davey. Thank you for your cooperation. We'll be in touch." He told the constable to report to Detective Constable McAfee and motioned for Watkins to leave with him.

Outside the crowd had thinned as people left for work. Declan ran his eyes over the remaining group. One short muscled man with a malevolent look caught his attention. The man looked away hastily when he saw Declan's appraising eye, raising the hackles on Declan's neck. "Your impressions of Haskitt?" Declan asked his sergeant, watching the man sidle away.

"Hiding something, I'll bet," Watkins answered. "Bit of a crush on the victim, I'd say. Wonder if he stalked her?" He rubbed his eyes. "What did the station want?"

"No confession from the Rogan woman. I told them to let her stew a bit and release her." Declan watched the muscleman cross the street and enter a flat down the block. Good, house-to-house would find out who he was. "We need to get the mother's details from her, do a notification so we can get the formal ID tonight."

The aroma of fresh-ground coffee reached the men from the cafe across the street.

"But first let's get a cuppa to go, Watkins."

Cursing under his breath, Tommy Clay turned onto the busy Cowley Road, walking briskly for fifteen minutes to the triangular junction known as The Plain, which marked the branching of the Cowley, Iffley and Headington roads, all leading to those suburbs of Oxford. Tommy paused beside the Victoria Fountain for a long line of small cars and large, spewing buses to pass, before crossing during a brief break in the late-morning traffic. Purposefully continuing on his course, he passed the entrance to Magdalen College's outdoor theatre on the River Cherwell, crossing over the bridge but ignoring the river's punters pushing along the quiet water with long poles, trying to catch a breeze. He carried on to the Botanic Garden, past laboratory buildings and a massive stone arch. He finally turned off onto Rose Lane, his destination the field behind Merton College.

It had become a hazy, warm summer day. He stopped to light a cigarette, inhaling deeply, getting his bearings. Merton Grove's playing fields were bordered on the north by Dead Man's Walk, an ancient passage for Jewish funeral processions, separated on the south from Christ Church Meadow by the wide avenue known as Broad Walk. Once the walk had been planted with elm trees, but a bout of Dutch elm disease had killed most of them. They were replaced by plane trees in the mid-seventies, but the enormous stump, more than nine feet wide, of one progenitor still remained. This was Tommy's objective, and as he approached, he was happy to see the fine weather had beckoned to many others as well, who were spread out over the green: single sunbathers, couples in various stages of courtship, and most of all, the nannies, sitting clustered together on blankets with heads together gossiping, as their small charges ran free and unnoticed in relative safety.

Tommy Clay, devotee of organic foods and exercise, newly interested in the merits of meditation, had clipped, short brown hair, shorter nails, and no visible tattoos to spoil the spotless image he desired to project. The casual observer immediately noticed that he worked out with weights, the sculpted muscles of his arms and chest highlighted by his clinging T-shirt. Lighting a second cigarette from the stub of the first, one of the few pleasures he allowed himself without regret, he settled in the shade of the plane tree nearest the elm stump.

When the police had knocked on his door in their house-to-house half an hour ago, Tommy had been prepared for them. It had been impossible that morning to live on Magdalen Road and not notice their presence, from the early-morning blue lights and sirens that woke the inhabitants to the crime scene tape and gathered crowd of gawkers outside the roped-off building. When he'd gone across to the Magic Cafe for his usual morning coffee, one of the waiters filled him in on the murder of that lithe brunette he'd watched so many times. That plainclothes guy whose eye he'd caught had sussed him out, he was almost certain, but he had been determined to remain calm and not let his anxiety show, and it had gone well. The plod had been brisk and officious, and after determining Tommy had not seen nor heard anything unusual, he had left.

There was always the possibility his past wouldn't come up, and he could get away from the spotlight. Even as he reassured himself on this point, Tommy felt fear knot in his intestines.

As soon as they'd gone, he'd come out to reach his special spot, like an itch demanding to be scratched. Leaning back against one side of the huge tree stump, happy to watch the group of children climbing over and around it, he felt a surge of hunger center in his groin, uncoiling the tension. He'd memorized a definition of desire by Albert Camus he'd come across in a book of quotations in the prison's library: "The warm beast . . . that lies curled up in our loins and stretches itself with fierce gentleness."

That guy knew what he was talking about, Tommy thought, stretching himself languorously, wondering if there was one among them today who could be coaxed to sit with him. He closed his eyes, picturing himself carefully exploiting a child's imagination to gain its trust. And then they would wander off together into the deeper woods, where he would fulfill his promise to show the child how his pretty bird could grow.

CHAPTER SIX

"Very nice sort of place, Oxford, I should think, for people
that like that sort of place."
— George Bernard Shaw, *Man and Superman*

12:30 PM

Val stood in the doorway, quivering like a cat before launching herself toward Nora and gathering her in a huge hug. As both women burst into tears, Nora was aware of Simon moving back into the hallway to give them some privacy. Val had called when they were just a few minutes out of Oxford and told them to meet at her flat.

"Oh Val, I'm so sorry," Nora said, rubbing her friend's back.

Val tightened her hold on Nora and cried into her hair, rocking back and forth. A few moments later she gulped and pushed Nora away, pulling tissues from her pocket and sharing them.

"Simon, come in. I promise I won't lunge at you," Val said, giving him a damp hug before turning back to Nora. "Look at you— you've got a football in there." She reached out to caress Nora's baby bump gently. "You look wonderful," she pronounced.

"And you look tired and worn," Nora said, taking in the dark circles under Val's eyes and her splotched complexion. "How about I make us all tea?"

"Sounds good," Val said, linking arms with Nora as they entered the apartment.

It was the same layout as Nora's on the floor below: a large main room with an opening in the far wall looking into a strip kitchen, one bedroom and a small bathroom. The flat showcased

Val's textile designs: bright, textured wall hangings; a colorful blanket shot through with satin ribbons, thrown over the back of the couch; heavy, theatrical trim bobbing from a lampshade.

Nora settled Val and Simon on an overstuffed sofa and went into the small kitchen. "What happened with the police?" she asked.

"They asked me a ton of questions, then I had to wait a hundred years for my statement to be transcribed, and after I signed it they let me go—with the usual warning not to leave the area," she added in a heavy tone. "They'll be here shortly to get Janet's address. I hope it's not that dark-haired detective, he creeped me out."

"Why?" Simon asked.

Val shrugged. "He came in at the end just before they let me go. He had this way of looking into me instead of at me." She closed her eyes for a moment. "It doesn't matter as long as he finds out who—hurt Bryn."

Nora returned with three mugs of tea on a tray and a tin of buttery shortbread she'd found on the counter. "Lottie's?" she asked, and when Val nodded, Nora added for Simon's benefit: "She makes the best shortbread you'll ever eat."

"She's my partner at the co-op," Val said. "You'll get to meet her soon; she's a doll."

"So who's this horrible detective?" Nora asked, pouring for everyone.

"A slick inspector named Barnes, and his sidekick Watkins," Val explained.

"At least it's not Watson," Simon said with a wink.

"Trust me, this guy's no Sherlock," Val said.

Nora leaned across the table and took one of her friend's hands. "Don't worry, Val, we've got your back."

Nora took Simon down to her flat to turn on the air conditioner and give Val a few moments to herself. She unlocked a blue door thick with coats of paint from previous tenants, and they passed a coat closet and entered the cheery main room Nora had always liked. The back wall was lined with bookshelves, and windows along one wall looked out into the garden, letting in bright light. Shelves crammed with more books ran underneath them. On the left side, a pass-through counter piled high with mounds of unread catalogues gave a view of the tiny kitchen.

"It all looks new to me after not being here for a few months," Nora said, sitting down at a bleached pine table near the counter. She'd updated her recycled sofa with floral slipcovers which, along with a plaid wing chair, sat around a low table facing the garden. "I was comfortable here," she said to Simon as he wandered over to the bookshelves.

"I can see that," he said, looking around him. "Great light, too. But my, you do have quite a book collection."

"I told you I was a biblioholic," Nora cautioned. "It's a disease—but don't worry. I'll be storing some and giving others away. I won't make you drag all of these back to my suite at the lodge."

Simon flashed a smile and reached for a book.

"That's the bathroom," Nora said, pointing to a closed door at the end of the hallway. "And that's my bedroom." She had no idea why saying this should make her avert her eyes. She changed the topic. "I bloody well hope they realize Val had nothing to do with Bryn's death."

"They'll figure it out the right way, I expect," Simon answered.

"I wish I shared your faith in the police," Nora said, noticing Simon's hands as he paged through a book on Oxford history. They were the hands of an artist, with long slender fingers, tanned from the summer sun at the lake.

Nora knew he was glad to be back in Oxford, a town he hadn't had time to explore well when he'd had a show of his paintings mounted here over two years ago. He had told her of his fascination with the ancient golden stone of Oxford, wanting to capture the dramatic alteration in color on the Bodleian Library and the Sheldonian Theatre according to the light and time of day. They and the dozens of colleges, bookstores, pubs, and cathedral spires were all perfect fodder for sketches he could turn into paintings back in Bowness.

"I can just see you in your studio trying to recreate Oxford on canvas," she said, receiving a slight smile in return. She must be certain to give him the time he needed for himself while he was being so helpful to her, and to Val. "Sorry to drag you into this. That's why I should have come alone and let you come in a week or so to help me pack."

Simon shelved the book firmly and stood looking down at her. "Nora, I wanted to be here—to help you, and to be here with you as Val goes through this. I'm going to use the loo."

Nora prickled. She knew Simon was a good man, but she felt compelled to keep him at arm's length. That was only right in her situation, wasn't it? She looked at the familiar flat that had been her home for the last six years, thinking back to Paul's death.

Their time together had always been severely constrained by his job at the Ministry of Defence. Eventually her engagement had felt like a convenience, an expected step after over a year of dating. Five months had then passed without firm marriage plans or even a ring. She met his parents for the first time at his memorial service; it had not been a binding experience.

The permanency of death caught all of them in its grip that day, the realization that son and lover were lost to them forever. His mother murmured behind her black veil that Paul mentioned Nora often but had never brought her down to Cornwall to meet them. The implied criticism filled Nora with guilt, although it was Paul's work that had kept him from coming home. His father, taller than Paul and with a wild look of surprise in his eyes, had briefly touched her shoulder and told her to keep in touch. She knew she would never see either of them again.

The bathroom door opened. "All set?" Simon asked.

"Yes, let's get back to Val." Nora stood up and impulsively gave him a brief hug. "I don't deserve you, Simon Ramsey," she said, gathering up her keys. "But I'll take your friendship any day."

Declan and Watkins were reaching to knock on the door to Val Rogan's flat when a small woman and a tall man rounded the stairwell and joined them.

"It's on the latch," the woman said, pushing the door open. Another lesbian friend? Declan thought. The small woman had wavy auburn hair and eyes more green than blue behind wire-rimmed glasses; the tall, slender man had sandy hair and deep blue eyes. Declan scrutinized the loose tunic and skirt the woman wore, perceiving she was not plump but actually pregnant. Curiouser and curiouser, he thought, following the pair into the apartment and down the hall with Watkins trailing behind. Val Rogan stood waiting for them in her sitting room.

Once the introductions had been made, Val opened her address book and gave them Janet Wallace's phone number and address. "I'm coming with you to tell Janet," she pronounced.

"I'm afraid that's not possible," Watkins said.

Simon Ramsey spoke up. "Detectives, would you happen to know Detective Sergeant Ian Travers from Cumbria CID? He was in Oxford on a course you gave this spring and speaks highly of you, Inspector Barnes."

Declan did indeed remember the Cumbrian detective. He had been impressed with the young man's desire to bring the most modern techniques back to his rural area.

"I recall him," Declan answered, wondering where this was going.

"Ian is a close personal friend, actually soon to be my brother-in-law," Simon said. "I'm quite certain if you were to call him he would vouch for me and for Nora. We'd be happy to follow you to Janet's house with Val."

"It's just that you're a complete stranger to Janet, Inspector Barnes, and this news is going to devastate her. She and Bryn were very close—she needs someone around her who knew her daughter. Please say I can come with you," Val pleaded.

"I'm sorry, Miss Rogan," Declan answered. "You've been instructed not to leave the area; it's totally against police procedure."

"Look, Inspector," Nora Tierney paused, meeting his eyes and smiling warmly, "What if Val rode with you? That way she would be in your custody the entire time." Her green eyes flickered as she toned down her sarcasm.

This one would be someone to watch, Declan decided.

"And surely Simon and I could follow you in our own vehicle? I mean, if you left right this minute, and the very next, we decided to visit Chipping Norton, there isn't any reason why we couldn't—isn't that right?" She pushed her glasses up her nose and smiled appealingly, this time without guile, and he realized she was trying to find an out for them all.

"I suppose . . ." In his hesitation he lost, for she proceeded to gather up her bag in a rush.

"There you go then," she said, shepherding Simon toward the door. "We will just happen to be behind you and Val and arrive at approximately the same time to visit Janet Wallace. Of course we'll stay to support her after you deliver your news and have to rush back to Oxford to pursue her daughter's murderer. There's nothing in that your superiors could object to, and Val will be in your company the entire time."

Declan was amused by this small powerhouse and allowed her to hurry them out, leading them all down the stairs. Val locked her flat door and joined them. When they reached the street, Watkins unlocked the police cruiser, and Val took her seat in the back. The two men paused to watch the Tierney woman.

Simon Ramsey hastened toward an ancient Celica. Nora threw Declan a somber smile and a quick "thanks" with a dip of her head, acknowledging his acquiescence as she climbed in.

"Quite a manipulator, the American woman," Watkins declared.

Declan had to agree with him. As far as Val Rogan went, he didn't really want to have her with him in Chipping Norton. But the ride would give him a chance to observe her at leisure. And at least he had made his point that she was a suspect.

Chapter Seven

*"I confess that when I first made acquaintance with
Charles Strickland I never for a moment discerned that
there was in him anything out of the ordinary."*
— W. Somerset Maugham, *The Moon and Sixpence*

1 PM

Dr. Ted Wheeler sat at his desk and closed the proof book from
his daughter's wedding. He felt great satisfaction and only a
hint of uneasiness after finally filling out the order slip from
the Miles Belcher Studio. He had been putting off the difficult
task of choosing the two poses he wanted for his rooms at Exeter College since yesterday's meeting. Ted's rooms looked out
on the sprawling ancient chestnut trees of the Fellows' Garden
in the shadow of the Radcliffe Camera. He had already chosen
the exact spot the photos would occupy on a bookshelf near his
favorite window. That way, every time he glanced out, which he
did often in the course of his day, he would see the two most important people in his world. He scrutinized his choices one last
time as he sipped a mug of Lapsang Souchong tea, the smoky
scent conveying a touch of the exotic. Little was exotic in the
daily life of an Oxford don, but his was the life he preferred.

The first picture was of his daughter, Kathleen, wearing her
mother's satin slip of a dress, a white rose coronet across her
crown. She was beaming happily and holding her bouquet of
white and pale, pink roses with one hand, her new husband with
the other. They looked pleased, as though they had invented the
state of matrimony, standing proudly in front of the vivid, rich

colors of the stained glass in Exeter Chapel. He supposed he should amend his thinking about his family to include a third important person now, giving himself points for the effort he had exercised in warming up to Derek during the engagement.

Ted reached for the next student essay on why the heroine in *Rebecca* is never named. It was a strange custom he'd been expected to embrace: blithely accepting someone relatively unknown into the intimate family circle, at the same time giving him total responsibility for his precious child.

A man of comfortable patterns, proud of the small family he and his wife, Jess, had created, Ted wished they could have just continued on as they had been. Each of Kath's milestones had been a special delight to him and to Jess, and they had even made their peace with Kath living on her own, regarding it as part of her learning and growing. She was living with a nice girlfriend, working as a registrar at The John Radcliffe Hospital, when this chap Derrick suddenly appeared one Sunday at dinner. Soon Ted had the feeling an uncontrollable force had washed over all of them.

Ted remembered walking around the house singing James Taylor's "Steamroller": *"Well, I'm a steamroller baby, I'm bound to roll all over you . . ."* Jess had not been amused. It seemed Kath's choice had pleased his wife, and he supposed he should trust her feminine instincts. It was true the lad seemed industrious: a radiological sonographer, whatever that was, with a decent income. But as far as he was concerned, young Derrick still had to prove himself by the way he treated Kath in the months to come.

The other photo was of his Jess, her blue suit and filmy hat the color of robins' eggs in the spring, taken in front of the chapel's famous *Adoration of the Magi* tapestry. The muted colors glowed behind Jess, springing her into bold relief, and he gazed with fondness at the familiar face. A bout of guilt assailed him at the dismal thought of deliberately hurting this sweet woman who had helped him raise Kath and rise to his position at the college. He had dreaded this for years, and with an effort to numb himself, he pushed the ugly thought to the back of his mind.

Ted had worked hard at reinventing himself from humble beginnings to a don in English literature and considered himself fortunate to be tutoring and lecturing about his favorite Gothic writers of the nineteenth and twentieth centuries. Ascetic looking in a way many of his female students found appealing, he was unaware of how attractive he was. He was a conventional man who liked knowing what was expected of him. His passion for his subject of study overcame even the most jaded student, filled his lecture halls and gave his tutorials a certain cachet. He took notice of those students who caught his enthusiasm for Wilkie Collins or Daphne du Maurier.

But lately he'd felt off track, events interfering with the usual order of his life even beyond the unsettling upheaval of the wedding. He'd found himself having absurd fantasies and then dwelling on past mistakes. Ted shook his head to dispel his gloom. Everyone was entitled to his private thoughts, memories and fantasies included. It was a point he always championed; any form of censorship was abhorrent to him. But along with this, his ability to compartmentalize his past had been threatened, and his very existence had been shaken along with it.

Miles Belcher had struggled through a busy Saturday morning, made more hectic without his assistant. Thank goodness there wasn't a wedding portrait today, he thought, flipping through the appointment book for the next week. It started out slowly but got busier as the week progressed, and he unreasonably blamed the dead girl for causing him added stress.

When the uniformed officer had arrived at Miles' door this morning, a frisson of fear had trickled down his spine at the sight of the copper. After establishing that Bryn Wallace was indeed Miles' employee, the constable had broken the news of her death, indicating a detective would be calling in the near future to get "background information" on the deceased.

He hadn't fooled Miles. "Helping the police with their enquiries" was a well-known phrase that meant "being questioned down at the station." But when Miles protested that he was merely the woman's employer, the PC had hastened to assure him he would be interviewed either at his flat or at the studio. Miles had smiled his toothy grin at the young man, announcing in a courtly manner that he would be available at their discretion. Best to be cooperative on all counts. He reached for the telephone.

No need to have the plod spending time with him when they should be out looking for the blighter to blame for this terrible event. Even though this PC had been annoyingly discreet when it came to the details, Miles had formed a mental picture of the crime scene, determining Bryn had probably brought her death upon herself with her dark good looks and variable love life. He sighed as he dialed. There was work to be done, no matter the circumstances.

"Terry? Miles here . . . Good, and you? . . . Look, I seem to have lost my assistant rather suddenly, and I was wondering if that nephew of yours had found a position yet?"

At The Artists' Co-operative, which she had started with Val Rogan, Lottie Weber wrapped a birthday gift that the gentleman leaning on the counter had bought for his wife. She was pleased he'd chosen a piece of her pottery, a large bowl with three different glazes that had taken her three tries before getting the effect she wanted.

Aerosmith sang about their Ragdoll on the radio while Lottie wrapped the bowl in bubble wrap before settling it in a nest of unprinted newspaper in the bottom of the box. Today she'd chosen to wear dangling silver sunflower earrings, which bobbed against her neck as she kept time with the song. She knew they complemented her skirt with its blue background and large yellow sunflowers. She'd added a bright yellow tee that strained across her large bosom. "Which paper would you like to use?" Lottie pointed behind her to three rolls of decorated wrap hung on dowels.

"The blue one with the stars; that's her favorite color," the man said.

"And you could write on the card: 'You are my favorite star!'" Lottie enthused.

The man shrugged. Some people just didn't get that relationships took work and careful attention, Lottie thought, tearing off a hunk of the paper. It was like her pottery. She started out with a lump of clay and molded it into shape, but if she overworked it, her bowl would collapse into itself. You had to use finesse, just the right amount of pressure. Lottie loved the earthy smell of the unbaked clay, the way the wheel spun and her fingers massaged what had been a square lump into a recognizable object.

She wrapped the box and added a blue and silver ribbon bow. "There you go! Your wife should be very pleased with your choice. Please come again."

The man thanked her and left. The smile faded from Lottie's face. It was quiet in the co-op now. The other artisans on duty today were out to lunch. The co-operative had a rotating roster of artists who manned their own stalls and helped shoppers in any stall. Lottie preferred to keep the co-op open at lunchtime, when working people might pop in for a gift, just as this man had done.

Behind her, from a small fridge, she took out a chilled diet soda and her wrapped sandwich and settled down to her own lunch, one foot tapping in time to the music. She'd made two sandwiches that morning, on the off chance that Val would be in to join her, but that hadn't happened. Silly to think it would. She wondered what Val was doing at exactly that moment, and bit into her salami sandwich.

In an expensive contemporary flat out west along the Botley Road, Cameron Wilson checked his profile in the triple mirror over his bathroom sink. For a moment he thought he detected a hint of sag, just there at the corner of his eyelids, and experimentally put tension on either side of his temples, tightening the skin around his eyes and lifting away his frown lines. If you do only one thing, a plastic surgeon he'd met had remarked, get an eye job. It takes away the tired expression characteristic of aging, freshening up the face. Best start saving for that one.

Dropping his hands, he examined himself critically, judging his blonde highlights could go another week, scrutinizing himself the way the lens of the camera did every time he donned one of the expensive suits he modeled. Posing for magazine advertisements for a well-known designer, affecting a nonchalant, casual manner, he had become associated with the designer's clothes, and Cameron knew once his face started to fall, so would his career, his travel, and his comfortable income.

Cam fancied himself a Hugh Grant type, smarter because he would never consider lopping off his trademark floppy bang as old Hugh had recently done for a film, a bad move in his opinion. And his eyes were better shaped than Grant's, he decided with one last look in the mirror, none of that downward droop giving him a hangdog look. Satisfied with his appearance for the moment, he checked his stash to see just how much of a good time he could have tonight at The Coven. The place would be jumping, mostly non-students vibrating to the lasers and lights, enveloped in clouds of smoke. A popular DJ was on tap, and his appearance would guarantee a dance floor filled with sweet-smelling young women, navels pierced and on display, shaking their booties and everything else they owned in his direction.

Bryn had always refused to come to The Coven with him. After taking up with that lesbian, Val Rogan, and her artsy crowd, she'd gone on occasion to The Blue Virgin. One look in there had convinced him he needn't return—too much sex and not enough drugs was his estimate. He'd rationalized when she'd broken off with him that Bryn's action was proof positive she was rather immature. He'd also felt certain she would regret her decision to dump him. When that hadn't happened, he'd made a decision to settle things. He could handle the rejection of a foolish girl leaving him for another man; what he couldn't stand was being trumped by a dyke.

CHAPTER EIGHT

"Before the murder I was grateful to live where I live,
to work where I work—for all the happy facts."
— Rafael Yglesias, *The Murderer Next Door*

1:30 PM

Detective Sergeant Douglas McAfee paced restlessly outside Bryn Wallace's flat, waiting for the SOCOs to pack up and leave. He had barely made the height requirement for joining the force, and as such, was known for his upright posture. A young man impatient to rise up through the ranks in the Criminal Investigation Department, he discovered that the thorough, routine parts of murder investigations didn't provide him with the stimulation he had anticipated when he set his sights on becoming a detective inspector. He would have liked to be the family officer on this case, just to experience that angle, but the job had been given to Watkins because of his seniority. McAfee consulted his watch for the fourth time in ten minutes, chastising himself for expecting the plum parts to fall into his lap. He needed to become proactive, to deliver something that advanced the investigation instead of grousing like an adolescent, if Barnes and his superiors were to take more notice of him.

He continued his pacing, this time with renewed purpose. As he paused to collect his thoughts, he saw the constable posted on the entry door allowing the postman to enter the lobby, where the man began slipping mail into the tenants' boxes.

"You there!" he called. The postman thrust a set of letters through one of the slots. McAfee strode toward him, holding up his warrant card. The young officer had always wanted to do that.

"Let's see what you have for Bryn Wallace," McAfee said.

The man scrutinized McAfee's ID, then thumbed through the stack he was holding before handing over the few items and having McAfee sign a receipt.

Now he'd clinched it, McAfee thought, labeling the evidence bag containing the victim's mail, careful to hold it by just one corner. Inside was a general circular announcing the opening of a new day spa in Cowley, a credit card bill, and two personal letters: one of ivory, watermarked paper, the address written with an elegant hand; the other a bright, lime-green note card printed in metallic gold ink. Certainly one of these should provide a clue to someone in the victim's life, with the added bonus of giving him something interesting to pursue in his own line of inquiry. Even if it proved a dead end, he would garner points for his initiative. McAfee smiled in silent satisfaction, industriously jotting in his notebook.

The Old Vicarage stood next to St. Mary's Parish Church, circa 1500, five minutes from the town center and just down from a row of picturesque, gabled almshouses with mullioned windows that lined the path to the church. It was the site of a popular bed and breakfast owned by Susan and Anthony Ross, managed and inhabited by Janet Wallace.

It was Janet's favorite position in a long line of work to provide support for herself and her only child, Bronwyn. As hostess she provided booking duties and checked people in, but did none of the heavy housework. Managing allowed Janet to meet people and to stay involved in the modern world, something on which she prided herself. She'd learned how to use a computer to take bookings, and with her own comfortable suite in the building provided rent-free, she had enough left from her wages to enjoy bus trips to Stratford with a local theatre group.

At the sound of the bell, Janet moved into the hall to open the door. She had the same fine facial structure as her daughter but not her height. Her feathery hair, once light brown, now sported wings of white at the crown. Her sharp brown eyes saw a police car parked outside. Janet was like a dog on alert, even as she strove to be welcoming.

"Valentine! What a wonderful surprise!" she said cheerfully, her face lighting up. "Welcome to the Old Vicarage," she said to the two men with Val.

As a Celica pulled up behind the cruiser, Janet looked from one man to the other as they withdrew their warrant cards and introduced themselves. Her puzzlement changed to alarm when she realized her daughter was not among the unexpected guests. "What's going on?" she whispered, her crisp look wilting.

One of the detectives gently took her arm. "Perhaps we should go inside, Mrs. Wallace," he said.

CHAPTER NINE

"This is the reason why mothers are more devoted to their children than fathers; it is that they suffer more in giving them birth and are more certain that they are their own."
— Aristotle, *Nicomachean Ethics*

2 PM

Nora was in the kitchen making tea with Simon. "The Brit's panacea," she told him ruefully. The room was airy and tidy, overwhelmed by a large Welsh dresser filled with stoneware and china and with a setting for one at a small table. From the sitting room, the murmur of voices had become low and soothing, Janet's weeping controlled. Nora nodded to Simon, who carried in the full tray ahead of her. She took in the scene in front of her.

"Who would do such an unthinkable thing? She was so lovely, our Bryn, wasn't she, Valentine?" The muscles around Janet's neck and jaw looked tense. She clutched Val's hand as they sat next to each other on a chintz love seat. The men sat in armchairs across from them.

The room was low slung, with an inky beamed doorway that all of the men had to duck under to enter. Wide-plank floors softly reflected a few polished tables; three armchairs covered in crewel prints shouted the Shakespearean influence in the area. A wide casement window drew the eye to a small but well-tended garden with a petite pergola crowned with wisteria vines. Nora thought it was a place of tranquility now spoiled by the devastating news.

It had become humid as the noon sun warmed the room, and

Nora rose and cranked the casement open. The peppery-sweet scent of the wisteria wafted into the room on a mild breeze, accompanied by the melody of a song thrush. From a chair in the corner, Nora watched Watkins take notes as the inspector gently questioned Janet. He'd gotten through Bryn's state of mind, her work and her friends. When he asked about Bryn's father, there was a noticeable change in the red-eyed woman who had seemed to shrink into the sofa as the room became sultry.

"There is no Mr. Wallace, Inspector Barnes," Janet said quietly, drawing her frame to the edge of the couch with great dignity and leaning forward. "Wallace is my maiden name. The man who fathered my daughter disappeared when she was two days old—I never knew if it was because he was disappointed the baby was a girl or just felt trapped by the responsibility." Her voice trembled as she recounted the day she was to take her baby home, waiting for Allen Wesley to arrive.

"I was convinced he'd had an accident when he didn't come. I called my parents, but they hadn't heard from him. He wasn't from around here so I had no one else to call. My father finally took us home, to the flat he'd made us over our barn."

Her voice faltered, and she paused to take a sip of her tea. Nora's heart turned over for her pain. Janet cleared her throat and continued.

"He'd left the baby things we'd collected and the money we'd saved and just took his clothes. I was certain he'd panicked and would be back in a few days. It took six months with no news from him for it to sink in he wasn't ever coming back, probably a year before I admitted that to anyone else."

The inspector nodded sympathetically. "How did you divorce?"

A blush rose on the pale face. "We weren't married. I wanted a proper dress, not one made to disguise my pregnancy. I suppose that turned out to be a big mistake."

Nora caught her breath. She understood Janet Wallace more than she'd ever imagined she would. At least she was having her baby in a time where it was more common for a woman to raise a child alone. She could only imagine the struggle Janet had gone through almost thirty years ago.

Janet shrugged, smiling ruefully, and her voice got stronger as she summoned the mettle it had taken her to raise her child alone without a father. "Perhaps in the end it was for the best. We didn't really know each other well, and the pregnancy pushed us into thinking we should get married. Allen gave Bryn her long legs and dark hair. She had beautiful hair—I used to braid it when she went to sleep and all the next day she would have brown waves like a soft cloud around her face." Janet blinked rapidly, hurrying to get her story out.

"My parents helped me raise Bronwyn while I worked in a series of town shops and then the postal office before coming here. We had a good life, I think. We all doted on her, and I managed, although it was tough at times. She was always pretty, a delightful child, but on occasion melancholy. I thought it was because she never knew her father." Janet's eyes misted over, and she was lost to her memories again; the room's occupants shifted their positions, giving the mother time to compose herself.

Nora found Barnes' eyes on her and realized her empathy was showing. She looked quickly away, struck by the intensity of his gaze. He turned to Janet, and Nora heard him gentle his tone as he continued.

"And you've had no contact with him, no idea where Allen Wesley is now?"

Janet shook her head. "I decided he either made a new life for himself, or he died."

"Would you have a picture of him?" Barnes asked. There was a pause as Janet concentrated.

"I had one from when we were dating. Bryn used to keep it in her room; I guess she took it with her when she moved to Oxford."

"Bryn had a tin she kept old photographs in; it might be in there," Val offered.

"Right, we'll get it and have copies made." Barnes paused before asking: "Do either of you know if Bryn ever tried to find her father, to contact him in any way?" Both women shook their heads, but a look between Barnes and Watkins told Nora they, like she, wondered if Bryn's father could be a part of this equation.

Nora stirred and got up to take the tea tray into the kitchen. While listening to the questioning, she had been trying to figure out who might have had a motive to kill Bryn Wallace, but she was at a loss. Surely if her father had surfaced, he would want to reconnect with his daughter. What possible reason could he have had to kill her?

Simon followed her, and as he helped her load the dishwasher in the large vicarage kitchen, she saw him notice her frown and distant expression. His own expression turned to one of dismay.

"Oh, no, I've seen that expression before," he said.

"What expression?" Nora asked, eyes wide, handing him a dish towel.

"The one that says you're getting ready to poke your nose in where it doesn't belong," he answered good-naturedly.

Nora was sorry she'd ever told him her mother called her a "nosey parker." She noted he was trying not to sound stuffy, but still, she wasn't going to let him off that easily.

"That's absurd," she said with more than a hint of defensiveness. "I'm not poking, I'm involved. Val is my dearest friend, and this was her love. I'm just going to try to think of anything those two detectives out there may have missed. I have no intention of trying to solve this murder."

"You promise to leave the detecting to the professionals?"

"Of course. At least I mean to leave it to them . . . I'm just *thinking*—thinking can't hurt." Simon groaned as she rushed on. "How about a compromise? I'll only poke about if it seems Val is a serious suspect. You'll just have to be happy with that."

When they returned to the drawing room, the inspector had finished his questioning. Watkins spoke next, suggesting Janet Wallace travel into Oxford later to the John Radcliffe Hospital to formally identify her daughter's body that evening.

"Stay with me tonight, Janet," Val offered. "It will be late, and you won't be in any shape to come back by taxi."

When the woman murmured that she didn't want to cause any trouble, Nora stepped in. "At least overnight, Mrs. Wallace. You shouldn't be alone. We'll be happy to take you with us back to Oxford."

"It's probably the best idea," Barnes agreed. "You'll be required to testify at the inquest, and we might have a better idea when that will be by tomorrow."

Both detectives expressed their condolences again to the bereaved mother, and with Val accompanying them, they left to return to Oxford.

Val had already notified Janet's employers, who would be arriving shortly to take over her duties; they insisted she take off as much time as she needed. Not only was Janet a valued employee, but they had both known Bryn as a girl and were shocked at the news of her violent death.

"I'll need to pack a bag," Janet said but continued to sit.

Nora said, "No rush. Let's take a walk through town for a few minutes, Simon. I need to get in my daily constitutional." She raised her eyebrows in Janet's direction, and Simon understood she wanted to give the grief-stricken woman a few moments of privacy. As they left, Janet was leafing through one of a series of photograph albums she had compiled of her only child, tracing the history of the daughter she had loved and lost.

Chapter Ten

"Death is always the same, but each man dies in his own way."
— Carson McCullers, *Clock Without Hands*

4:30 PM

Charlie Borden was known to be punctual, in life and in the pathology lab. Therefore Declan was not surprised when, after returning Val Rogan to her flat, he got the call telling him Charlie was ready to review the postmortem with him. Declan directed Watkins to drive him to St. Aldate's Station, where he could pick up the MGB. He left Watkins combing through the initial reports and interviews that filtered in before they were logged into the Home Office Large Major Enquiry System computer network. It was a collation of information on similar serious crimes, and Declan wondered how long it took the person who created the system's acronym to get it to read HOLMES.

The John Radcliffe Hospital, Declan's destination, was known locally as "the JR" and had a newly built mortuary. Every accommodation had been made in the public areas to soften the harsh reality of its purpose. But in the pathology lab, the rooms had the sterile air, tile floor, and preponderance of stainless steel that spoke of areas washed down regularly with disinfectant.

Declan was not surprised to see the postmortem advance promptly.

"All set?" Charlie asked before dictating his assessment on the external exam of Bryn Wallace. He began by noting her height and weight and the location of her wounds. His assistant helped the pathologist roll her body onto its side as he examined her back and dictated his findings, then rolled her back. "Can you grab a pint later?"

"Maybe a quick one after the formal ID," Declan responded.

"Let's go then." Charlie picked up a scalpel and made the usual Y incision down Bryn Wallace's torso.

Declan sucked hard on the strong peppermints he used to help disguise the fetid odors of death. All of the worst smells he had ever experienced merged here, mingled with the rank metallic odor he associated with blood.

Declan considered the postmortem a source of vital information and didn't dwell on the gaping cavity and slicing of internal organs as the post advanced. He steeled himself to view the scene unfolding before him as if he were looking at a stage set. He thought it fantastical, the bright mustard yellows, blues and maroons of the body's interior contrasting sharply against the bloodless, almost translucent, chalky skin. It was all more startling than anything a Hollywood director could hope to produce.

Charlie grunted as the assistant helped him turn the body over one last time, and after inspecting the wound between Bryn Wallace's shoulder blades, he turned her back. Stripping off his gloves and mask, he finished dictating into the microphone suspended from the ceiling, while his assistant weighed her organs and prepared microscope slides prior to sewing the organs back inside of her. The pathologist beckoned Declan closer.

Stripping off his own mask, Declan wondered if Charlie's beard trapped the odors of the pathology suite.

"It would appear the posterior wound was the original entry site, just below the scapula. The slight downward angle indicates a small degree of height over the victim." Charlie indicated the area on Declan's back. "It was made with a large, thin, pointed blade, very much like the fillet knife missing from that kitchen rack. This sliced the pulmonary artery and punctured the lung, causing massive internal hemorrhaging into the body cavity, and it was the lethal injury."

Declan made several notes as Charlie continued.

"Two other stab wounds to the abdomen were not as deep, missing vital organs. The wounds to the dorsal aspect of the hands and arms were defensive. Here is what I surmise might have happened, and note I use 'surmise' and 'might have happened' deliberately."

Declan nodded. Charlie couldn't testify that this was exactly the way the murder happened, but years of experience told them it would be very close if not exact.

"The lass opens the door to someone she knows. They talk or argue, and she goes into the kitchen with the murderer following as the argument escalates. Her mistake was turning her back on someone she trusted. The knife was handy, the first wound made, and she spins around, instinctively putting her hands up across her face as the killer keeps lashing out, scoring two in the belly." Charlie sighed. "She would lose consciousness rapidly from the first wound, and the killer seems to have run out of steam, leaving the flat with enough thought to take the knife with him."

Or *her*, Declan thought, thinking of Val Rogan.

Charlie looked over at the well-formed slim body that had once been Bryn Wallace and shook his head. "She was a pretty one."

Declan agreed, going back a few pages in his notebook. "Charlie, the way the body was found this morning, did it look arranged to you?"

The pathologist scratched his beard. "I wondered that earlier. There was a symmetry to the arms and legs that would be difficult to achieve in a natural fall. Oh, one other thing," he said, consulting his own handwritten notes. "There was little external blood, except for the small slice across the radial artery, which left the spray across the cupboard and might have gotten the killer's clothes, but not much."

"Easily covered with a coat, then?"

"Yes, I'd say so. If the killer hid the knife in a pocket and threw a coat or jacket on, I doubt anyone passing in the street would know he'd just committed cold-blooded murder."

Declan raised his head. "You said he? Could a woman have done this?"

"Oh, I'd say so, if she were a bit taller than the victim, and angry enough. Wallace was 177.2 centimeters and was certainly taken by surprise."

"And stabbing is still the most common form of homicide in the UK," the inspector added as they headed for the changing room, where he put in a call to Watkins.

"Any joy?" Declan asked, pulling off his second paper suit of the day.

"We can go over a few things from the house-to-house that bear looking into. All done at your end?"

Declan visualized his first interview with Val Rogan in the entryway of Bryn Wallace's building. She had come up to about his chin. "Just finished. Say Watkins, how tall do you think Valentine Rogan is?"

CHAPTER ELEVEN

"Whatever crazy sorrow saith,
No life that breathes with human breath
Has ever longed for death."
— Alfred, Lord Tennyson, *The Two Voices*

6 PM

When the mortuary assistant appeared, Val stood up, then blanched as if she would faint. Quickly Nora rose and took her arm, lending support. She looked back at Simon, who urged her on with his hands, picking up a magazine in the waiting room and sitting down. Val wrapped her other arm protectively around Janet's waist as the three women were led down a hallway and into a room with muted lighting. They stood before a curtained window, Nora on the other side of Val. Low classical music was piped into the room, Mozart, Nora thought. The door opened, and Detective Inspector Declan Barnes joined them.

"How are you holding up, Miss Wallace?" Declan asked sympathetically. "Have a bit of a rest before coming into town?"

Janet nodded. Nora saw her eyes stray to the closed curtain, anxious about the formalities.

Declan nodded, and the assistant pulled a cord on the left side of the window. The curtains parted. On the other side of the glass, in a circular room, Bryn Wallace lay on a stretcher immediately next to the window, neatly covered up to her neck with crisp white sheets. A morgue attendant stood silently next to her body as if guarding it.

Nora saw Val look away, as if by avoiding Bryn's body she

wouldn't have to bring herself to confront this moment when loss would be undeniably confirmed. Nora followed Val's eyes, focusing on the cream walls and terra-cotta ring of indirect lighting that ran around the room near the ceiling. It was set up as a nondenominational chapel, with a basic altar holding a vase of flowers. The unimportant details imprinted on Nora's mind. She heard Janet suck in her breath, and Nora finally wrenched her eyes from the floral arrangement.

Even in death Bryn Wallace was lovely. With her chocolate eyes closed and her chestnut hair brushed and shining as it lay arranged over each shoulder, her face looked serene, her prominent cheekbones casting a delicate shadow. But on a closer look, Nora saw sophisticated lighting could not disguise the waxy look of death, the bluish tinge around her lips. Janet started to tremble, and Val grasped her tighter, squeezing her eyes shut. Nora couldn't tell which one of them allowed a small moan to escape.

"That's our Bronwyn," Janet finally whispered, and Val nodded. Declan started to close the curtain, but Janet stepped forward, raising one hand.

"Please, just one more moment," she asked. He dropped his hand and stood in respectful silence as Janet pulled Val closer to the window and gazed lovingly at her child.

Nora stepped back and met Declan's eyes. She narrowed her gaze, willing him to see how upset Val was, how hard she was hit with the reality that the woman she loved was lost to her. These were not the actions of a murderer. Why couldn't he see this?

Janet sighed. "Thank you," she said to Declan Barnes, moving away, allowing him to guide them back to the waiting room. Simon rose as they entered the room. Declan finished his instructions.

Nora, a consummate list maker, took notes for the women. Next to her, Janet Wallace stood erect, her hand tucked into

Val's arm. The older woman shared the same wan countenance as the younger, listening to Declan Barnes.

"Miss Wallace will be kept here while a perpetrator is sought. If there's an arrest shortly, the defense team has the right to request an independent postmortem, although in this case the results seem pretty straightforward."

"And if no one is caught on a *timely* basis?" Val asked, one hand on her hip.

Nora cleared her throat. This wasn't the time for Val to be snarky.

"Then an independent pathologist is called in, and those results are held for use by the defense when someone is caught. After the inquest the remains are usually released by the coroner, and you'll be able to plan your private funeral arrangements." With a glance at his watch, he summed up. "I'll need you to come to the station tomorrow to make formal statements and sign the identification papers, say about 10 in the morning? You'll be at Miss Rogan's flat, Miss Wallace?"

"She'll stay with me for a day or two at least," Val said. "You have the number. I gave it to you during the hours I spent at your station this morning." There was no mistaking Val's anger.

Nora moved closer to her friend and gave her side a small pinch. *Wake up! This is not the time to lose your temper with the lead detective.*

"All right, I think we're finished here." The detective ignored Val's tone. He handed business cards to all of them, including Simon and Nora. "I can be reached through St. Aldate's if any of you think of anything useful." He paused, then looked directly at Val. "And we'll continue with you tomorrow, Miss Rogan."

He turned to leave. Janet Wallace reached out and grabbed his arm.

"I'm counting on you, Inspector Barnes," she said in a firm voice. "Find the bloody bastard who killed my little girl."

Chapter Twelve

"In literal truth each of us has only one life to live,
one death to die . . ."
— Julian Symons, *The Name of Annabel Lee*

7:45 PM

Declan held himself to a quick pint with Charlie at the pub after gobbling down a pasty, then begged off to see what had come up in the department. By their usual agreement, they did not discuss the case in public, and Declan felt he had learned what he needed from Charlie at the autopsy. The finger still pointed at Val Rogan.

The night was sultry. Declan slung his jacket over his shoulder, walking back to the station, mulling over what he'd learned in today's crowded hours. The image of red-haired Nora kept surfacing; he felt oddly drawn to her, admiring the way she had supported them all through the long afternoon and evening. She had bottle, as his mum used to say, a kind of gutsy attitude, and he wondered how she would react as he investigated her friend. He suspected she could be tenacious and hoped she would understand the boundaries of a formal investigation.

He dodged crowds of map-reading tourists and throngs of summer students, glued together in packs that spilled over the narrow sidewalk into the road. Raucous shouts from pubs along the street punctuated the clamor of the audience entering the Old Fire Station Theatre to see this year's revival of *The Importance of Being Earnest.* He absorbed noises and colors intensely at this moment, recognizing that one part of dealing with death constantly was the deeper appreciation he gained for life, his and those of others. He hoped this kept him from turning callous. He certainly needed a curtain of distance but couldn't overlook that the victim had once lived and breathed.

Declan believed that to be successful in his hunt for Bryn Wallace's murderer, he had to know her well, her choices and her temperament. His competition was, after all, a ruthless killer. He would need to think and feel as she had, for only when he could see her life clearly would he know who had wanted her to die.

The cramped offices of the Criminal Investigation Department housed some twenty-four detectives in shifts, without benefit of air conditioning, and the August humidity in the building had risen to a level Declan deemed unhealthy for living things. As he slowly climbed the stairs, he saw a wilted-looking Watkins leaving the office, tie off, shirt collar hanging open, cotton material sticking to the sergeant's chest in a way that made Declan feel even hotter and more uncomfortable. He paused in the hallway as they came abreast of each other.

"You look as wrung out as I feel," Declan said.

"I'm for a shower in an air-conditioned room, and Julie better have it turned up on high," Watkins replied. "I just left a note on your desk."

"Anything important?"

"The bartender at The Blue Virgin confirms Rogan and Wallace met there last evening. House-to-house found a neighbor who heard arguing from the flat late last night, and a computer run shows a sex pervert living on the same street."

Declan raised an eyebrow. "Convicted?"

"After a bunch of complaints he finally got six months for exposing himself to children. Clean for the last four. McAfee left some of the vic's mail on your desk—two personal letters you'll want to see."

"Thanks, I'll check it out. Best leave it to me if you're family liaison on this one. The mother's staying with the Rogan woman in town. They're coming down at 10 tomorrow to give a statement. Get some sleep—I'll see you then."

Yawning and waving goodnight, Watkins left, leaving Declan to remember the Watkins' row last year over Julie wanting at least one room in their flat air conditioned, and her husband's declaration that she had "gone American." Tonight Declan envied him the pert Julie waiting at home in a cool bedroom, with a snack and who knew what else.

Entering his office with its regulation desk and solid chairs, Declan winced at the horrific yellow-green carpeting his predecessor had chosen. Someone had the gall to name it "Citron Au Vert." He knew the name because he had petitioned to have the carpeting changed the same day he was promoted to this office, only to be shown the voucher indicating that the carpeting had been too recently installed to be changed. He suspected it had been a joke of sorts, a kind of "Sod off, you poor bastard" from the retiring Baxter to whomever would have the misfortune of inheriting his headaches.

Declan hung his jacket over the desk chair, glancing through the glass partition into the next room to the white board set up at one end. A listing of known facts about Bryn Wallace had already been printed on the board. As they became known, more facts would be added to the compilation until several threads were connected and then more threads would weave themselves into a tight case that would let them prosecute their prey.

He turned his attention to the clear evidence envelopes on his desk. McAfee had used gloves on the originals to copy each, stapling the copies to the outside. Declan picked up the first one. The original was written on a garish lime-green card with a matching envelope; already he disliked the sender. The note was brief:

Bryn,

Why won't you answer my calls? I need to talk to you,

Cam

Interesting, he thought, noting the sender's address in his notebook. This must be Cameron Wilson, the former boyfriend, according to Val Rogan. He turned his attention to the second note, written on good-quality ivory stationery in an elegant hand:

My dear Bronwyn,

I must admit I owe you much more than mere words serve. Please know that I am acutely aware of that fact, and I will make certain to never let you forget me. I will be in touch.

Your humble servant, Ted Wheeler.

Even more interesting, Declan thought, turning to the return address. He was not surprised to see an Oxford college address; the prose and handwriting alone suggested it. He jotted Ted Wheeler's room number at Exeter into his notebook and wondered if this note didn't also hold a discreet whiff of blackmail about it. The office was stifling, and he fanned himself with a batch of interview reports from his inbox before settling down to read them. Forty minutes later he had them separated into two groups.

The larger batch he initialed and threw into his outbox for filing; a few he kept out, lining them up for re-reading before the morning team report and his interviews. He looked at Watkins' note and the statement from Althea Isaacs, the neighbor who had heard arguing. That must have been with Rogan. Declan checked his watch. It was after 9:30, but the subject indicated she worked largely from home and kept late hours. He was contemplating the merits of going over there before heading home when McAfee paused by the door on his way out.

"What did you think of the mail, sir?"

Fishing for a compliment, Declan thought. "Gold star idea, McAfee. Why don't you get the particulars on these blokes and we'll see them tomorrow afternoon?"

McAfee beamed at his superior. "Headed home, then?" he asked politely as Declan stretched and stood up.

"I've been trying to decide that. Do me a favor, will you, and call this number for me while I hit the machines? Ask Miss Isaacs if she would mind a brief interview tonight. If she isn't keen, don't press it. Just leave me a note, and I'll see you in the morning for report. Thanks, McAfee."

Heading down the corridor, Declan jiggled his pocket for change at the soda machine, wondering if he would be on his way to one more interview or home to open the windows and turn the fan on high in his flat, surely a steam bath after today's heat. He knew he was driven, but he was also tired from a very long day.

Chapter Thirteen

*"Once you have given up the ghost, everything follows with dead
certainty, even in the midst of chaos."*
— Henry Miller, *Tropic of Capricorn*

9:50 PM

Simon hefted their cases out of the back of the Celica, pulling
up the handles to roll them across the driveway. One was decid-
edly larger than the other. Nora carried a smaller flowered bag
and her purse.

"One thing that puzzles me about women is the amount of
gear you seem to need for even a simple trip," he groused as the
wheels of the large case caught in the gravel of the driveway.

The long day was catching up with all of them, Nora thought,
looking at the stone Victorian building that had been her home.
A renovation in the eighties had split the house into six flats.
She held the door open for Simon, helping him juggle the cases
over the sill. The pungent smell of Indian food met them in the
stairwell as they climbed up.

"Just how many stairs is this?" Simon asked, bouncing the
cases up the stairs.

"Asks the man who will be helping me pack and load." Nora
allowed herself to smile. She unlocked her door and the cool air
hit her like a wall.

"Put these in the bedroom for now?" Simon asked, rolling the
cases down the hall.

"Yes, thanks." She opened the bedroom door. "You sleep in
here, I've got the couch."

"We agreed I was taking the couch," he protested.

"Just as we agreed I would help with the driving?" she answered. "Really, it will be easier for me out here. I get up so many times at night I would keep waking you, and the bathroom is closer. Besides," she continued, "when I can't sleep I'll have all of those books to sort through and pack up."

The pale-blue bedroom was only big enough for a double bed and one long dresser, but there was a sizable closet. The headboard was of old brass, sadly in need of a good polish, and from each post hung an assortment of scarves and laces Nora favored. At the foot of the bed stood a pine chest. Nora lifted the lid and took out a much-washed, thin blanket, then had Simon place their suitcases on top of it, side by side.

"We can work out of our cases," Nora told him, opening the closet door and taking out a set of sheets. "I'll just steal one of those pillows."

Simon grabbed two of the pillows and followed her into the sitting room, adding them to the pile she made on the wing chair. "Are you taking that chair with you?" he asked. "It looks so comfortable and would make a great nursing chair." He immediately colored. "If you were, I mean, to decide to nurse . . ."

Nora laughed at his discomfort, her first genuine smile of the day. "I haven't decided yet, but it's a great reading chair, so I'd planned to take it and sell the couch." She arched her back and rubbed the small of it. "Simon, would you please run up and see if Val has Janet settled? I don't think I can take another set of stairs."

"At your service, Madam." He saluted her and left.

The flat was silent when he'd gone. Nora didn't know when she'd felt this exhausted, mentally and physically. Her back ached, and her feet felt swollen. She looked down and realized they *were*, her toes cramped sausages inside her shoes.

"Oh, cripes," she muttered, throwing herself onto the sofa after slipping off the offending shoes. She lay back and raised her head on one pillow and her legs on the other. Early this morning she had thought packing up her life to start another was an emotional event. After the horror of Bryn's murder, she realized moving was just a step in life's journey. Her plight shrunk to a mere wrinkle when she thought of the loss Janet and Val were facing.

Nora ran her hand over her growing belly. When she first found out she was pregnant, she had been bewildered, forced to closely examine her feelings about abortion, adoption, and single parenting. Then one day, a memory on the fringe of her consciousness became clear. She had been five years old, huddled in the tiny upstairs hall of the Connecticut house that held the doors to their bedrooms, bathroom and narrow linen closet, like a fist opening its fingers. Behind her parents' door, her mother's muffled sobs were overlaid with low murmurs of consolation from her father. Her highly anticipated little brother had died in the womb. Nora knew without a doubt how her mother would advise her.

She remembered lying in bed in Bowness that night, wakeful, exhausted by the tension of such weighty ruminations. One thing she had learned in her thirty years was that every action she took would have a consequence she must live with, good or bad, sometimes with results she could never have fathomed but would never forget.

She'd fallen asleep then, and when she woke in the morning she called her boss and told Mr. Jenkins she was quitting her job at the magazine to move to Bowness. She would live there and work on the second book in her series, living off her nest egg, having realized with a stunning clarity when she awoke that she wanted this baby.

The door opened, and Simon joined her. "They're settled in, although I don't know how much sleep either one of them will get tonight if they don't take a sedative." He lifted her feet and sat down, resting them in his lap, starting to gently massage them. "Your feet are swollen."

"Oooh, that's wonderful," Nora sighed. "I should protest but I want you to keep doing it."

"That's the kind of statement I like to hear from you," he teased, wondering if Nora meant to stick to sleeping on the sofa. "Would you like the bed tonight?" he asked.

"No, thanks, I meant it about being close to the loo. Can you hit that spot again?" She moaned appreciatively and closed her eyes. "Loos and little fat piggies—the joys of being pregnant."

"When I was small, my mum would give me twenty pence to rub her feet in the evenings." Simon described his mother's social work, which took her all over the county. "She had a way of convincing young boys to stay out of trouble by having better expectations of them. One summer she organized a weeding group. They earned spending money keeping gardens tidy for the elderly who couldn't do the work themselves."

"Simon, what a great idea," Nora said.

"She had T-shirts made up with a plant leaf on it that read: *The Weeders*. Some parents objected to the reference to pot, but it was clearly a dandelion, and the boys thought it was cool. Everyone benefited, and most of the boys stayed out of trouble when their parents were working that summer."

"Your voice shines with admiration for her. I'd have liked to know her," Nora said wistfully, placing her hand on her abdomen.

"She'd have loved you to bits," Simon answered. "May I?" he asked, his hand poised over her swelling. Nora nodded, and he delicately placed his hand in a tender gesture. "Have you felt her moving yet?" He ignored the glisten of tears he saw under Nora's lashes.

She cleared her throat. "I'm not sure. I get this feeling like soda bubbles popping, but I can't say if that's his waving about or not. Soon he'll get bigger, and then I bet the little bugger will keep me awake punching and kicking. At least that's what my book says."

"You called it 'he,'" Simon pointed out.

"I just feel it's a boy, but I didn't let them tell me at the sonogram. They said I could find out if I changed my mind." As Simon moved his hand away, she wiggled her toes. "Forget the pence, I'll give you a whole pound note if you keep on."

"I'd want to know the sex, but I'm not the one who's pregnant. Bet you a dinner it's a girl," he said, picking up a foot and tackling the heel.

"You're on." Nora sat up suddenly, whisking her feet down to the floor. "Simon, that poor woman—Janet must be devastated. To go through all of this," she waved at her swelling, "and all of the hell and delight of raising Bryn and loving her and worrying about her—and then to lose her irrevocably in such a horrible way . . ."

Simon put his arm comfortingly around her shoulders as Nora trailed off. "It's not the natural order of things for a child to die before his parent," he agreed. God, he was pathetic, in love with a pregnant woman and willing to take advantage of any opportunity to touch her.

"I hate to see Val so tortured by this. It's not enough to lose her love, but then to be considered a suspect is just too much." Nora looked up at him. "Simon, I'm afraid Barnes is missing something. He's concentrating on Val when he should be out there looking for the real murderer."

Simon rubbed her shoulder. "I'm sure it only looks that way. He's a professional, Nora. He'll be looking at all sorts of people and angles."

He felt Nora tense up. When she spoke, her voice was very small. "You—you don't think Val could have had anything to do with this, do you?" Before he could answer, Nora shook herself. "Forget it—I don't know why I even said that. I'm just so tired, you know?"

"I do know." He drew little circles on her shoulder with the hand he was using to support it, feeling Nora relax against him as they sat in silent contemplation.

Once her breathing became regular, he knew she had dozed off. Simon pulled his head away to look down at the sleeping woman he loved. In repose she looked vulnerable and delicate. This close he could see the freckles across her nose and the fine reddish hair on her arms. Her hands were small, too small for the big grabs she took at life sometimes, he thought. He had the sensation of wanting to protect her forever from the dangers of being out in the world, a foolish notion, he knew intellectually. But sitting here in the aftermath of the strange and sad day they had been thrown into, Simon wanted nothing more than to wrap her up, to cocoon her away from people like the one who had committed murder last night, so that nothing and no one could ever hurt Nora again.

Chapter Fourteen

"This is a true story but I can't believe it's really happening."
— Martin Amis, *London Fields*

10:10 PM

Heading down the hall toward Bryn Wallace's neighbor, Declan consulted the note Watkins had left: "Althea Isaacs, bl/bl Jamaican, 50's, lect/Trinity; hrd arguing near 12M." He decided Miss Isaacs was black, but the second "bl?" Of course, blonde. Declan rang the bell, expecting it to be opened by a statuesque black Juno with blonde cornrows, perhaps adorned with noisy stacks of bracelets covering one arm and a brightly colored silk wrap thrown over a shoulder.

The woman who opened the door was of medium height with short, curly black hair streaked with grey, wearing dark glasses even at this time of night and dressed in a sleeveless black linen dress and comfortable black flats. Althea Isaacs had a tasteful gold chain hanging down the front of her dress. The only other spot of color in her attire was her matching gold earrings. She smiled politely, looking cool but troubled, as he introduced himself and produced his warrant card, which she ignored. So much for preconceived notions, he thought.

"Please come in, Inspector Barnes."

Her educated voice had no hint of the lilt he'd expected. The door opened directly into her sitting room. She turned and led the way to two chairs set near the fireplace and slid in front of one chair, feeling it with the back of her leg, sitting as she pointed to the one opposite her. Declan sat, taking in the calm room decorated in soothing beige, cream, and gold without a jarring note. A ceiling fan kept the flat comfortable, and as he withdrew his notebook he took the opportunity to look around, realizing that except for stacks of DVDs piled on a back table, the only ornament was a jasmine plant that wound its way over the low table set between them, its sweet perfume reaching him as he wrote her name, the time, and the date on a new page.

"I appreciate your seeing me this late, but I'm sure you're aware time is so important in cases like this," he said.

"Of course. Time has little meaning for me anyway, and I want to help in any way I can—Bryn was a lovely girl and I am greatly grieved by her death." Isaacs' voice was composed but she cleared her throat after this speech and slid back deeper into her chair.

"How long have you been Miss Wallace's neighbor?"

"Since she moved in almost two years ago. I've been in this flat for nine years."

Declan looked around him. "It's very peaceful in here." Isaacs nodded in acknowledgement with a slight smile. "Did you know her well? Can you describe what kind of person she was for me?"

She flinched at his use of the past tense. "I knew her only as a caring neighbor. If the weather was poor and I didn't go out, she always made certain I had provisions. Davey from downstairs would bring her pastries from his bakery, and she shared them with me on many occasions. She didn't have loud parties, and her stereo was not usually kept on too late. I had no complaints."

Declan nodded in understanding. "And where do you work?"

"I lecture on Thomas Hardy at Trinity two days a week but work largely from here—I'm finishing a biography on Fanny Burney, an influence on Jane Austen and others."

He heard the pride in her voice and remembered the name from an enthusiastic literature teacher in school. "Satire was her specialty, right?" he ventured.

Miss Isaacs nodded and smiled. "I'm impressed, Inspector."

He smiled back. "I understand you heard arguing last night from Miss Wallace's flat. Can you tell me what you heard, from the beginning?"

"I've been going over and over it in my mind all day—I know it's important. The stereo was on low, later than usual for Bryn, but I decided she must have had company. I was working in here at that time. I heard raised voices just before the 11:15 chime—my mantel clock chimes every fifteen minutes. I have acute hearing, and it was the first time I've heard arguing from her flat."

Declan leaned forward. This must be the argument Val Rogan admitted to. Could you hear anything that was said or identify the voices?"

"Not really. I mean, there were two voices and both were female registers, so I assume it was Bryn and another woman. But I couldn't hear distinct words and I wasn't trying to."

"Of course not," he reassured her. "How long did the argument last?" The timing here would be important.

"Not long, less than ten minutes, I'd say, and then it was quiet. I thought I heard the flat door open and close, but the arguing started again before a quarter to 12, only lower this time. It was distracting to me, so I went into my bedroom—I couldn't hear it in there—and put in my earplugs and went to sleep. I always sleep with earplugs due to the traffic noise," she confided, then added wistfully, "I'm sorry I did that now. Maybe if I'd heard something extreme I could have helped Bryn, at least called the police, and she might have been revived." Her voice was stricken with regret.

"Don't feel that way, Miss Isaacs. From the injuries she sustained, it would appear her death occurred quite rapidly." Declan hoped she wouldn't press him for details.

"I see. I guess that might be considered a blessing," she said sadly.

"Can you tell me anything else?" Declan's mind was racing ahead. He had enough evidence in his mind now to ask Val Rogan to bring in the clothing she had worn the previous night.

"Not that I recall. I sleep soundly with the earplugs, but of course that poor boy screaming got through them and woke me. The stereo was still on when I went to my door. When I opened it, he was there, crying hysterically, telling me to call the police. I did that immediately and tried to calm him until they arrived. I didn't go into the flat."

"What exactly did Mr. Haskitt say to you?"

"He was crying, and he kept saying, 'She's gone, she's really gone' over and over. I made him tea, and he eventually calmed down enough to tell me he'd gone up to her flat because her stereo stayed on all night, the same song repeating, and he was concerned she had fainted or was ill. The police arrived then and took him from here. I do hope he's all right?" she inquired. "It must have been terribly upsetting for him."

"Yes, I think he's quite recovered by now," Declan answered, remembering the eagerness Davey had exhibited when being questioned. "Did you by any chance see any visitors when they left? Perhaps you were putting your garbage out?" he asked hopefully.

Her quick smile broadened as Althea Isaacs took off her dark glasses. Opaque lenses stared blankly at him, and Declan knew he was truly exhausted not to have figured out Watkins' second "bl" referred to her blindness.

CHAPTER FIFTEEN

"Even in our sleep, pain that cannot forget falls drop by drop upon the heart . . ."
— Aeschylus, 5 B.C.

Val Rogan closed her bedroom door after checking on Janet, who finally slept after taking the sedative Val pressed on her. Janet had wanted Val to take one, too, but Val had her own way to unwind.

She took a carved wooden box from a desk drawer to the sitting room window, cracked it open, and in a minute was blowing smoke from her hastily rolled spliff into the still night. Val became maudlin at first, a crying jag seizing her as she squeezed out all the tears she thought her body could possibly produce, softly sobbing into a pillow so she wouldn't wake Janet.

After a few minutes she blew her nose and wiped her swollen eyes, relighting her joint and inhaling deeply, hoping for enough distance from her pain to sleep for a few hours. Janet would need her over the next few weeks; it was a responsibility she felt keenly. Every time she closed her eyes she felt Bryn urging her to take care of Janet. Val shuddered, stowed her box, and threw herself onto her couch.

She was fortunate to have Nora and Simon around her just now. Simon had a quiet strength she found calming. And dear Nora was like a sister.

Val thought with fondness of her fourteen-year-old half-sister, Louisa. The girl was too young to be a companion, but perhaps in the future they would grow closer. This immediately led to thoughts of Louisa's mother, May Rogan, her father's second wife. Lloyd Rogan's sudden death two years ago had only widened the breach they had been unable to cross in more than fourteen years.

She supposed she and May had reached an impasse. At one time they both had tried, for her father's sake, to learn to be friends. Val's mother had died when she was so young that Val's memories of her were shadowy at best, so she knew she didn't feel May was taking her mother's place. It was just that May was so involved in—May, and how others saw her.

Val remembered confiding to her father that she was homosexual and her stepmother's reaction at dinner that night when he'd explained the situation to May. "Oh?" May had said at first, as though she didn't understand the meaning of the word. Then "OH" again as she did, unable to stop the look of disgust that crossed her face. An argument escalated from there, with Lloyd unable to calm the women.

Val clearly remembered taking her glass of ice water and throwing it at May's pretty face, wishing she could squeeze her hands around that slender neck instead. Her temper had gotten her into trouble on more than one occasion, and this would not be the last time.

May was shocked and ran into the kitchen; Lloyd Rogan ran after her instead of berating Val, and she'd heard him pleading with his wife in low tones. Shortly after that they had returned to the table, May sitting in a dry chair.

"I'm sorry, May." Val had stiffly apologized before her father had had to ask.

May had accepted her apology. "I have some news of my own, Val. Perhaps my hormones are out of whack. You see, I'm pregnant!"

Val was stunned. She saw her father's radiant smile and was glad she was leaving soon for art school.

The arrival of Louisa had kept May involved and busy and out of Val's affairs. The two women arrived at a cool truce that let them function when Val came home for holidays. Val could even admit she had enjoyed watching her little sister grow. Right now Louisa was the only part of Lloyd Rogan still available to her.

Now she wondered if she should call May to let her know about Bryn's death. After heavy rationalization, she decided she would only become angry if May acted less than sympathetic, which was a distinct possibility. It was news that could wait.

Turning on her side, trying to doze, Val caught sight of a gaily striped hat box that stood on a chair in the corner of her sitting room. It contained a straw schoolgirl's hat with a black velvet ribbon and a bunch of lilacs sewn at the bow. Val had bought it as a gift for Bryn and planned to give it to her when they took their favorite stroll following the steps of Alice Liddell at Christ Church's Poplar Walk. "My own Alice in Wonderland," Val had called Bryn. The hat seemed to mock her happy mood of only days before, representing the promise of a future rescinded in a heartbeat. She closed her eyes against the sight and waited for exhaustion to overtake her.

Chapter Sixteen

"It might be an old and old-fashioned city, with inconvenient build-
ings and narrow streets where the passersby squabbled foolishly
about the right of way; but her foundations were set upon the
holy hills and her spires touched heaven."
— Dorothy L. Sayers, *Gaudy Night*

Saturday

9:15 AM

Declan felt his entire team's eyes on him as he discussed the
direction of the investigation into the murder of Bryn Wallace.
The morning sun was bright, streaming through the windows in
the promise of a lovely day. The accumulation of heat and sweat
would build up as the day ran on. Watkins, McAfee, and the
other members of his squad looked fresh and unwrinkled as they
drank their coffee or tea, some munching bacon butties from the
canteen, the scent starting juices going in Declan's stomach.

The case was fresh enough that no one had yet complained
about working through the weekend, and he had their full attention as he brought them up to speed, pointing out relevant items
listed on the white board and detailing the information they had
gathered on Bryn Wallace and on the manner in which she had
been killed.

"Today I'll want Val Rogan's fingerprints taken and compared
to those found around the knife rack. I have her bringing in the
clothing she wore that night."

"Sir?" asked a tentative voice. It was McAfee, in a tone that
suggested he was hoping he was not going to make a fool of

himself. "How will we know the clothing she brings us is what she actually wore?"

"We have a witness from The Blue Virgin who gave a full description of what should be in the bag before we ever open it," Watkins said.

Declan handed out murder books, compiled with known information to date, then discussed his own movements and impressions. He made eye contact with the newest member of his team, a female detective who had just made constable grade and was still green. He smiled briefly in encouragement, but not too much. It was a fine line he walked each and every day. "I'll be taking formal statements in the morning from Rogan and Janet Wallace with the assistance of DS McAfee once the fingerprinting is concluded. DS Watkins will be family liaison and will try to get more background from the mother."

Heads nodded as he consulted the notes he had written at 8 that morning when he'd arrived, fresh and anxious to get this day underway. He had fallen soundly asleep once he'd gotten home from his interview with Althea Isaacs. During his morning shower he'd planned his strategy, plotting an avenue for his team to explore.

"We have to cover all our bases, but in my mind our prime suspect is the Rogan woman. In the afternoon I'll see the boy again, the one who found the body, as well as the pedophile living on Wallace's street. Watkins, when you finish with the mother, head out to interview the two men Bryn Wallace received personal notes from yesterday. The forensic reports will start coming in, and I'll want to be notified of anything deemed important." He glanced over at the duty officer. "The rest of you see the duty officer. I'll want you to go back to the people you missed yesterday in the neighborhood. More should be home on Saturday. We're looking for any sightings of someone entering or exiting Wallace's building between 11 and midnight Thursday night. And don't forget the cafe across the street; they stay open late. I think the inquest will be scheduled by tomorrow. It would be nice to have something concrete to report before the chief gets anxious we're bollixing this show. Any questions?" Declan concluded. The team dispersed, and Declan turned his attention to getting breakfast. He needed fuel to stoke his furnace. This was going to be another long, hot day.

CHAPTER SEVENTEEN

"For some time now they had been suspicious of him."
— James A. Michener, *Chesapeake*

10 AM

Immediately after arriving at St. Aldate's Station, Bryn Wallace's mother and partner were fingerprinted. They both had visited the flat at times, and their fingerprints, they were told, would be used for exclusion. Nora knew only Janet's would be excluded. When she explained that she had been in Bryn's flat, too, she was added to the list. She did not miss the stony look Simon shot her before she was led away to be fingerprinted and to give a statement. When she had insisted on accompanying Janet and Val to the station, he had insisted on accompanying her.

The constable in charge described the procedure to them before their fingertips were rolled in ink and pressed firmly onto a card. They were given a creamy goop to tissue off what they could of the ink before washing up. Afterward they were ushered into a corridor off the interview room where Simon was allowed to join them. Nora noticed he was reading a magazine he'd taken from the lobby.

"Sudden interest in *Police Gazette?*" she asked. "Handcuffs and billy clubs?"

He turned another page, ignoring her. So he could get in a snit. This human side of Simon was reassuring to Nora.

The hall was lined with wooden benches, and a watchful sergeant manned a long desk at the end closest to the lobby. A dank odor of wet mops and cleaning fluid lingered, unsuccessfully masking stale smoke and pungent perspiration. Nora saw their seats were adorned with a multitude of graffiti in a mixed media of pen and knife scratches. They displayed the usual initials, catchy phrases, and profanity, with one reference to the consequences of sin.

"I do hope they won't be taking mug shots today—no make-up," Val joked unsuccessfully as they waited.

Watkins called Janet in to take her formal identification statement. Val waited with Nora and Simon outside the interview rooms, pacing the small corridor restlessly, arms crossed over her chest. "Why am I trying to discard the feeling that what happens in the next few hours could determine my entire future?" she asked, stiffening as Declan appeared at the head of the hall.

"I'll do the quickest interview first," he explained. "Miss Tierney, please come with me."

"It's Nora," she insisted, standing up, not missing Simon's brief snort.

Chapter Eighteen

"The girl was a real pest. 'I think it's terrible,' she said."
— Donald E. Westlake, *High Adventure*

Inside the interview room, Declan had Nora settle in and introduced her politely to McAfee, who explained the recording process. He asked how she knew Bryn Wallace and about the last time Nora had been in her flat.

"It would have been last spring, when I came back to Oxford to resign from my job and close up my flat." She succinctly explained about moving to the Lake District to work on her children's books, leaving out personal information.

Declan was interested in getting information on Valentine Rogan and hoped Nora Tierney would answer his questions without holding back. He remembered her actions at the hospital last night. She had been angry he suspected her friend, and had clearly supported Val Rogan. When Nora asked for water, McAfee stopped the taping and left to fetch it. Declan cast an eye over the woman opposite him.

Her high spirits and wide arm movements in speech gave the impression, at times, of someone bigger. She had the fair, freckled skin of a true redhead, and for her small frame, she was carrying her pregnancy well. She also had a habit of pushing her glasses up her nose, and when she wasn't waving her hands, she rested them gently across the small protrusion of her belly.

Declan wondered if Simon Ramsey were the baby's father, and if not, where the real father stood with Nora. Or maybe she had been impregnated from a lab; she might be a lesbian herself. She looked up just at this moment and caught Declan looking at her, returning his inspection calmly. He took in her earnest expression, deciding which approach would go down best, all the while acutely aware his questions would be recorded for posterity if Val Rogan were arrested.

He took this opportunity to ask her a few questions he did not want recorded. "When is your baby due?"

Nora Tierney's face lit up. "Christmas."

"Quite the present for you and Mr. Ramsey."

"Simon's not the fath—" She caught herself and sat up straighter. "My baby's father is really none of your business, Inspector."

"Fair enough."

At that moment McAfee returned with water bottles for all of them, but Declan knew the atmosphere in the room had changed. "Right then. Moving on from Miss Wallace, how long have you known Valentine Rogan, Miss Tierney?"

"We met when I moved into the same building, over six years now."

"And how would you characterize your relationship?" Declan felt McAfee stir behind him.

"We're very close friends," she said, not giving him the clarity he sought.

"Would you have any idea what might have caused the argument between Val Rogan and Bryn Wallace on the night of the murder?" He could see by her puzzled look that this was news to Nora Tierney.

"No, but surely all couples argue from time to time." She shrugged. "Lesbian or otherwise."

"I didn't realize you had firsthand knowledge of lesbian activities, Miss Tierney." He sat back, waiting for her reaction.

"I don't. I'm not a lesbian, if that's what you're implying," she snapped. "What does that have to do with anything?"

A knock on the door admitted a constable, who whispered to the sergeant. McAfee nodded and bent down to Declan's ear, relaying the message.

"Are you aware there are brown stains on the sleeve of the blouse your friend was wearing the night Bryn Wallace was murdered?" He had the satisfaction of seeing the color drain from the woman's face.

"Blood?" she asked.

"We're having it tested. But you seem awfully certain your friend didn't murder her lover."

The woman leaned forward. "Val would never hurt Bryn. She loved her."

"You know the saying, Miss Tierney? 'Heaven has no rage like love to hatred turned?'"

"'Nor hell a fury like a woman scorned,'" she finished. "Congreve. But Val was not scorned."

"Ah, but she does have a temper, does she not? I saw a flash of it myself last night at the mortuary. Who knows what might happen in a moment of unguarded rage. Do you really know?"

He watched Nora bite her lip and knew he'd hit a truth. "What were you afraid of last night when you tried to calm her down? That she might implicate herself?"

"No!" The woman's frustration flowed from her. "Can't you believe two women can love each other? Or are you too prejudiced to understand that?"

Declan sat back. "It has nothing to do with bias of any kind. Surely you're aware that even in a hetero relationship we scrutinize the boyfriend or husband in a murder investigation."

Nora grimaced at this truth.

"I'm asking you about Miss Rogan to learn more about Bryn Wallace," Declan explained. He was getting little joy from her answers and had the distinct impression she was playing with him. He found the challenge Nora Tierney represented stimulating and grudgingly gave her points for being so assured of her friend's innocence.

"Of course you can ask if you really think it will help," she replied.

Behind him McAfee slurped his water. "It must have occurred to you it would appear she was the last person to see the victim alive. I'm trying to find out as much as I can about her to, well, to eliminate her from our inquiries, as it were." That was true enough on one level, he thought.

"Eliminate her? That's why she had to bring in the clothing she wore that night? Inspector Barnes, even the general public has read too many Agatha Christies not to know that very action means you consider Val a suspect worth investigating." Nora shook her head in annoyance and pushed her glasses up her nose. "There is just one thing you need to remember."

This wasn't going at all the way he had thought it would although he was enjoying the verbal sparring. He decided to play along with her. "I'll bite, Miss Tierney. Just what is it I need to remember?"

Nora stood and leaned toward him, her small hands lying flat on the tabletop. "The last person to see Bryn Wallace alive wasn't Val Rogan. It was her murderer."

Chapter Nineteen

"I must compose my face and push the fear and doubt
beneath the skin."
—John Hersey, *White Lotus*

11 AM

Enjoying brunch in the backyard, Ted Wheeler looked with pleasure upon the rows of delicate pink, yellow, and mauve zinnias clustered with white daisies. His wife was really a wonderful gardener. He sipped a second cup of green tea. According to the porter, a detective named Watkins had called for him at Exeter and said he would try again. Ted's stomach had calmed down, and he was almost able to pretend everything was as it had been. He had written to the woman. He hadn't decided what to say or how to act, but that would come to him in time, no doubt. He just needed to stay calm.

Ted smiled across the wicker table at Jess, deciding the streak of grey hair coming in at one corner of her forehead gave her an exotic look. She was still a striking woman. Middle age had softened her features, giving her a benevolent air that added to her character. He thought back to their early married years, the tiny flat, and the three flights they'd climbed up every day. Jess had never complained about going out to work and had done so cheerfully, as he took classes and wrote papers to get his doctoral degree. She had always been confident of his eventual success, always encouraged him, even at times when his poor beginnings threatened to trip him up. He owed her his allegiance.

Kath and Derrick were coming to dinner later. Certainly he

was mellowing if he was looking forward to seeing them together, he decided, pleased he had managed to jump that hurdle of the new husband. There were grandchildren to look forward to now, little Kaths running around, and the cycle of their lives would continue. He leaned back in his chair with great complacency, feeling the sun warm his face.

Beside him, Jess opened the paper, and with her exclamation, he felt his tranquility rapidly dissipate. "Ted! That lovely girl from the Belcher Studio has been *murdered*!"

Inside the penthouse flat of a large contemporary building that overlooked Botley Stream, Cameron Wilson waited for the detective who had called earlier in the day; he'd said he would be dropping by with a few questions. After a quick hit, his imagination was in overdrive. He pictured the man driving out of Oxford centre and west along the Botley Road, maybe planning where he would stop for lunch, turning onto Prestwich Place, the new lane leading to his building.

"Posh," the detective would think as he parked.

Cam checked one last time to be certain his stash was properly hidden. The morning newspapers had the conspicuous headline "Former Model Murdered in Magdalen Road," adding an extra jolt of heartburn to his hungover morning.

He had read the article with growing fear gripping his stomach and immediately anticipated this visit; his story was prepared. All he had to do was stick to it, and they would never find out he had been on Magdalen Road that night.

CHAPTER TWENTY

"No one could really like Jimmy Jamison, but that should come as no surprise."
— Jack Galloway, *The Toothache Tree*

11:15 AM

Declan decided to let Val Rogan stew while he and McAfee left to do two quick interviews, knowing her anticipation and anxiety would be heightened by several hours spent waiting in a stuffy police station, just soaking up the atmosphere, as it were. As they parked outside Tommy Clay's building, he pictured the woman back at the station getting more and more annoyed. He knew she was aware of her position in this case, and he hoped the long wait with too much time to think would persuade her to tell him the truth. And while she was thinking, he could be tying up a few loose ends. One of those loose ends was the bloody blighter who stood defiantly in front of him.

The two officers followed Clay into his flat, where Declan questioned him carefully. He had gone over the notes from the PC who'd done the house-to-house and looked now for discrepancies in Clay's answers. While the man's usual behavior did not include a background of murder, he was still a suspect to be examined.

Declan's belief that pedophiles were the lowest of the low had made this visit disagreeable from the start. The man before him represented a cancer upon society as far as Declan was concerned, preying on youth's innocence and destroying it in the process.

Although he had been surprised by the barren feel of the small flat, just down the road from Bryn Wallace's more imposing building, Declan was totally unimpressed with the pugnacious man who chain-smoked as they questioned him. So far his answers had been consistent.

"So you're on the dole, Mr. Clay?" Declan asked.

"Not even. I'm a lucky budgie, my auntie left me something in her will."

Declan made certain McAfee was taking notes. They would have to investigate his claim of an inheritance that let him stay idle since leaving prison. "And your plans are?"

"Don't have none yet, do I? Just trying to get my pins under me, like. I'll sort out something soon enough."

I bet you will, Declan thought, grimacing inside. "I think that's all, Mr. Clay. Please call the station if you remember anything that might be of help. Don't leave the area without notifying St. Aldate's. And we'll be checking your alibi."

"I still don't see why you big guns had to come and talk to me. I told that other bloke yesterday I only knew that girl by sight." The cloak of indignation Clay wore was obnoxious. "You're just bothering me 'cause I was in gaol."

"Strictly procedure, Mr. Clay," McAfee answered as they stood to leave, but the man would not be placated, stopping them at the door.

"I know what you're about then," he sneered. He pointed his finger at Declan's chest, stopping just short of jabbing him. "I'll never lose the label. Hundreds of thousands of people involved, millions of dollars spent every year on the porn industry, yet you righteous plods will only condemn me—remember me—because I was caught."

Declan drew himself to his full height and looked down at the man, this time not bothering to mask his loathing.

"You were caught exposing yourself to *children*. What stays between adults in the privacy of their homes is just that—

private. You violated that right of privacy when you took your sexual perversions and inflicted them on innocent children."

And turning on his heel, he pushed McAfee out of the flat, slamming the door behind them.

On the other side of the closed door, a wide smile spread over Tommy Clay's face. He had greatly enjoyed rankling the big detective who dressed too well for a copper, in his opinion. They would have to leave him alone now; to do otherwise would smack of harassment. He would love to slap a suit on them. His alibi for Friday evening was solid: he had been having his future told by Miss Odessa across the street, waiting outside for his turn, smoking as usual. She would confirm that at 11:45 he was sitting across from her in the patchouli-scented room where she did her readings. She had given him his full fifteen minutes' worth until midnight.

When she told him during her reading that she saw him coming into unexpected money in the near future, he had known it was fate that he had been waiting on line outside Miss Odessa's that night. He'd seen the woman leaving Bryn Wallace's flat at 11:25, a fact he neglected to mention to the plod. Why should he help a queer bitch out? It was the bloke who had entered the building four or five minutes later, and whom he'd recognized, who would be his gold mine, and he threw himself across his bed to ruminate on the best way to approach his quarry.

CHAPTER TWENTY-ONE

"The meal had the ill-subdued restlessness of a headquarters' mess on the eve of the battle."
— Richard Gordon, *A Question of Guilt:
The Curious Case of Dr. Crippen*

11:45 AM

Nora and Simon stood with Janet on the steps of St. Aldate's police station. Janet hadn't spoken much since her interview ended, and it was clear to Nora that Janet hated leaving Val behind as much as she did.

They walked up St. Aldate's, pausing for Janet to examine the raised perennial beds of the War Memorial Garden, lost in thought. When she finally spoke, it was to say: "When Bryn was a baby, I thought of all kinds of excuses I would tell her for why she didn't have a father. One of my favorites was that her father had died in the war, any war." Janet sighed.

"What did you eventually tell her?" Nora asked.

Janet shrugged as they moved on. "I told her the truth—somewhere she had a father, but I had no idea where he was or what he was doing. My father did a fine job of being a stand-in when she was little. I was very fortunate to have both my parents' support, but my dad spent a lot of time with her when she was young."

Nora glanced at Simon, who met her eyes with a sympathetic look. She would miss her own father's support for her child, something she hadn't dwelled on before.

They continued to Christ Church, where they watched the

bowler-hatted college custodian checking IDs. They looked
down the long drive to its pepper-pot tower and the majestic
cloisters of Christ Church Cathedral. "Would you like to go in?"
Simon asked Janet.

Janet considered this. "No, I think what I would really like is
a good cup of coffee."

"I know just the place," Nora said, escorting them across the
street to the corner of Pembroke Street, where St. Aldate's Coffee House stood open.

It was a cool, peaceful oasis after the bustle of the outside
street, and with encouragement from Simon, Janet ordered her
coffee and a bowl of home-cooked soup. After they'd ordered,
Nora checked her watch.

"Val said she would call us as soon as she's through," she said.

"I expect it will be lunchtime at the station, too, so they might
not get to her until later," Simon predicted.

Beside him, Nora snorted. "Oh, please. Barnes will make her
sweat until he's good and ready to talk to her. He's probably out
somewhere having a three-course meal on the taxpayer's dole."
She sipped a glass of ice water.

"You're right, Simon, it will be a while," Janet said. "Perhaps
after we finish here I should go back to Val's flat. I need to call
some cousins, and I suppose I should call the vicar. I can at least
make some preliminary funeral preparations."

"And take a nap," Nora said. "You need to keep your strength
up."

"I could say that about two people at this table," Simon said.
He was promptly rewarded with an elbow in his side.

After dropping Janet home and using the bathroom, Nora paced her small sitting room. "I feel like those books are looking at me with guilty spines," she told Simon. "I should be packing, but I just don't feel like it."

"That's natural," he said. "You're worried about Val. I could make a start, if you like, and you could nap."

Nora considered this, then shook her head. "No, let's get out of here." She slung her quilted bag over her shoulder. "I need to walk and think."

Simon drove them into the town centre and scored a parking spot on Broad Street, right across from the curved end of the Sheldonian Theatre, built for Oxford University ceremonials. Nora guided him past the railing containing the stone busts of the Emperors' Heads to the stone-paved Old Schools Quadrangle. The traffic noise dissipated; there was an atmosphere of calmness. Discreet signs requested silence. Nora walked the quad with Simon at her side, letting the peacefulness of the area flow through her.

She was thankful Simon didn't interrupt her. He walked beside her, silently reading the names of the original schools of the University that were painted in gold above shadowy doorways. What was Val going through? Was Janet on the phone right now, crying out her news to her relatives? When would the inquest be? Who had killed Bryn Wallace and why? Nora's thoughts went round and round until she found they'd stopped in front of the Radcliffe Camera, its spherical gracious form mirroring her circular thoughts.

"You have to take an oath to be a reader at the Bodleian Library, did you know that?" she asked Simon. "They have all of these original books and manuscripts that go back to medieval times, and you merely swear you won't deface them or take them away or light them on fire, and that's pretty much their security code."

"Sounds pretty amazing in modern times," Simon admitted.

"It's because they have faith the majority of people will value the history contained here," Nora explained, aware that the heat of the afternoon had made the back of her neck perspire. She searched through her bag for a coated rubber band. "When I was a student here I read the original newspaper reviews of Wilkie Collins' *The Woman in White*—it gave me goose bumps." She tied her hair up in a ponytail. "We should have the same faith in those we love."

He nodded. "But not be blind to their faults," he said. "You glow when you talk about old books, you know."

"Just as you must glow when you visit a museum and see old masterpieces," she countered. Was he telling her to keep her mind open that Val might not be as innocent as she thought?

They walked on in silence while Nora contemplated this awful thought, exiting on Catte Street and approaching Hertford College. Connecting two buildings on opposite sides of the street was the ornate corridor known as the Bridge of Sighs for its resemblance to the original Ponte dei Sospiri in Venice. They lingered in the alleyway, admiring the architecture. Nora wondered if Simon was aware this was traditionally a favorite place to become engaged. Why would he? Why was she even thinking about these kinds of things? She felt a wave of misgiving pass over her. One minute she was worried Val might be capable of murder and the next she was thinking of engagements? What was wrong with her?

"Simon, why do people revere historical things like paintings and books but have so little regard for the humans who produced them?" Nora knew her tone was disturbed. She suddenly felt out of energy. There was just too much to take in all at once.

"I don't know why humans act like that, Nora," Simon said, taking her elbow. "But I do know that you need air conditioning and a lie down."

Chapter Twenty-Two

"Now, what I want is, Facts."
— Charles Dickens, *Hard Times: For These Times*

2 PM

Davey Haskitt was not at home; Declan left his card tucked in the door saying he had stopped by. He had McAfee check in with the team conducting interviews on Magdalen Road: nothing of interest had surfaced. Watkins said he felt Cam Wilson had been nervous but hadn't established Wilson had been stalking Bryn Wallace.

It was nearly 2 when Declan arrived at the station after a hasty ploughman's lunch with McAfee at a pub in Cowley. McAfee had ordered the same thing as Declan had, and the inspector had felt his actions were being shadowed. The young man was eager for a promotion; whether he had the intellect and skill to pull it off remained to be proven.

Checking with his team in the incident room cost Declan another forty-five minutes while he sorted incoming information. Just as he was wrapping up, Debs delivered copies of the transcription of the song playing in Bryn Wallace's flat when she was found dead. Debs' research indicated the song, "No Matter What," was written by Andrew Lloyd Webber with lyrics by Jim Steinman for their musical *Whistle Down the Wind*. Declan recalled the show had not been a success. But when Boyzone recorded the song, it had become a huge hit. "Record of the Year in the U.K. in 1998," he read out loud as McAfee followed along on his copy.

"Blimey! Why do you suppose this was on?" McAfee asked.

Declan put his copy in the folder he planned to take to the interview room. It was after 3; he was finally ready to call Val Rogan to the interview room.

McAfee trailed behind him, starting to hum. "Sir, I think I know this one—" McAfee took a deep breath.

Declan turned and silenced him with a dark look before the constable could break out into full song. "I heard the melody in the flat, McAfee. I don't think the entire station need be subjected to your recital." He raised one eyebrow and continued on to the interview room.

McAfee caught up, refusing to be downhearted. "That's all right then, sir. Mum always said I was tone deaf anyway. But it must have some significance to someone, right?"

Declan paused with his hand on the door to the custody block, where prisoners on remand awaited disposition. He would pick up tea from the kitchen there; they would undoubtedly need something to drink during the lengthy interview he planned to conduct with Val Rogan. "I quite agree, McAfee, and presumably that person would be our murderer."

CHAPTER TWENTY-THREE

"Except for the occasional dry question, he left the talking to her,
waiting while she fought out the difficult words."
— Wallace Stegner, *A Shooting Star*

2:50 PM

Val looked at her watch with the oversized William Morris face
for at least the thirtieth time, plucking at the ribbon running
through the edge of her shirt, a Val Rogan Original. It was silk-
screened with a waterfall design in a multitude of colors: aqua,
blue, green, purple, all competing for attention, with strips of
vintage ecru lace set into the design and a band of old shell buttons running around each cuff. The soft confection stood in direct contrast to Val's short, spiked hair and slim, boyish figure.

The wait after lunch was unbearable in this stark room, with its
table and chairs nicked and scratched from years of use and abuse.
The walls were a dull color she would have described as putty,
and the lino tiles on the floor were swirled with mocha and tan,
crisscrossed with scars from chairs hastily scraped back.

She had picked at the chicken from a lunch salad they'd brought
her, and the smell of the Caesar dressing emanating from the bin
was turning her stomach. This was bloody ridiculous. Barnes was
deliberately leaving her to get agitated, hoping to trip her up. She
remembered Nora's words to her as she'd left: "I know you didn't
do this. Just stick to the facts and you'll be fine."

But she wasn't fine, Val thought ruefully. She was anything
but fine. She was tired and keyed up and in pain knowing that
Bryn Wallace would never be a part of her life again.

Val kept replaying their last evening together, trying to think what she might have missed that would point to someone, anything to indicate who might have killed Bryn. The only ripple in the night had been the way it had ended, their silly argument that was just a disagreement, really. And that had been sorted out when she left, hadn't it? Or was she kidding herself? Were there layers to Bryn Wallace she'd known nothing about?

Val sat up straighter as she heard footsteps and muffled voices coming in her direction; she ran her fingers through her cropped hair as the door opened. A smiling Inspector Barnes entered, followed by Constable McAfee carrying a paper tray he set down on the table between them. While McAfee busied himself at the recorder, Barnes picked up a covered cup of tea from the tray, loosening his tie as he settled in. This did not bode well for a brief interview, Val decided, and she sighed audibly.

"Sorry to have kept you waiting, Miss Rogan, but it was unavoidable," he said smoothly, handing her a cup of tea. "Not like home," Declan nodded toward the cup of tea, "but always good this time of afternoon, even in this warm weather, although we're lacking biscuits to go with it. What are your favorites? Personally, I'm keen on HobNobs."

The personal approach, then, Val thought, designed to put me at ease. "Shortbread," she answered briskly, immediately picturing Simon enjoying Lottie's buttery confection yesterday. Dear Lottie, who was taking care of everything at the co-op in her capable manner. Val eased the lid off the milky brew, deciding it wouldn't be in her best interests to demand her tea with lemon. She blew on the hot liquid while the detective dictated the date, time, and names of those present for the benefit of the recording.

"Now then, Miss Rogan. First things first. I'll need verbal answers to my questions. The recorder can't see a nod or a shrug, just to remind you. Let's start at the beginning." He shuffled papers in the folder in front of him.

Val nodded anyway, adding, "Fine" for the tape, her clear voice without a trace of the tenseness she felt. She darted a glance at the young constable, sipping tea and labeling a clean sheet in his notebook, who was sitting next to Barnes. Val flashed on a memory of watching a *Mystery* series from which she had learned that any missing pages from a detective's notebook had to be accounted for; she wondered how they managed that feat. It meant they couldn't ever scribble or write a grocery list, at least not on company paper. Her thoughts were wandering away from her when she realized Barnes had asked her a question.

She looked up. "Sorry?"

Declan repeated his question carefully. "For the record, please state your name, current address, and occupation."

She did so, feeling foolish for losing her concentration before they'd even started, feeling the need to explain. "Sorry—I haven't had much sleep since, well, since we got the news about Bryn."

Declan was pleasant but capitalized on this extraneous statement. "You must have been very upset."

A warning bell went off in Val's mind. Was that a leading statement? A fishing expedition? She met his look squarely. "I'm devastated," she said.

"How long had you known Miss Wallace?"

Val spent the next few minutes describing how she and Bryn had met. She spoke carefully, afraid to say anything that could be interpreted as a motive for murder. The tea in front of her was already developing a filmy coating on its surface.

She saw the constable watching his superior intently as the inspector smoothly guided Val back and forth between topics, interjecting questions about her work and family. Val explained the details of her art co-operative and discussed her partner, Lottie Weber, who worked in mosaics and pottery. She described textile art she created as silk-screened wall hangings and clothing, with additions of vintage laces, ribbons, and embroidery. McAfee scribbled a note at her grimace when she told him what was left of her family.

"I only have a stepmother I'm not close to and a half-sister I would like to be closer to," she said, immediately regretting the flippant remark.

"Your stepmother," Declan consulted his notes. "May Rogan? She keeps your half-sister away from you? Why would that be?"

He said it mildly, but to Val it had the sound of unearthing an unsavory character flaw of hers.

"She denies it, but I'm sure she thinks Louisa will become a lesbian if she hangs about me too much." Val smiled regretfully. "But I fail to see what my stepmother's opinion of me has to do with Bryn's death." She wasn't about to let him get off track too easily. He could misinterpret extra information there was no reason for him to know. It had happened in too many movies for her to fall for that. A bead of sweat rolled between her small breasts; she fancied Declan knew she had a tiny gold bar piercing her left nipple. And that young constable hanging on his boss's every word annoyed her. A hot spot of temper flared behind her eyes.

"Just background information," he assured her, adding, "It would be good to get some on Miss Wallace, too. Your friend Nora Tierney had only met her once. You, on the other hand, had an intimate relationship with the victim, and you may have information that could help me find her murderer." He looked her in the eye disarmingly. "You do want to assist in finding her killer, Miss Rogan?"

Very smooth, Val thought, feeling trapped and then irritated at herself for letting him get to her. She hated him poking voyeuristically into her private life, and Bryn's too, but if she didn't answer his questions, he would interpret that as her having something to hide. She returned his look, wondering what he was really thinking behind those grey eyes as she answered him. "Of course I want to help you find Bryn's killer."

"Then help me get to know Bryn Wallace so I can find him— or her."

Val flinched slightly at the feminine pronoun, her throat tight with rising anger. Declan had backed her into a corner where she had no choice but to help him, and becoming belligerent wouldn't help the situation. "What do you want to know?"

"Everything you can tell me about Bronwyn Wallace."

Half an hour later, a knock on the door interrupted Val's description of Bryn's typical day. She had already communicated what she knew of Bryn's past life and had described their life together since becoming partners.

McAfee opened the door and took the proffered paper, glanced at it, and handed it to Barnes, who skimmed it rapidly.

Val was bone tired and shifted on her chair, rolling her shoulders and twisting her neck to loosen up the tight muscles, thinking the interview really hadn't been that bad after all. It had to be over soon. Once she had started describing Bryn's passion for photography, Val had gotten caught up in making certain the detective understood what a creative and talented person Bryn Wallace had been. Her face lit up when describing Bryn's skill at capturing reality in a snapped moment. But she was exhausted. If she could go home right now, she might actually be able to sleep for a while.

"It seems the inquest is scheduled for Thursday. As the last known person to see Miss Wallace alive, you'll be called as a witness." Declan stated these facts impersonally, then suddenly changed the subject. "What can you tell me about the argument you two had that night?"

Val momentarily speculated on what he was holding back from his report. As she digested what he had asked, her positive mood evaporated. She felt the color drain from her face. She kept her gaze directed into the cold teacup she held. Stalling for time to think, she raised the cup to her lips, letting a few drops of the stale liquid wet them. It was fruitless to deny it when she'd been the one to tell him they'd argued. Val felt an unpleasant tremor course through her. How could she convince him the argument had been meaningless in the context of their entire relationship? But then, that context, when they'd argued, had not included murder.

"It was a simple disagreement," she answered.

"Miss Wallace's neighbor heard raised voices," Declan insisted.

Val sighed, wondering how to describe their conflict. "We were discussing the time frame for moving in together. When any two people disagree, there are likely to be raised voices. It was all settled when I left."

Declan made a note. "Which one of you was hesitating?"

Nicely done, inspector. "Neither of us. We were committed to each other and to living together. It was merely a timing situation."

"But that still meant one of you wanted to do it sooner than the other," he persisted.

Val thought of changing their points of view to take the onus off her, but that seemed foolish when she didn't have anything to hide. No, better to stick to the truth. Her father had always taught her that, hadn't he? "Bryn was very independent. She insisted on paying her half and just needed a bit more time to save money."

Declan nodded as though he understood completely, but she knew he didn't really understand anything. "All right, you had a simple disagreement. Then what?"

"I don't know, we both calmed down, and she finally explained that she thought she'd be getting a bonus at work but it wasn't coming through. She had definite opinions about keeping things on an even keel as far as money was concerned. I saw her point of view, agreed to a postponement, and left."

"Then why did you return and argue again a few minutes later?"

Val let her puzzlement show. "I'm not sure I know what you mean. I didn't come back until the next morning."

Declan changed tactics again. "Why did you put the stereo on so loudly before you left?"

"I put it on when we were first talking."

The detective seemed about to challenge this but instead reached into his folder and thrust a printed page in front of her. "What is the significance of this song?"

Val looked surprised but read the page. "It's on the same disc I put on the stereo. Is that what you mean?" She looked up in confusion. The detective's grey eyes were steely; the young sergeant avoided her glance.

"This song was playing on repeat for almost five hours after the murder." The detective kept his voice firm and emotionless. "I repeat the question, Miss Rogan. What is the significance of this song to you and the victim?"

Hot tears traveled down her cheeks. "She had a name. Her name was Bryn Wallace. And a song that had significance for us is on this disc, but it's a different song. This disc is the soundtrack from *Notting Hill* about two unlikely people getting together." Val brushed the tears away impatiently with the back of her hand and struggled to compose herself. She would not let him get to her. She must remain in control. The weight of being under suspicion settled heavily around her shoulders.

Sandwiches were brought in as dinnertime approached. Val forced herself to swallow part of hers to fill the noisy void in her stomach before Declan started in again. An hour after that, even he was looking tired. She hoped he was about to let her go, but a knock at the interview room door changed everything.

Again it was McAfee who opened the door and glanced at the paper. He shrugged and handed the missive to his superior, who read it and raised one eyebrow. It must be important to garner such a response, Val thought, but Declan ignored the paper and instead asked her yet again about the last dinner she had shared with Bryn.

"Tell me once more about this dinner. You did the shopping for Bryn, who worked until 5 that day, correct?"

Val nodded, then remembered the tape. "Yes."

"And you arrived at her flat when?"

This was absurd. The detective knew by now the precise times she'd gone to the loo that day. Val felt the demon Temper fighting to be released, contained for the moment in the headache gathering just behind her eyes and spreading to her temples. "We arrived together around 6:30 after meeting at The Blue Virgin." It was a litany she recited well.

Declan nodded as though she were performing for him and knew her lines. "And then?"

"I did as she directed, chopping and slicing and generally helping her to prepare the dinner." Val pictured their shared glass of wine during the preparations, their easy laughter. Her head throbbed.

"Which knives did you use?"

"The ones on a magnetic strip attached to the side of the end cupboard. Look, I can't believe this is helpful to you to go over and over the same ground. I'm trying to cooperate. I even brought you my clothing, as asked." Val's voice rose in frustration and tiredness, her temper rearing its ugly head even as she tried vainly to stomp it down.

"Your clothes will be tested, but I won't have those results for a day or two. This paper," Declan said, tapping the typed sheet of white A4 that rested just out of her reach, "confirms that your fingerprints were found in many areas of the kitchen, with a great concentration on the remaining knives and the rack."

Val answered stridently, "What the hell did you expect? I've told you over and over I used those knives. It would be awfully difficult to chop and slice with my bare fingers." Val couldn't keep the sarcasm out of her voice.

Declan stood and stretched his back, looking down at her with a distinctly annoyed expression.

"Yes, they would be expected to be there." He looked down at her. "It would be most unusual if they weren't there, after your stated activities."

"Then what exactly is your point?" Val asked through clenched teeth.

"If I were a murderer who used a knife and had the presence of mind to take it with me, I would also wipe down the rack. But if *you* were the murderer, there was no need to do that. Indeed, it would be suspicious if it were wiped, so you left your fingerprints to support touching the knives earlier."

Hot anger knotted Val's stomach and seethed through her. She stood up, slapping her hand on the table in front of her and shouted at him. "That has to be the stupidest, most convoluted thinking I've ever heard! You're saying I'm a suspect because something I told you was found to be true? You bloody-minded bluebottle!" She paced back and forth on her side of the table in agitation, not caring if her behavior was exactly what he hoped to provoke.

"A bit of a temper, Miss Rogan?" Declan asked mildly. "DI

Barnes leaving the room at 19:15," he dictated and stalked from the room.

Left alone with the young constable, Val noticed him stealing looks at her as he pretended to study his notebook, which pushed her buttons yet again. "What? You think you're looking at a murderer? Well, if this is what a murderer looks like, then soak it up, baby!" She collapsed sulkily into her chair, not caring if her temper had gotten her into trouble.

Declan re-entered. "DI Barnes returning at 19:25. Miss Rogan, I feel it would be in all of our best interests if you were to spend the night in Her Majesty's holding cell to continue to assist with our inquiries in the morning."

CHAPTER TWENTY-FOUR

*"It seemed to me that I had just gone to bed that Monday night when
I heard the telephone ringing and had to crawl out again."*
— Mary Roberts Rinehart, *Miss Pinkerton*

7:30 PM

Nora pushed food around her plate, noting Simon and Janet
picking at the Indian take-away in the same desultory fashion.
There had been no news from Val, and the walls of Nora's flat
seemed to close in on her tonight.

"She must be exhausted," Janet said. There was no need to
specify who she meant. "I know she didn't get even the few
hours sleep I got last night after I took that pill."

Simon tried to reassure them without much success. "Maybe
they got started later than they thought, and it's just taking a
long time. Or maybe they've taken a dinner break."

Nora gave Simon a brittle smile. He could be irritatingly
cheerful at times, always the optimist, but she shouldn't take her
anxiety out on him. In any case, Janet wouldn't be served by her
jumping down his throat. "I expect that's it. I'll do the dishes,"
she said smartly, gathering up their paper plates. The chicken
masala she usually enjoyed lay heavily on her stomach, and she
felt the desire to go to sleep immediately. What she needed was
to move around and get her oxygen going. "Let's go for a walk,
shall we? It's cooled off, and I'll bring my cell phone."

Janet agreed, closing up paper cartons of leftovers and joining
Nora in the tiny kitchen. She handed the cartons to Nora, who
stowed them in the refrigerator. Janet laid her hand on top of the

one Nora was using to hold the door open.

"I see now why Val admires you. You're a very caring person—you remind me of my Bryn."

Nora smiled at the woman's candor. "That's a lovely compliment. And I think it's very good to talk about Bryn, so please don't hesitate to speak about her. After my father died, my mother and I were determined not to let a day go by for the first few months when we didn't somehow mention him. When I was a little girl, trying to understand my grandmother's death, Dad told me we carry our love for the person in our hearts. Every time we thought of Nana she would live again for that moment. I find it a very healing way to think." Nora's throat tightened with emotion. She closed the refrigerator door.

Janet nodded in understanding. "How did your father die?" she asked.

Nora hesitated. "He drowned in a sailing accident," she replied, leaving out the details burned into her memory. A teenaged Nora had preferred her newest boyfriend's company over her father's invitation to sail that summer night. A sudden squall capsized his tiny boat. In her memory she saw the crowds that had gathered up and down the beach by the time she returned home. Their flashlights were fairy beams, crossing and crisscrossing each other over the surface of the moonlit water. Her mother had tried to remain calm, and then there was a shout, and everyone started running in the same direction. Nora and her mother had stood rooted in the sand.

Nora carried around the firm conviction that if only she had gone with her father, the two of them could somehow have made it back. She had learned to deal with it but had never forgiven herself completely in the past thirteen years. It was the reason she had learned not to discount the potential significance of seemingly unimportant decisions she made every day.

"Sudden death is always worse," Janet commiserated. "One has no time to accept the idea, or to say goodbye." Both women were silent, joined for a moment in understanding the depth of the other's pain.

"Right then, all set for that walk? I've even put my trainers on." Simon filled the doorway with his lanky frame, his hair, badly in need of a trim, falling over his forehead. His smile was infectious, his blue eyes crinkling at the corners. He reminded Nora of a large, affectionate puppy, and she let go of her ghosts to join him.

They were at the door of the flat when Nora's cell phone rang. She dug it out of her skirt pocket in delight. "Val, all set for leftover curry? . . . What? You can't be serious! . . . Yes, of course I will, but . . . let me write it down . . ." Nora had been rummaging around in her bag as she spoke and pulled out her notebook and pen. "Set, go ahead—27875, got it . . . as soon as we hang up. Stay safe."

Nora hung up and started to dial a number, anger pinching her mouth. Her hands shook while trying to punch the buttons as she explained. "Our pal Barnes decided Val needs to stay at the station tonight to help with their inquiries—what crap! I'm to call May Rogan to get their family solicitor to send in someone local."

Simon took the phone from her, consulted her pad, and dialed the number, handing the phone back to her. Janet hovered in obvious distress.

Nora spoke in a rush. "May Rogan? This is Nora Tierney, Val's friend . . . I'm afraid I have some sad news to pass on, and Val really needs your help . . ."

CHAPTER TWENTY-FIVE

*"Every family has relatives they don't talk about and others about
whom they rarely stop talking."*
— Chaim Bermant, *The Patriarch*

8 PM

May Yates Rogan digested the news of Bryn Wallace's death with
mixed feelings. While she felt true repulsion for her step-daughter
Valentine's lifestyle, she acknowledged the importance of the role
Bryn played in Val's life. Her late husband would expect her to
help Val. Lloyd Rogan had loved his first daughter deeply.

May reclined on a brocade sofa, considering what her course
of action should be. She sipped a good port and flipped through
television shows, settling on an *A Touch of Frost* repeat as she
polished her nails. David Jason was perfect in the role of the di-
sheveled, cursing detective, although she would never have him
in her house. She pushed away any thought of acting quickly,
distastefully imagining the gory details of her stepdaughter's
homosexuality. Val could sit in gaol for one night as a sort of
penance, she decided, blowing on her wet manicure.

May had adroitly kept Val at arm's length during her four-
teen-year marriage, but she had truly been in love with Lloyd
Rogan and grateful to him as well. When they met, Lloyd was a
widower of many years who came equipped with a sixteen-year-
old daughter. May's devotion to him had been genuine. Lloyd
had given May stability and an elegant lifestyle just when she
thought she was too old to be taken from the shelf and dusted off. Then had come along a lovely child of their own, sweet

Louisa, and May had created a comfortable home and been a delightful hostess for Lloyd's business dinners, knowing how to present an attractive stage for these events.

In turn, Lloyd had been generous to her and a wonderful father to Louisa, when lulls in his busy law practice permitted it. At his death, May found he had thoughtfully left them financially comfortable with insurance that paid off the mortgage on their townhouse in Holland Square. This was of immense significance and a relief to May. She loved their home and its fine furnishings, the heavy satin drapes and well-polished antiques, the silver, the oil paintings, as much as she loved the neighborhood and its status. Not everyone could claim celebrated author P. D. James as her neighbor. Brief interactions on the street between May and the sprightly, grandmotherly writer were mentally recorded and then repeated at the frequent charity luncheons and teas May attended. Really, the only wrinkle in her marriage had been her inability at times—just at times—to hide her distaste of Valentine and her "friends." A frown crossed her brow at the thought that she would probably be surrounded by them for the next few days.

With grim determination and a sense of selflessness, May decided that if respecting Lloyd's wishes meant staying in Oxford for a few days, she would rise to the occasion. Louisa seemed fond of Val and would expect to be included—fine, as long as Louisa didn't get involved in Val's bohemian lifestyle. It was warm in London and socially sluggish right now. May brightened at the thought of a jaunt to Oxford as a welcome diversion. They would stay at the posh Randolph Hotel, of course, and perhaps shop for clothes for Louisa. She would pack her new navy suit for the funeral, assuming there was to be one, hoping they wouldn't all have to traipse into the wet countryside when a suitable site could be found among the many revered chapels of the University.

May sipped her port. She had no idea if Bryn Wallace even had family to bury her. She had met the young woman only once and had spent the occasion sizing Bryn up and trying hard not to let her imagination run wild. She'd never gotten near any personal conversation during the awkward meeting.

Frost ended, and May determined it was now too late for a solicitor to get Val out until the morning. Smoothing her cool blonde hair, she reached into a gilt table beside her and flipped through her address book, hazel eyes searching for Harvey's number.

Harvey had been Lloyd's partner, and May was confident he would recommend a capable solicitor in Oxford for Val. There was always the chance that if she sounded upset enough he would make all of the calls for her. Her father used to tell her she had rigid thinking and a closed mind, but May never understood that. She admitted to a low tolerance for frustration, allowing her to feel justified taking any actions to make her life easier. Mostly she felt clever. Why feel shame or guilt for exploiting a situation to gain as much as possible for oneself? May knew she was not a deliberately mean person, but she was definitely a self-serving one, possibly egocentric at times. All this was wrapped up in a pleasant-looking package, with the occasional capacity for compassion that kept her from appearing too brittle. She knew this was the quality that had attracted Lloyd. Her ruminations were interrupted when the phone was answered briskly by a deep, masculine voice, and May rapidly shifted gears.

"Harvey?" May's voice trembled slightly and got husky. "I need your help."

CHAPTER TWENTY-SIX

*"Painfully hungry, achingly sleepy, hot, uncomfortable, ignored,
Esteban had given up even crying."*
— Oliver La Farge, *Sparks Fly Upward*

Sunday

8 AM

Val spent a sleepless night in the cell block on the first floor of St. Aldate's Station. Normally detainees were housed in the basement of police stations. The unusual location of the cells at St. Aldate's required a special lift that let out directly into the secure car park on the ground level; this lot was accessed through fifteen-foot-high remote-controlled metal gates.

Val knew this because throughout the long night the gates banged and slammed. Their hollow clanging reverberated in her ears while she listened to the sounds of others being brought into the block to sleep their drugs or alcohol away. The unfamiliar noises, coupled with thoughts of things crawling over her in the dark, kept her awake. She was reminded of the time she'd been in a car accident and had to stay overnight in the hospital. Then, too, she'd been kept awake by the continuous activity cycle of such an institution.

At least she was in a tiny cell by herself, a holding room of sorts. The guard passed by every fifteen minutes, ruining any chance at privacy. The metal slab with a thin mat that passed for a bed had quickly turned to stone beneath her as the hours passed. Val became inured to the mixed scent of disinfectant trying to mask body and urine odors. Her skin was covered in a dusty mix of grime and perspiration she desperately wanted to shower off. Her clothes clung to her in annoying places, the thick denim seams of her jeans rubbing her raw between her slender thighs. She thought her odious breath would kill a mouse.

She'd felt a mixture of embarrassment and shame when she realized she wasn't going to be allowed to go home. The young sergeant had done his superior's bidding, escorting her quickly to a desk so she could make her call and then checking her into the cell. She had used her call to reach Nora, who could tell Janet what had happened and reach May for a solicitor. But no one had showed up to get her out, and she had had too much time during the night to think. The detective had indicated she was not being formally arrested for Bryn's death—not yet—but it was only a matter of his putting together a few loose ends, stringing them into a loop he could tighten around her.

Now that morning had come, Val's nerves were stretched taut; her muscles were painfully stiff, and her back ached. Memories of Bryn caused fresh bouts of pain, alternating with anxious stabs of fear that left her cold and clammy. She was glad her father wasn't around to see her now.

While she had no idea how this horrible story would end, she knew for certain that when it was over, Bryn would still be dead. She would have to face life without her—if she had a life to face at all after Barnes was finished with her. She didn't pray often and had stopped trying to decide whether she believed in a Higher Being or not; the jury was still out on that one. In the last few days she suspected she had chosen to believe mostly when it was convenient or necessary. She closed her golden eyes in exhaustion, slumped against the wall, and silently asked anyone who might be listening for help.

CHAPTER TWENTY-SEVEN

"To have a reason to get up in the morning, it is necessary
to possess a guiding principle."
— Judith Guest, *Ordinary People*

8:15 AM

Nora waited for Simon to finish showering. Last night she'd fallen into an exhausted sleep on the couch, one ear waiting for the ringing phone. Janet had promised to call her the moment Val arrived at the flat, regardless of the hour, but no call had come. As much as May Rogan had promised to help, Nora questioned the woman's dependability.

And then there was Val's temper, which, Nora knew, surfaced when Val was tired or frustrated, and she was certain Val had been both by last night. Even though she had no alternative, Nora felt she had run out on Val yesterday at the station, and the thought disturbed her. She sighed and looked out her back window onto the peaceful garden. It was too early for tenants to disturb the slick grass or inhabit the scattered chairs, but a few butterflies were enjoying the cosmos. A lone grey squirrel ran across the expanse of shimmering lawn, sprinkling the dew. It was clear and sunny, without the intense heat and humidity of the past few days.

Nora had missed the spring bulbs this year due to her stay in the Lake District. They were her contribution to the garden, but she knew she wouldn't see them again if she stayed in Bowness. The next tenant wouldn't know Nora Tierney was the one responsible for the fragrant purple hyacinths, yellow and white daffodils, and blue scilla that poked up in early spring. This, she knew, was silly thinking. She didn't own this house or garden; she was definitely on the verge of becoming mawkish.

Simon whistled in the shower, his unquenchable spirit amazing Nora. She considered herself an optimist, but Simon had a bottomless well of good cheer and patience. That quality had served her well when she was embracing the idea of her pregnancy. There had been times this summer in Bowness when his encouragement and support had let her see herself and her child living happily in that naturally majestic place. This trip was supposed to be a bridge to that future, but instead it had been filled with death and confusion. The garden blurred in her vision as she returned to thoughts of the hellish night Val must have spent in an uncomfortable cell. Nora knew Val must barely be able to believe the events that had crowded in on them in the past three days, for she could hardly believe them herself.

Who could have wanted to murder Bryn Wallace? Despite her moment of doubt, she did not believe it could be Val. Bryn's murder had not been a random act of violence, a car-jacking or purse-snatching gone awry. This was an act of anger and deliberate malevolence, perpetrated by someone Bryn Wallace had let into her apartment late at night without a thought to her own safety.

She thought DI Barnes had been sympathetic when he'd interviewed Janet, but he seemed blind to Val's innocence. Nora's love for Val, coupled with her anger at the person who deliberately took Bryn's life, gave her plenty of motivation to find out who was really to blame for Bryn's death. Simon would just have to stuff it if he didn't approve. She looked for her pad, tucking her hair behind one ear. Nosey parker she might be, but she was damned if she was going to let a murderer go free.

CHAPTER TWENTY-EIGHT

"The relevant questions, as it happened, came by chance."
— Sybille Bedford, *A Compass Error*

8:40 AM

Declan Barnes woke suddenly in his Headington flat, the dream dissipating quickly but leaving its imprint of a carnival scene, bells and whistles clanging noisily, while knives hurled toward a green-eyed girl with red hair who rotated on a huge striped wheel. He heard her saying, "You know she didn't do this," as the man throwing the knives turned to him, but his face became the clock Declan saw as his eyes popped open, and the telephone continued to trill. He snatched up the receiver, clearing his throat and sitting up in the big bed, thinking maybe it was time for him to get a dog. All as he said, "Barnes here."

It was the weekend duty sergeant, letting him know Val Rogan's solicitor was asking to have her released. He was surprised this call hadn't come during the night. He had spent part of the evening wondering why he'd detained Val Rogan in the first place, feeling off his pace in that interview, distinctly annoyed with himself.

"Who's she got? . . . Jeff Nichols, huh? Okay, let her go, just make sure she knows not to leave Oxford proper without letting us know where she's going specifically and why. And tell him she has to appear at the inquest Thursday."

"Got it, Dec. Anything else?"

"Watkins or McAfee in yet?"

"Watkins left to give her a lift home. But McAfee just came in."

"Ask Watkins to call me when he gets back, and put McAfee on." Declan got out of bed, holding the portable phone to his ear while he turned on the shower. He was brushing his teeth when McAfee came on the line.

"Mornin' sir."

Declan spat noisily into the sink. "I've decided to do a few interviews before coming in, probably the boy again, the don, and Wallace's employer, but maybe not in that order. Please get the morning briefing done. The duty sergeant will help. Tell Watkins I want him to cover that art co-operative Rogan runs. They have Sunday hours for the tourists. He's to see what everyone there has to say about Val Rogan and her relationship with the victim. He's just gathering background information on the victim if anyone asks, nothing to get anyone's back up. I'll meet you both back in the incident room this afternoon. Keep in touch if anything surfaces. I'll be at Belcher's."

"Absolutely, sir. No problem."

Declan did not miss the thrill in McAfee's voice at being assigned the morning briefing, even though it would be a formality at this point. As Declan stepped under the hot water, planning his day, he realized he often did his best thinking in the shower and wondered what the department's shrink would make of that.

After calling to set up his first interview, which he decided would be with Miles Belcher, Declan ran a cloth over his black leather wing tips. Today his housekeeper, Mrs. Tinker, would clean his flat, and he must remember to leave her weekly cheque on the console table. Tink had been "doing for him," as she called it, for four years. He would arrive home tonight to clean sheets, the lemony smell of the furniture polish she used with a heavy hand, and his shirts ironed and hanging in the closet. Declan rarely saw her unless he happened to return to his flat during the day. They communicated mainly by notes. Hers were brief and motherly: "Your blue button-down needs replacing, collar too frayed." They were always written in a large loopy hand and signed, "Regards, Mrs. Tink." On occasion he left her little treats he found during the course of his week along with her cheque, as he knew the value of keeping her happy and appreciated her efforts. Then she would be extravagant with her thanks: "Thank you very much for thinking of me in your busy day. Those chocolates were too good for Mr. Tink. I've hidden the box in the broom closet, where he would never look, and will enjoy one a night with my evening cuppa. Regards, Mrs. Tink."

Leaving the flat, taking the stairs down two at a time, Declan left by the back entrance that led to the mews where he garaged the MG. It was a good omen he only had to slam the door once. While he buckled his seat belt, he hoped this smooth start to his day would continue.

Ten minutes after negotiating the morning traffic, he pulled up in front of the The Miles Belcher Studio of Photographic Portraiture. Driving in Oxford was a challenge even for the initiated, one reason so many people rode bicycles or took buses. Parking on the yellow line in front of the shop, he placed his "Police" card on the dash. Then he extricated himself from the low car and checked the road. It had become part of his detective's instinct to be acutely aware of his surroundings, a way to enhance his security and control.

This was an elegant part of Oxford, the trendy shops and boutiques along Little Clarendon Street beckoning locals and tourists with enticing windows. At the far end of the street he could see a cluster of antiques shops. His ex-wife, Anne, had liked to browse there on the rare days they spent together during their brief marriage. Now she was remarried to a headmaster and living happily in Harbury. Declan knew he had not been the best companion and was genuinely happy for her.

This was part of a detective's lot, he mused, as he opened the glass door and started up the lushly carpeted stairway to the first-floor studio. The long hours and uneven routine had always left Anne, and every other woman since then, feeling neglected. When he finally was physically present, they accused him of being someplace else mentally. It was true, he'd come to see—spot on if he were being honest. Every time he was wrapped up in a violent-crime investigation, he felt he was in a race with Evil, what Nietzsche termed "good tortured by its own hunger and thirst." Even when he wasn't out working the case, he was mulling it over in his mind, sorting evidence and supposition. Declan wondered what kind of woman would see his work as something he was bound to do, driven to do, and would accept it as part of him.

Reaching the door with its elaborate gold lettering, Declan decided Miles Belcher must be living up to his successful reputation. A bell tingled as he entered a reception area lined with attractively worn, brown leather love seats. There were a few discreet side tables piled with glossy international fashion magazines. Decorated in the style of a posh Edwardian gentleman's club, the room contained a bubbling fountain nymph in one corner, and in another, a stuffed pheasant under glass on a round, walnut table. Brass eyeballs, dimmed, softly lit the thick burgundy carpeting and ficus trees with shiny leaves. All that was missing was a brandy snifter.

The only bright lights were reserved for mini-spots focused directly on framed blowups of Miles Belcher's favorite clients, scattered across the walls in lieu of hunting prints. University dons in sub fusc mingled with hearty town councilmen and tweeded church vestrymen; groups and wedding parties represented old Oxford families, Anglican prelates, and successful business owners. Declan knew these were deliberate choices to assure the viewer that Miles Belcher took no side in the centuries-old rivalry between town and gown, a stance that netted Belcher the largest possible audience.

By maintaining his connections with the university, Belcher could add graduated students to his province, possibly even a lucrative college contract, while remaining part of the town circle. Declan wondered how long Miles Belcher would feel it was necessary to keep him waiting after he'd called him into the office on a Sunday. He turned at the sound of firm footsteps coming down the hall.

The man who appeared looked Declan up and down as he came into the room, paying particular attention to his shoes. He must have passed inspection, for the man smiled toothily and stuck out his hand in greeting. "Miles Belcher. How can I help you?"

In return, Declan took in the man's gangly limbs and straw-colored hair draped in an artful Warhol imitation over his forehead. He was dressed in black jeans and a white tuxedo shirt, cuffs hanging loosely over his large hands. The front studs rakishly opened to reveal a large piece of amber hanging from a leather thong, resting in the middle of a sparse patch of pale chest hair. It was not a pretty sight.

"DI Declan Barnes, we spoke earlier," he said, flashing his warrant card.

"I thought you might be a walk-in; those good shoes threw me off. The plod is usually not as well shod." Belcher grinned at his pun, then rearranged his features. "You've come about dear Bryn, I know. Oh, the poor girl, one simply cannot believe it!" Belcher used his long arms extravagantly, large flourishes punctuating his speech. "It's so difficult for one to believe she is really gone . . ." His voice fell to a respectful hush.

Declan took in the man's sorrowful face and low voice and wondered irreverently if Belcher's father had been an undertaker. The photographer ushered him down the hall, past studios on either side, into his private office at the end of the corridor. One wall was all windows, providing an expansive view of the grand neoclassical buildings of the Oxford University Press directly across the road. Declan took a chair opposite the photographer, who dropped dramatically into his black leather swivel chair, twisting himself from side to side as he continued to rant.

"She was so alive, so real. A beautiful girl, or . . . was she disfigured?" One hand leapt to cover his open mouth, his eyes wide open in horror, reminding Declan of a bad audition for drama school. Yes, Belcher was exactly that—stereotypical and a raving drama queen.

"I'd prefer not to go into details, Mr. Belcher. I'm sure you understand the necessity for restraint." Declan smiled politely. Restraint was probably not a word Miles Belcher used often. The inspector opened his notebook, getting down to business. "How long did Miss Wallace work for you?"

"I pulled her file when your constable came by with the tragic news." Belcher consulted a purple folder that sat on his desk. "We celebrated her first anniversary with me in April. I brought in pink iced cupcakes from Maison Blanc for tea time." He looked genuinely distressed, his animated face turning down at the corners, eyes reddening in preparation for tears.

"Right then," Declan said briskly. "And what exactly were her duties?"

"She was indispensable, Inspector, a true right-hand man, or should I say, woman?" He grinned again at his own levity, then cleared his throat and continued gravely. "Specifically, she assisted me with photographic layouts and studio lighting and, of course, the more mundane parts of the business: ordering sup-plies, making appointments, delivering proofs." He paused, then added, "She was always very good about bringing me a café au lait in the morning, nothing chichi for me that early."

Declan decided the man was incapable of not centering the conversation on himself. "You were close friends then?" He thought he added no particular emphasis to "friends," but Belcher didn't see it that way.

"We certainly weren't intimate, if that's what you mean," he answered testily.

"But you were privy to some details of her personal life?" De-clan persisted. "As a confidante, I would think, working closely together."

"Well, yes, to a certain extent." Belcher let the statement stay until Declan raised one eyebrow in question, and he elaborated. "I knew her when she modeled, actually shot her twice when she was with Cam Wilson. They looked so good together. Of course, she broke up with him when she came to work with me, and there was no one special I'm aware of until Valentine Rogan."

Now they were getting somewhere. Declan asked, "How would you characterize that relationship?" He waited with pen poised over his notebook.

Belcher took his time, stroking his chin in thought. "I would say they were committed. Bryn certainly seemed smitten. I be-lieve they were talking about moving in together."

"You've met Miss Rogan ?"

"Oh, yes, many times over the past months. I've seen her at The Artists' Co-operative and now and again at art shows. She's very talented in textile work." He leaned across the desk as though they were not alone, as if to impart wisdom he didn't want overheard. "Oxford is really a small town, Inspector, once one gets to know it well."

"Yes, I live in town myself, Mr. Belcher. Can you tell me anything about a bonus Miss Wallace was supposed to get?"

Belcher's face darkened. It was the first time Declan had seen him lost for words.

Finally Belcher's expression cleared. "That would be her Christmas bonus?"

"I don't know, was she up for anything else?" Declan waited to see if Belcher would look him in the eye.

He did. "Not that I'm aware of."

"Was there any change in Miss Wallace's moods or behavior that you noticed over the last few months?"

"Let me see . . ." Belcher hesitated.

Declan had the distinct impression the photographer was deliberating how to answer. There could be an opportunity here if he played it right. What was Belcher hiding?

CHAPTER TWENTY-NINE

*"Della Wetherby tripped up the somewhat imposing steps of her
sister's Commonwealth Avenue home and pressed an energetic
finger against the electric-bell button."*
— Eleanor H. Porter, *Pollyanna Grows Up*

9 AM

Louisa Evelyn Rogan stacked clothing onto her carved four-poster bed, adding her journal to the large pile of books she was taking to Oxford.

She enjoyed spending time with Val, who was super-cool, and looked forward to comforting her. Even though her mother hated it, Louisa loved it when Val called her "Lou," and she'd been trying to convince her friends at school to use the nickname.

Louisa thought she understood how much her sister had cared for Bryn Wallace. Poor Bryn, to die in such an awful way. Murdered, her mother had said, not providing any additional information, but she'd heard her mother tell a friend while talking on the phone that Val's paramour had been stabbed. An online search of the Oxford papers had given few details, other than that the killing had taken place in Bryn's apartment. That didn't stop Louisa from filling them in with her vivid imagination. She wondered if Bryn had felt pain or fear as she faced her killer, picturing different scenarios of her death. Bryn had been one of the most beautiful women Louisa had ever seen in real life, just walking around normal-like and not a bit stuck-up. If she'd been stabbed in her heart, would it have hurt worse or just caused her to die faster? What was her last thought as she lay dying, or did she faint, not knowing she wasn't going to wake up?

The girl shivered and started sorting the clothes into piles, switching her thoughts to the trip to Oxford. This trip would definitely be a chance to get closer to Val. Although Val had been away at school for much of Louisa's early childhood, she remembered shared holidays with long walks in Kensington Gardens with their father. They would search out Peter Pan's statue, where Lloyd Rogan would pretend to swipe one of the bronze rabbits for her. She missed her father, who had called Louisa his Little Princess and Val his Big Princess. It was something she and Val had in common, this sadness over missing their father. Now she would be sad for Val, too, and would share her hurt over Bryn's death. Shared pain lost some of its sting, Louisa decided in a moment of adult clarity. She desperately wanted to show her sister she could be more to her than just a kid.

There was a soft knock on the door, and her mother came in, smiling at the sight of Louisa's industriousness. May Rogan nodded, approving of the neat stacks of clothes, then hesitated, taking in the high pile of books.

"Do you need to take so many books, dear? I don't think we'll be in Oxford for more than a few days."

Louisa's face fell. "But Mum, Val needs us now. We should be there for her—it's the only chance I'll get to be with her before term starts. I can leave half of them home if that helps." She started to sort through the books, rationalizing she could always buy more in Oxford if she ran out. Anything to keep her mother in good spirits about going to see Val.

"Take them, darling, we'll manage them somehow if they're important to you." Louisa recognized her mother's martyr-like smile as she patted Louisa on the shoulder before leaving the room. The girl sighed and turned back to her packing, diminishing the number of books slightly in a compromise, for she was fond of her mum. But she wondered if her mother knew just how foolish she seemed to others at times. Or maybe everyone else didn't see her mother the way she did.

She sat heavily on the bed. Sometimes she felt as if she had some kind of special vision, an intuition about people and their inner feelings. "Hidden agendas" one of the psychology books she'd read had called it, when a person said one thing but really meant something entirely different. Maybe she could use this talent to seek out Bryn Wallace's killer. Then her mother would have to stop treating her like a child, and Val—well, Val would be so grateful, Louisa would have her eternal respect and loving thanks. Louisa wanted more than anything to be accepted for something she had done to help someone else, something un-selfish and totally daring.

She reached for her cell phone, hitting the speed dial for her best friend.

"Diana, guess what? I'm going to Oxford to find a murderer."

Chapter Thirty

"I'm afraid there's been a change of plan,' Mr. Eliot said."
— Susan Minot, *Folly*

9:30 AM

Nora hung up her phone in relief.

"That was Janet," she told Simon. "Val's home. She took a shower, gobbled down some tea and toast, and was asleep before her head hit the pillow. She has to see the solicitor this afternoon. Janet's insisting on going with her. I guess that's a good idea."

"I agree," Simon said, drying his hands on a towel after washing their breakfast mugs. "Val could do with a little mothering right now."

"And Janet will love doing it," Nora added. She'd been sitting at the table after breakfast, jotting notes and trying to recall what Val had mentioned of the other tenants in Bryn's building.

Simon looked around her sitting room. "I guess we could start packing up some of this." He walked down the hallway to the large closet. "You said there's packing material in here?"

Nora was intent on her notes. "Um-hmm—tape, brown paper and flat boxes we can tape up."

"Good idea." Simon returned with a load that he dumped on the floor, startling Nora and causing her to look up. "As long as you don't lift anything heavy." He held up his hand to stifle her outburst. "Enough notes. You take the tape. Where do you want to start?"

Nora reluctantly closed her notebook and cleared the table. "If I put a sticker on anything I'm taking, could you wrap or box it? Especially the artwork; you'll know how to do that better than me. Anything without a sticker I'll store." She pulled a pack of colored stickers from her bag.

"Very organized," Simon said. "I don't suppose you have any of Lottie's shortbread tucked away to speed the process? A man needs to keep his strength up." Simon took down a framed vintage movie poster and a small watercolor Nora had tagged and moved them to the table.

Nora shook her head doubtfully. "I know I need to feed you to get work out of you, Simon, but I don't have any left." Nora's mind turned ideas over quickly. "Lottie's covering Val's hours at the co-op today, and she always has some with her. We could always stop in there on the way to Bryn's building." She knew this would not be seen as enough of a compromise, and she was right.

"And we would go to Magdalen Road because—?" he asked, starting to wrap the poster in bubble wrap.

"Just to poke around." Nora said this lightly and very reasonably, pushing her glasses up her nose.

Simon looked up at her. "You're joking, right?"

Nora's chin came up. "Not at all. I think we should talk to Bryn's neighbors and see if anybody heard anything. And we could try to talk to that boy downstairs who found the body."

Simon set his mouth in a straight line. "I think we should leave the detecting to the police." He attacked the bubble-wrapped package with a roll of packing tape.

"Because they're doing such a bang-up job," Nora retorted, immediately regretting her annoyance with Simon. Why couldn't he see they needed to be proactive and not sit around filling boxes? "You can stay here and pack. I can go to Magdalen Road."

Simon's retort was cut off by the ringing of his cell phone. "Ramsey," he said, listening hard. Nora saw his face light up and thought it must be his sister, Kate. "That's great . . . yes, I have the number. How's Darby? . . . I see . . . I'll let Nora know . . ."

Nora used the loo while Simon filled Kate in about Val's predicament. When Nora returned he was off the phone, looking through his wallet.

"Everything okay?" she asked. "What were you to tell me?"

"Darby misses you, the little traitor. Kate had to take him to her room to sleep. But the news is—aha!" He triumphantly held up a business card. "Nigel Rumley called."

Nora's stomach lurched. Nigel Rumley was the publisher who'd expressed an interest in her book. She and Simon were to meet with him later in the week. If he took on her books, she could relax about finances a bit. "He called on a Sunday?" She held her breath.

"He wasn't certain when we were coming to town, and once Kate told him we were already here, he wanted to up our meeting."

"Oh," Nora breathed out. "I thought you were going to say he decided not to meet us."

"To the contrary. He wants to run up to Scotland to see his daughter in a play and asked if we'd meet him at his office today."

"Great!" Nora said. "We'll go see Rumley. And then we can go straight to Magdalen Road."

CHAPTER THIRTY-ONE

*"It's a fake,' said the Russian leader, staring down at the small
exquisite painting he held in his hands."*
— Jeffrey Archer, *A Matter of Honor*

10 AM

Watkins found The Artists' Co-operative without difficulty,
walking up St. Aldate's and turning right onto High Street after Carfax Tower. Located in the undercroft of the University
Church of St. Mary the Virgin, the downstairs area once had
held the university's centre for administration and ceremonial
events. It drew visitors to climb the one-hundred-and-eighty-
eight-foot spire-topped tower, which dated to the late thirteenth
and early fourteenth centuries. Many would linger to catch their
breath by visiting the co-operative downstairs.

The detective was directed by signs and the sound of the Beatles singing "Lady Madonna" to a huge rectangular room where
rows of stalls ran along each wall and a center cube held twelve
more stalls. Wide walkways separating the rows made browsing
easy, while clerestory windows near ground level let in a surprising amount of light. Each stall established its individuality with
brightly painted walls and gay displays in a visually startling
jumble of color and texture. One stall displayed landscape watercolours and one was hung with the usual still-life bowls of fruit in
oils on canvas, but that was the extent of traditional art forms.

The other stalls held a profusion of handmade items: blue,
green, and yellow pottery, sponged and glazed; loomed shawls in
soft, fluffy wool and angora; wood carvings of small animals and

larger pieces designed as outdoor sculpture; tooled leather belts and soft, capacious backpacks. A display of wind chimes by the door tinkled gently in the breeze from a ceiling fan. Some were fashioned from strips of copper and steel, others from tiny metal tubes that plinked off-rhythm from the Beatles' CD. Julie, his wife, had mentioned she'd bought gifts here last Christmas.

Watkins turned to a checkout desk next to the door, and the rather plump woman who sat behind it, tapping her foot to the insistent beat, looked up, laying aside the tray of colored beads she was sorting, her foot still in motion. The woman wore her black, wiry hair tied away from her face with a calico bandanna, emphasizing the roundness of her features. Her tight denim skirt was decorated with shiny beads sewn in a paisley pattern, and tooled leather slides on her surprisingly small feet, with neatly painted pink toenails, rapped in time to the music. Her red T-shirt was a size too small, hugging her large breasts, drawing the sergeant's eyes to the outline of her prominent nipples.

"Can I help you?" She stood, scrutinizing his warrant card as she sized him up, her foot still snapping to the beat. "I'm Charlotte Weber, and please, no spider jokes, I've heard them all," she said with a giggle, shaking a handful of beads. "Call me Lottie. How can I help you?"

"I understand Valentine Rogan is one of the owners here?" Watkins asked.

"Yes, but she's not here right now." Lottie Weber jiggled the beads she held and swayed to the music. "There's been a death in her family." She stopped moving and raised her hand to her mouth. "Of course, that's why you're here."

"I'm trying to get background information on Miss Rogan and her relationship to the deceased. How many of the people here knew Bryn Wallace?"

"I've met Bryn, of course, since she and Val were partners,

and I'm Val's partner, too, here at the co-op." Lottie scanned the room. "Perhaps Alicia knew her, down there at the end by the silver jewelry, or Justin, with the wire sculptures."

"And those who are not here today?" asked Watkins.

She shook her hand again, the beads making a soft clicking sound against each other. "I'm not certain. She came by sometimes to meet Val after work. Bryn had a show here a few weeks ago, so everyone saw her work but didn't necessarily know her personally." Lottie dropped the beads back into a bowl and reached under the counter. She brought out a red plaid tin, lined with foil and containing shortbread, the buttery sweet smell hitting the air as she opened it. "Any news about who might have killed her?" She offered him a piece, one hand rapping a beat lightly on the counter.

Watson shook his head. "Not yet." The detective dipped into the tin. "Thanks." The buttery confection almost melted in his mouth. "Tell me your impression of Miss Rogan's relationship with Bryn Wallace," Watkins said, chewing on his shortbread.

Lottie picked up a broken corner from a cookie and ate it with gusto. "I'd say Val was totally smitten with Bryn."

"Did you notice any change lately? Any cooling off or negative remarks about Wallace?" he asked. "This is great stuff. Thanks."

"My trademark." Lottie waited while he took another piece then slid the lid back on the tin. "No, I didn't see or hear anything to indicate there were any problems at all." She picked up a pen and tapped on the counter with it. "I need to get back to work if we're done here."

McAfee finished reading over the HOLMES report, then walked into the hall, where he ran into Watkins just coming back into the station. McAfee asked the sergeant about the co-operative and Lottie Weber.

"Bit of a Mexican jumping bean, that one, but an excellent baker," Watkins said.

He described speaking with Justin and Alicia; neither artist had more than a nodding acquaintance with Bryn Wallace, although both spoke highly of her photographs. Watkins showed McAfee the listing he'd come away with of the other members of the co-op. "I'll go divvy up the work between the team members."

McAfee nodded. DI Barnes was still out, and McAfee felt at odds. He stopped at the computer desk and leafed through the printouts of background checks that had been compiled. Detective work was often such a grind, routine interviews conducted for any bit of information, slim leads followed up in hopes of a break in the case. Nothing much here, he thought, flipping through and scanning pages. Then a name and an alias caught his eye, and he smiled in satisfaction. Today's gold star was staring him right in the face.

Chapter Thirty-Two

"Unlike most people, Konrad Vost had a personality that was clearly defined: above all he was precise in what he did and correct in what he said."
—John Hawkes, *The Passion Artist*

Declan drove away from the Belcher studio through the narrow, twisting streets of Oxford, scores of one-way roads causing him to take a circuitous route to reach Exeter College. It would have been faster to walk. More than once he had to slow down for yet another American tourist stepping off the curb after looking the wrong way. But he supposed if he were to travel to America he would have the same difficulty, so perhaps he should be more generous in his criticism.

Thinking of America brought Nora Tierney to mind. He speculated about what she had done this morning. Probably commiserated with her friend Val Rogan about the horrid inspector who'd kept her in gaol overnight.

He liked her spirit and the way she wasn't letting her pregnancy keep her on the sidelines, that spark of what he had to call impudence, which he usually found annoying. He'd watched her fight to stay in control and remain courteous at her interview. It distracted him to think of her. Why *was* he thinking of her? It wasn't natural to be attracted to a pregnant woman, yet Nora Tierney seemed to be popping up in his thoughts often lately. How could that be? It was tough enough for him to have any kind of female relationship at all. This was ridiculous. He must really be losing it.

Parking on Turl Street, using his dash card again, Declan stepped over the high sill of Exeter's thick door and back into another era. The cobblestone walk was uneven, the rounded stones high and easy to stumble over, their edges smoothed from foot traffic since rebuilding in Victorian times. He knew from years of living in town that a portion of the undercroft of the college's great dining hall dated from 1314. Declan wondered if Nora Tierney would enjoy a personal tour of Exeter, and if she did, if she would leave her illustrator behind. He doubted Ramsey was the father of her child, although there was something proprietary in the way the artist treated Nora. Yet during her interview, Nora had described their relationship as "friends working collaboratively."

He stopped at the porter's desk to show his warrant card and was directed across the quad to Ted Wheeler's rooms. Wheeler had been less than thrilled when Declan had phoned to arrange to see him, dismay evident in his voice. Declan had said little to the don, only that he needed help with questions regarding a recent incident. On the phone, the don had not asked "what incident," which had been surprising in itself, as though he had expected Declan's call. Wheeler had immediately suggested meeting at the college, and Declan didn't know whether this was because he didn't want Declan to see his home or because he wanted to keep knowledge of the interview from his wife. At this point, it didn't matter; he could insist on seeing Wheeler's home down the road if it proved necessary. Better to take his measure of the man first.

The trees in the Fellows' Garden were filled out and leafy, the flowers blowsy with late blooms as Declan made his way around the sacrosanct piece of green lawn, admiring the dominant chapel as he turned into the correct stairwell. Even at the height of summer, students clustered around the quad, taking special classes or tutoring.

In answer to Declan's knock, Ted Wheeler called out, "Come in." The don looked up from his desk, standing when he saw the detective. At first Declan was reminded of a lean monk out of his robes, for Ted's hair was thinning in a pattern reminiscent of a Franciscan. The habit the don had of clasping his hands in front of him added to the impression.

Wheeler looked at Declan's warrant card as the detective introduced himself, the don's bald pate glowing red with embarrassment which spread to the tips of his ears. Interesting, Declan thought, although from experience he knew many people disliked the police on general principle, a form of discrimination he'd found persisted across class lines.

"Might we sit down, sir?" Declan pointed to chairs set in front of Wheeler's large desk.

"Of course, where are my manners," the man said, almost physically gathering his wits about him. "Please, do sit, and tell me how I can help you."

"I understand you knew Bronwyn Wallace?" Declan dove right in.

There was no mistaking the redness now, though Wheeler's face took on a sorrowful look. "The poor girl. I read about her killing in the papers yesterday. A true tragedy."

"How did you become acquainted with Miss Wallace?"

Wheeler's answer was quick. "My daughter married recently, and we used the Belcher studio. I'm certain you already know Miss Wallace was his assistant."

"I see. So your relationship was purely professional?" He smiled pleasantly, trying to put the man at ease.

"Of course. I'm probably old enough to be her father." Wheeler laughed nervously, overlooking his use of the present tense.

Declan nodded again, looking around the large room, which was filled with bookshelves crowded in a pleasing jumble. The large window overlooked a huge chestnut tree that let in dappled light. "Did she ever visit you here?"

There was a perceptible pause before Wheeler answered. "She delivered the wedding proofs here. Later she picked up our selections, because the college is closer to the studio than our home, and I was the last one to make my choices. I still hadn't decided when she came the second time. Very difficult when the photographs were all remarkably well done."

A good answer, Declan thought, but instinct and perception told him there was an unspoken layer. "Can you tell me if you wrote this note and what it's about?" He reached into his jacket's inner pocket and withdrew a copy of the note Wheeler had sent, handing it over for the man's inspection.

For a moment he thought the don was going to faint as the blood rapidly left his face, and he swayed forward. Wheeler stared stupidly at the paper in his hand, making a great effort to compose himself. "Yes, I wrote the note. I was extraordinarily pleased with the work and Miss Wallace's service. It's a simple thank you." His voice quavered.

Declan took the copy back. "Rather effusive, no? Even for an English lecturer?"

He consulted the note and read out loud: ". . . I owe you much more than mere words serve . . . acutely aware of that . . . will make certain to never let you forget me." Declan raised one eyebrow in question and sat back to wait for an explanation. A heavy silence pervaded the room.

A range of emotions flitted across Wheeler's face, mainly fear. He wiped his sweaty palms on his pants leg and swallowed dryly. His eyes took on a hunted look, his nostrils dilating.

Declan kept quiet. Most people had difficulty with long stretches of silence.

Finally Wheeler drew in a deep breath, and Declan saw his

look change to one of resignation. "I repeat, it is a thank you note for someone I held in deep regard." His voice held a note of firmness.

Declan didn't buy it. He slapped the paper against his thigh. "You know, I got the impression when I read this that you might be trying to blackmail Miss Wallace."

"Blackmail? How absurd!" Although his voice was indignant, Wheeler clenched his hands together to steady them. "About what?"

Declan leaned closer to the man. "You tell me, Professor."

A brisk knock at the door was followed by a young man entering the room, a bulging backpack over his shoulder. He stopped sheepishly when he saw the two men. "Sorry, sir. The porter said you were in today, and I've a question about my essay." He turned to go.

"No need to leave. I was just going." Declan rose, tucking the note back into his pocket. "Thank you for your help, Dr. Wheeler." Declan's gaze locked on Wheeler's eyes as he handed over his card. "You can reach me at this number if you think of anything else—important. I assume you know not to leave Oxford."

CHAPTER THIRTY-THREE

"You will rejoice to hear that no disaster has accompanied the commencement of an enterprise which you have regarded with such evil forebodings."
— Mary Wollstonecraft Shelley, *Frankenstein*

2 PM

Simon and Nora sat at Val's table, sharing a late lunch Janet had prepared while Val slept. Simon had thought he'd have to peel Nora off the ceiling from excitement after their interview with Nigel Rumley. When Janet called them about a late lunch Nora agreed to come home for a good meal and to see Val. At least for the moment she seemed to have forgotten her determination to visit Magdalen Road.

Now Simon wolfed down Janet's steaming shepherd's pie. Janet watched him eat with a bemused expression on her face, apparently thankful one person enjoyed her cooking. Val had arrived at the table last and pushed around the mashed potatoes, meat, and peas. Nora, too, had hardly touched her food; she seemed too giddy to eat.

"We should be thankful for some fine things that happened today," Janet said, putting her fork down. "Val is home, and Nora and Simon have gotten wonderful news. Tell us, Nora."

Simon enjoyed seeing the sparkle in Nora's eyes, the slight flush on her cheeks as she recounted their meeting with Rumley. From his stately antiques-filled office to his argyle socks, Nigel Rumley was a character in his own right. But the interview had turned out better than either of them had expected.

"I admit I was gob smacked, as you Brits say. We signed a note for a proposed contract that will be reviewed by Simon's lawyer and his agent, but it's for three books in the series, with first rights to expand in the future. We have a date for the next one to be submitted, and the galley proofs for the first should come in six weeks. I'll have both of those things done and out of the way before the baby is due."

Val grabbed her friend's hand. "That's just wonderful, Nora. You must be so pleased. And Simon, good for you, too."

"By the time we get back to Ramsey Lodge, it should be ready for signing," he said.

"And with the advance arriving soon after that, I'll only have to dip into my savings occasionally," Nora added. "But how are you feeling, Val?"

Simon saw concern etched across Nora's face.

"Honestly, I feel like I'm moving through a vat of pudding. It's all so unreal, like I'm living someone else's life," Val said.

Janet patted Val's hand. "It will be all right."

Simon helped himself to another biscuit. "This is delicious, Janet. Thank you for including us."

"I've always enjoyed cooking," Janet said, "and Bryn was an excellent helper and student. She was more adventurous than I am, though. I tend to stick to old favorites."

Val put her fork down. "If you'll excuse me, I need to get ready to see my favorite solicitor," she said with an attempt at wryness.

Simon finished his biscuit, watching Nora. He saw deep worry knitting her brow. Janet noticed it, too.

"We'll get it sorted out, somehow," Janet said, rising as Val left the room.

"Let me, Janet," Simon said, helping her stack dishes. "I almost feel guilty enjoying that meal."

"No need to, Simon. Bryn would understand, and Lord knows

I do. The living need to go right on living. It's what my dad told me like a litany after Bryn was born and we were alone."

Simon was struck by the phrasing of Janet's statement. It almost sounded as if Janet knew Bryn's father had died. He saw by Nora's pensive expression that she had also tucked away this thought. She nodded in agreement and said: "And we need to conserve all of our energy right now."

Simon groaned. "Don't tell me you still want to go to Magdalen Road? What for?"

He watched Janet pick up on an impending argument. She ducked into the kitchen with a pile of plates. "I'll just load the dishwasher."

"What for? For finding Bryn's murderer, that's what for," Nora said without missing a beat. "I've told you I won't leave Val's future to police who are already convinced she's guilty."

Simon knew he had to tread carefully. Nora was fiercely independent, and he had no real claim to her movements. Still, he could not stop himself from commenting. "And you think speaking to Bryn's neighbors is somehow going to make a difference?"

"It might." She got up from the table. "And I mean to make a start. If it bothers you so much, I'll get permission first from the police."

She bounced up to help Janet as Simon sat back in exasperation. There would be no stopping Nora now. She would make her lists, and ponder, and rationalize. All he could do was try to stop her before she got in over her head.

CHAPTER THIRTY-FOUR

"It may take time to get over an obsession, even after the roots have been pulled out."
— Booth Tarkington, *Rumbin Galleries*

2:15 PM

The Covered Market was pure retail theatre, Declan thought, with its mix of boutiques, food stores, high-end jewellery, and low-end T-shirts. It was mid-afternoon, and his stomach growled. He ducked into a small cafe and ordered coffee and a pastie.

Fortified, he walked past the showy flower stalls, pausing to watch the butcher hang a whole deer to age alongside the rabbits and steer already swaying from the rafters. Declan walked carefully on the uneven cobbles to his destination, The Cake Shop, pushing through the crowds window-shopping or munching on warm cookies. He knew the shop closed early on Sunday but judged he had plenty of time left to push and nudge Davey Haskitt a bit.

Pausing outside the bakery's large, glass window, he looked past the display of an Alpine village executed in fondant and icing to watch a woman seated on a tall stool. She was fashioning miniature people in lederhosen to populate the re-created town.

Inside he asked the woman behind the counter for Davey Haskitt and was told he was on a break. When he showed his warrant card, the woman raised the pass-through and directed him out back. The baking area, now dormant but coated with a fine dusting of flour, was rich with the sweet mixed odors of sugar, vanilla, and cinnamon. Declan ducked around a tower of empty cooling racks and found Davey lounging on an upturned crate, smoke from his cigarette curling away into the fresh air.

"Nice day, Davey."

The lad turned at his name, surprise in his expression fading when he recognized the detective. "What'd you want then?" he asked, rubbing the stump of his smoke out against the crate and throwing it into the road.

Not quite as pleased today, Declan noted. Davey seemed older, more insolent, and the detective thought that perhaps his being this close to a murder had toughened him. But then being close to a murder affected everyone in its circle in some way. "You had enough of being the center of attention?" he asked.

The boy shrugged. "Still dead, isn't she? No matter what . . ." He cut himself off and looked away, suddenly interested in the state of his fingernails, scraping flour out from underneath a few.

"No matter what . . ." reverberated in Declan's memory, and he recalled where he had heard that phrase before. It was from the lyrics of the song playing in Bryn Wallace's flat when her body was discovered. "No matter what, Davey?" he prompted.

"Nothin'," Davey said sullenly, closing the topic.

Declan sat down on a crate next to him after carefully dusting it off. "Davey, it must have been a rough experience to find Miss Wallace's body like that, especially since she was a good friend of yours."

The boy nodded but kept his head down.

"Is there anything new you've thought of now that a few days have gone by? Anything at all that you might have forgotten to tell me?" Declan loosened the knot in his tie. "It could be important in finding her killer."

The boy shook his head and lit another cigarette, blowing smoke out of one side of his mouth, keeping his silence.

Declan stood, fighting down annoyance. "Why do I get the feeling you're holding back, Davey?"

Davey wouldn't meet his eyes. He inhaled deeply one last time, chucking the butt into the street. He rose and checked his watch, muttering: "Have to help close up shop now."

He pushed past Declan into the bakery, leaving the detective wondering what Davey Haskitt was hiding and what buttons he could push to find out.

When he got back to the office, McAfee was hanging about. "Any joy?" Declan asked.

"Nothing of interest at the co-op according to Watkins, but I've found something I think you'll find interesting." He followed Declan into his office, pointing to a few sheets of paper placed front and center on his crowded desk.

"The background checks, sir. Nothing at all on Allen Wesley, the deceased's father; he seems to have fallen off the face of the earth. But Cameron Wilson, her former lover? It seems his real name is Melvin Wilmot, and under that name, he has form for cocaine possession." McAfee straightened up.

"Interesting. Very much so, McAfee." Declan tapped the sheets on his desk while he thought. "Get this Wilmot's mug shot and one of the pervert, Tommy Clay, and have the team take them around Magdalen Road for idents. We're looking to see if they were hanging around Wallace's flat. But be careful," he warned the young man. "Clay will be the first one to cry 'unfair' if we're not scrupulous. Don't mention either one of their backgrounds."

"Yessir, understood." McAfee whirled around, almost running over the female constable who had started to enter the office. "Oh, sorry, Debs," he said.

The woman shook her head at his retreating back. "In a hurry to make Inspector, that one," she said with a smile. "You have a visitor, sir. A Miss Tierney asked if you had a few moments."

Declan raised his eyebrow and put on a face of annoyance. "Have her wait ten minutes while I look over this pile on those handbag snatchings and then bring her up. Thanks." He made himself sort dutifully through his pile, pondering what was behind this visit from Nora Tierney.

CHAPTER THIRTY-FIVE

"Pardon me for interrupting whatever it is that you might better be doing just now. Having got this far, I hope to grow on you."
— Paul West, *Tenement of Clay*

4 PM

Nora waited patiently downstairs to be summoned up to Declan Barnes' office. She'd implored Simon to drop her off and then run to pick up more packing supplies. Nora felt she would make more headway with DI Barnes without Simon's presence.

She knew she hadn't fooled Simon, but he was gentleman enough to play along with her charade after she announced her intention of visiting the inspector. She'd pointed out she was safe enough inside a police station. Simon must be mellowing, she thought, because he'd finally caved and hadn't nagged her about coming here.

Nora had her notebook out and was perusing her jottings when a shadow fell across it, and she looked up to see Declan Barnes standing over her. She stood quickly, thrusting her hand out in greeting.

"Thank you for agreeing to see me, Inspector Barnes," she said.

He led her upstairs. When they reached his office, he pointed out a chair and settled behind his desk. "Have you some information for me?"

She smiled. "I don't have information as such. Actually, I was hoping to get information from you." She pushed her glasses up her nose.

Declan leaned back in his chair, linking his hands behind

his head. "That seems highly irregular, Miss . . . Nora. Usually I'm on the receiving end in an investigation. It's best to leave the policing to us, and I'm not really allowed to discuss the case with an outsider."

Nora thought he sounded almost apologetic and pressed her point. "Oh, but I'm hardly an outsider. Val Rogan is my friend. I know her better than you, after all, and let's be honest here; we both know she's in your sights for killing Bryn Wallace. I'm out to prove she didn't, and that will leave you to find the real murderer." She thought she'd explained this very well and sat back in satisfaction.

"So you're not prepared to find the murderer for me?"

It took Nora a moment to realize he was teasing her. "If you insist, I'd be delighted. Hire me on," she parried, looking him straight in the eye.

There was a moment of silence as they appraised each other. "What are you interested in knowing, Nora?" Declan finally asked.

She flipped a few pages over in her notebook. "I've made a list of people I can interview, starting with Bryn's employer, her neighbor, and the boy who found Bryn's body."

Declan sat up in consternation. "Perhaps you missed me telling you to leave the detective work to the professionals."

Nora's chin rose a few inches. "Perhaps you missed me telling *you* I'm going to prove my friend didn't commit this awful murder."

"If you meddle in my case," Declan said through clenched teeth, "I can have you arrested for interfering with an investigation."

Nora had the feeling Declan Barnes was poised to ask her to leave, but before he could, she flashed him her broad smile and, raising one eyebrow in mock imitation of his habit, held both wrists out for future handcuffing.

A swift knock at the door was followed by Debs entering. "Sorry, sir, but DS Watkins has a suspect in those computer thefts and needs a word."

Nora hastily dropped her arms.

Declan stood. "Tell him I'm on my way. Miss Tierney, I'm sorry but we've been having a rash of laptop thefts in town, and I must be involved in this." He escorted her to the door and down the stairs without further commentary.

Nora noted he had lapsed back to "Miss Tierney" and wondered what he would have said or done after her flippancy if they hadn't been interrupted. She turned at the doorway before stepping outside.

"Thank you for your time. I promise to try very hard not to get in your way, Inspector Barnes."

He looked at her, and his annoyance seemed to waver. "I'm merely concerned for your safety, Miss Tierney," he said. He turned on his heel and left, but not before she saw the concern written on his face.

Chapter Thirty-Six

*"Wilson sat up very straight. This was the first letter she had
ever written in her life and she wished it to be correct in
every particular."*
— Margaret Forster, *Lady's Maid*

4:45 PM

At home at last after a long day, Cameron Wilson scrubbed his
makeup off and stepped into the shower. He'd been shooting
on location outdoors, in the gardens of Kelmscott Manor. Normally it was closed on Sundays, but most of the staff had showed
up anyway, ostensibly to clean. They and everyone else who had
heard about the shoot had turned up in droves to watch him and
two female models drape themselves dramatically over William
Morris' simple grave in the churchyard.

While the light and weather had been perfect for photography, the shoot had required long and tedious staging sessions,
dressing changes in a cramped caravan, and poor-quality food
from the caterer. The other models were new to him. Cam chatted them both up, but with little result. In the end, the hours
dragged on in truly tiresome fashion. The only redeeming note,
he decided, was that the clothes hung well on him, as usual.

As Cam, hungry and tired, toweled dry in his own comfortable bathroom he thought again about some other way of earn-
ing income before his looks faded. He'd toyed with the idea of
managing other models, but the prospect of scheduling and ex-
ecuting contracts for others held little appeal. Those headaches
he was happy to leave to his own manager.

He threw his towel in the hamper and slipped into comfortable sweats, padding barefoot into the sleek kitchen, modeled after Jamie Oliver's television set right down to the aqua Smeg fridge. Pouring himself a cold glass of mineral water, he added a squeeze of lime and dropped the wedge in, turning to admire his contemporary flat and its glossy furnishings.

This was the fruit of his labors, a visible reminder of his long days sweating under layers of out-of-season clothing and heavy makeup. Each item in his home had been chosen with care. Even the Picasso print, "The Maids of Honor," had been meticulously framed and hung as a focal point over the fireplace, not because Cam was fascinated by the many paintings within a painting or because it was based on a Velazquez of the same title, but because the bright scarlet and butter-yellow colors in the work exactly matched the throw pillows scattered on his sofa and chairs.

Mixed textures of leather and suede, glass, and chrome gave him a perpetually cool feeling, providing the right background against which to display himself. Flopping down on his leather sofa with today's mail, he sorted out the junk and circulars. That left three bills, a postcard from a friend hiking in Kendall, and a small plain white envelope without a return address.

Cam took a long swallow from his glass and put it down on the floor beside him, debating the merits of going out for dinner or having a takeaway at home in front of the telly. Curious, he tore open the anonymous white envelope. Inside was a stiff, white card, an invitation to yet another party, he assumed. But as he pulled the note out and read it, his stomach plummeted, taking his hunger with it.

He sat up quickly, knocking over his water glass, sweat breaking out on his freshly scrubbed brow. The water ran unheeded under the sofa, the lime wedge stranded on the pile of his handwoven Kirman.

A square of poster board had been crudely cut to fit the envelope. It was printed in pencil, all capitals, and simply read:

I SAW YOU THERE. MEET INNER BOOKSHOP MONDAY 11 AM.

Cam stared at the missive for a few long seconds, his mind racing over the implications of the message. With a shudder, he dropped the card as though it burned his hand.

Declan lounged on his worn leather sofa, a well-thumbed address book open on the walnut coffee table alongside a Styrofoam container from his Indian takeaway. He brushed naan crumbs off his chest and dialed a London colleague, muting the television.

"Willis—Barnes here—how goes it at the Met? . . . Not interrupting anything important, am I? . . . Listen, I'm coming up blank on a background check in a murder case, and I wondered if you could suss it out on your end. Might be too old to be on computer, but worth a shot . . . Excellent, my shout next time I'm down there . . . A punter who lived for a while in Chipping Norton, disappeared about twenty-eight years ago. Name of Allen Wesley."

He hung up, settling full-length on the couch, his feet propped up on one arm, his head on the other. Taking the remote off mute, he scanned the evening's offerings, settling on a Monty Python rerun for background noise. Pulling his briefcase up on his lap, Declan took out the files on Bryn Wallace, re-reading the interviews from the residents of Magdalen Road. He had the tantalizing feeling an important sliver of information was just out of his grasp.

CHAPTER THIRTY-SEVEN

"Mary sometimes heard people say: 'I can't bear to be alone.'
She could never understand this."
— Monica Dickens, *Mariana*

5:15 PM

Nora hit Althea Isaacs' buzzer in the lobby, waiting for a response on the intercom. Nora had gone down to Davey Haskitt's flat first but had come upstairs when there'd been no answer to her knock.

"Yes?"

"Miss Isaacs, I'm Nora Tierney, a friend of Bryn Wallace and Val Rogan's. Would it be possible to speak with you for a minute?" There was a long pause. "I'm not a reporter, just a friend."

Finally the woman said, "For a minute, then," and hit the release. When Nora reached her flat, Althea was waiting at her door, the chain on.

Through the gap, Nora glimpsed Althea's dark, smooth skin, complemented by her pale yellow pantsuit. "Thank you very much for agreeing to speak with me." Without her dark glasses, Althea's blindness was immediately apparent.

"What did you want to see me about?"

Nora decided to be direct. "Val Rogan is my best friend, and she's under suspicion of murdering Bryn. I'm trying to prove she didn't." She didn't mention she would also like to find the killer. "Could I ask you a few questions about what you heard that night?"

Another moment of hesitation, and then the woman seemed

to make up her mind. "You'd better come inside."

Althea took off the chain and led Nora to the same sofa Declan Barnes had occupied, sitting down herself after feeling the rim of her chair with the back of her leg. "You're American, Miss Tierney, from somewhere in New England?"

"Please, call me Nora. And you're right, I grew up in Connecticut."

Althea Isaacs smiled. "Brilliant! It's a hobby of mine, puzzling out people's accents. I'm Althea. Now that's all sorted, what can I do to help you? I met Valentine a few times and thought her quite pleasant. Oh! I do hope I'm not the reason she's under suspicion."

"Why would you think that?" Nora asked.

"Because I told Inspector Barnes I heard arguing from Bryn's flat the night she died. And it sounded like two women."

Nora chewed her lip. No wonder Declan Barnes had rushed to judgment on Val. He had a witness to the argument between Val and Bryn.

"Can you tell me exactly what you heard?"

"Of course. There was a brief period of music, and then two voices, both female, rose in argument."

"How long did they argue?" Nora asked, jotting in her notebook.

"About ten minutes. Then it was quiet. I thought all was well until about a quarter to 12 when it started again, only this time the voices were much quieter. I'm afraid I went into my bedroom at that point, where I couldn't hear it, and went to sleep. I told the inspector I wear earplugs to sleep due to the traffic noise because my hearing is so sensitive."

Nora considered what Althea said. "Val admits she and Bryn had a mild dispute but insists it was patched up when she left."

"I'm sorry, I don't know quite what to say, except I distinctly heard two arguments."

Nora thought hard. "The first argument, which we presume to be the one Val took part in, began around what time?"

"11:15." Althea was firm. "I'm certain about the time because my mantel clock chimes every fifteen minutes."

"All right," Nora said. "Bryn and Val argue from that point, for about ten minutes you said?"

Althea nodded. "If even that long."

"Which brings us to 11:25. Then there was a second argument about quarter to 12?" Nora leaned forward in her chair. "Althea, that's twenty minutes later. Could it have been someone different the second time?"

Althea nodded quickly. "I did tell the inspector I thought I'd heard the flat door open and close after the first argument ended. Maybe it was your friend leaving?"

"Did you hear it open to admit someone else?" Nora asked. Had she found a major clue Declan Barnes had missed?

"No, I didn't," the blind woman admitted reluctantly. "Let me think a moment."

Nora held her pen poised in midair as Althea concentrated. She couldn't wait to tell Simon what she'd unearthed.

"Wait!" Althea said. "I forgot I went to the loo just before the second argument—I might have missed a second visitor to the door."

"Not a visitor, Althea," Nora said grimly. "A murderer."

Chapter Thirty-Eight

"If a man insisted always on being serious and never allowed himself
a bit of fun and relaxation, he would go mad or become unstable
without knowing it."
— Herodotus, *The Histories*

7 PM

Nora drove the Celica on its last voyage, Simon beside her. To-morrow she would turn it in for the Volvo that Simon had examined and pronounced sound. She was keyed up and hungry.

Val rode in the back with Janet. She had insisted they take Janet out for drinks and dinner. "We can toast Nora and Simon's book news, too. Jeff Nichols told me to get a good meal and a good night's sleep, and I plan to do both." She checked her watch. "Louisa and May should be getting the train right about now."

"What's your plan with them?" Nora asked.

Val made a face. "I suppose I'll have to thank May for getting me Jeff Nichols. I told her I'd bring Janet to the Randolph tomorrow to meet her. Will you two come along?" Val caught Nora's eye in the rearview mirror. "Please don't make me inflict her on poor Janet alone. Even Lou isn't enough to counter that experience!"

Nora laughed. "What do you say, Simon—up for a bit of running interference for Val?" She made a left at the foot of the Banbury Road and turned into the driveway of The Old Vicarage.

"Absolutely," Simon said. "I've always wanted to play footie."

Nora parked, and they entered a honeyed stone building with mullioned windows, draped lavishly with wisteria.

"It's lovely here, Val," Janet said as they were led to their table in a corner. The dark fuchsia walls were covered with oil paintings. Soft lighting reflected the patina of the antique furnishings, while discreet classical music in the background enhanced the polished feel. "Much more elegant than my parsonage," Janet declared, scanning the tall menu placed before her. "I haven't been here since my teens. I came for a bank holiday with a group of friends, and we had high tea, right outside in that lovely garden, gossiping and laughing over the silliest things. It seems like a lifetime ago," she said wistfully.

"After enduring meeting May, Janet's going to go home until the inquest," Val explained. "There are neighbors and friends she wants to see. I admit I'm curious to see how May will behave."

"In terms of you?" Simon asked.

Val nodded. "If she's not properly sorry for me, or for Janet, I may well earn the murderous title Barnes wants to give me."

"Shh, don't say that." Janet patted Val's hand.

May Rogan always had such a hard time with Val, Nora thought, and worried about her influence on Louisa. Could May have decided to eliminate Bryn Wallace? Val's stepmother certainly had the financial resources to hire someone to do her dirty work if she were enraged enough. Of course, killing Bryn wouldn't have changed Val's lifestyle. There would always be someone lining up to fall in love with her golden-eyed friend. But would May have been perceptive enough to consider that? Aloud, Nora asked, "How was your meeting with Nichols, Val?"

"Dad's old partner came through for me. I feel better after talking with him, like someone believes me."

"We all do, Val," Nora said, feeling a twinge of guilt for the few moments she'd doubted her friend.

"He also told her to get back to normal activities until this is all settled," Janet added, patting Val's arm.

"That's why I'm going to stop at the co-op after running Janet home tomorrow. There might have been developments in the approvals for the new building, and it isn't fair to leave Lottie shouldering everything alone."

"Lottie's a dear," Nora said.

"She's such a dependable colleague. I owe her so much. I should have invited her along tonight." Val's eyes darkened. "I feel so guilty having a nice dinner out with Bryn gone."

The table's occupants were still until Janet spoke up. "Val, if Bryn were here she would be coaching you from the sidelines, urging you to live while you have the chance."

Simon pushed his empty dessert plate away. "That was an incredible meal."

The quartet lingered over coffee and pudding. As Janet excused herself to find the ladies' room, the others turned once again to the events that brought them all together.

"I still have no idea who would have wanted Bryn to die," Val confessed. "I think I'm numb to the reality of it."

Nora immediately pulled out her notebook and heard Simon unsuccessfully stifle a sigh. "I'm determined to look into this, Val," Nora said. "You can't go on being a suspect while the real murderer walks around enjoying life. I've made a list of a few people I'm going to talk to over the next few days—"

Val interrupted her. "Nora, that could be dangerous, and I've already lost someone I love."

"Thank you, Valentine," Simon threw in.

Nora was prepared for their opposition. "I'm not going to be in any peril just talking to a few people. I can't believe you and Janet don't want to know what really happened." She pushed her glasses up her nose. "Besides, I've already started. I went to see

Declan Barnes today and then to see Bryn's neighbor Althea Is-sacs. Barnes wouldn't talk about the case with me, of course, but I got Althea to remember a very important point."

Nora related her theory that a late visitor came to Bryn's flat after Val went home. "I know it's upsetting, but Val, it's a real possibility."

Simon had remained silent during her explanation, but Val's excitement showed. "Finally, a reasonable explanation that doesn't include me."

"Can you think of anyone who might have visited Bryn that late?" Nora asked. "Was she expecting someone?"

"Not at all," Val said.

Janet rejoined the table. "Janet, I was just going to ask Val to think back to her time at the station last night," Nora said. "Val, did you hear anything relevant, any names that caught your in-terest or seemed connected?"

Val considered this as Janet spoke up. "Nora, I appreciate what you want to do, especially for Val, but you have a child on the way. None of us wants you to endanger yourself."

"I promise I'll be safe, Janet. I've almost convinced Simon to come with me for more interviews tomorrow—" Nora broke off and gave Simon an appealing look.

"My friend, you can be so manipulative at times," Val said.

Simon cleared his throat as he composed a reply. "I think I'm the last one who'd want to see Nora in jeopardy. But I've also seen that once she becomes determined about something she won't let it go." He kept going even as Nora put her hands on her hips. "So when I can be available to accompany her, I will. Against my better judgment, I might add."

"You couldn't resist adding that last bit, could you?" Nora teased.

"Absolutely not," he answered.

"Last night I did hear something," Val said. "I didn't think much of it at the time, but now that I'm concentrating—"

Nora leaned in, pen poised over a clean page. "Yes, go on."

"Don't get your knickers in a twist, Yankee. But when I was being escorted to my overnight accommodations, the officer at the desk congratulated that young sergeant for going through Bryn's mail."

"I would think that's standard, Val," Simon said.

"I know, but at the time I was chucked off at the invasion to her privacy. Anyway, he asked, 'Any joy, McAfee?' And my escort answered along the lines of: 'Not till we've checked out Wilson and Wheeler for a connection.' And then he shut up like he shouldn't have said that in front of me, but I think he meant Cam Wilson."

Even Janet sounded interested. "Bryn dated him. I met him once and wasn't impressed. She talked about him for a few months, and then he suddenly wasn't in the picture, and she said they weren't seeing each other anymore."

Nora scribbled away.

"Bryn told me she outgrew him. They weren't together when we met," Val said. "But that last night she did mention he'd been calling and bothering her."

"But who's Wheeler?" Simon asked.

Val answered him. "I've no bloody idea."

Chapter Thirty-Nine

"The Assistant Commissioner was careful of his appearance before meeting men younger than himself."
— Graham Greene, *It's a Battlefield*

Monday

10 AM

Louisa Rogan brushed her silky blonde hair until it shone. On the train up last evening, as her mother read the latest issue of *Vogue*, Louisa had given thought to what she would say to Janet Wallace when they were introduced. "I'm sorry your daughter was murdered" wasn't the way to go. And she wanted to be sincere. She knew the pain of sudden loss from when her father had died. *Our* father, Louisa corrected herself, smiling at the thought that Lloyd Rogan connected her by blood to Val.

She wished she could see Val more. As a small child she hadn't been aware of the distance her mother put between them. When she got older and more observant, Louisa recognized her mother treated Val almost as she treated Louisa's school friends—polite and pleasant, but rather patronizing and aloof. Her mother was prone to let cutting remarks fly at Val, too, remarks Louisa noticed never occurred when their father was home.

The girl sighed. May did have moments of true caring, especially toward Louisa, and even enlightenment at times, but that was not her typical reaction to situations. Her mother was who she was, and Louisa was old enough to wish for change but not expect it.

She sat back and wondered how she could possibly get away

from her mother today to begin her search to help Val. She rummaged through her train case, debating whether to let her hair hang loose or to wear a black velvet Alice band. Louisa opted for the headband, hoping it would prevent her mother from constantly whispering "brush that hair off your face" during the meal.

In the second of the two elegant connected rooms, May Rogan finished the last touches to her makeup before slipping into her clothes. She had decided a demure cream silk blouse with gold buttons worn with black dress slacks would be appropriate and flattering. May always presumed she would be inspected by the people around her, at the center of the spotlight as it were. She leaned close to the mirror, examining her facial lines and the slight sag of middle age that appeared despite her best efforts to control it with facials, toning exercises, and cream imported from Switzerland.

Stepping back to check her full-length reflection, May was satisfied, flicking a stray hair into place. She stifled a yawn while changing purses to match her outfit. May didn't care for an early start to her day, but she did like to control events when possible. She had told Val to bring Janet Rogan to the Randolph for their meeting. Afternoon tea might be considered too twee, so a late breakfast it would be, the better to leave the rest of her day free for the shops. She would still impress Janet with the hotel's pedigree. Celebrities stayed there when in town, and several films had shot scenes at the hotel as well. Upon arriving in her suite last night, May had decided it must be the same one Sir Anthony Hopkins had occupied during the filming of *Shadowlands*.

The only drawback was the noise of the traffic, but everything had its faults, and a small flaw in presentation was unlikely to faze Janet Wallace. She pictured Bryn's mother as a country-woman in tweeds and wellies, working as she did at a bed and breakfast in the Cotwolds in a truly distasteful job, having to change all those strangers' sheets and to clean up after them. Not for her, a life of picking up after others. One of the perks of being financially stable was a biweekly housekeeper, "for the heavy work," she confided to friends. She hoped the poor bereaved woman would appreciate being treated to the splendor of this revered hotel, although May was quick to remind herself that once the funeral was over, it was doubtful she would ever see Janet Wallace again.

An hour later, Cam Wilson was outwardly composed, knowing he looked put together. Inwardly he quaked as he browsed the shelves at The Inner Bookshop. What was he supposed to do? What if he were recognized? How would he know the person who had sent him the note? And more importantly, did he really want to?

He knew his actions on the night in question had put him in jeopardy. He had no choice but to see what this person wanted. If it was blackmail, and Cam shuddered at the thought, he might be trapped for life. He checked his watch for the fourth time and tapped his foot impatiently, just as a voice whispered in his ear.

"Fancy a coffee?"

Cam whirled around to see a short, muscled man with clipped brown hair and a neatly pressed shirt. The man was smiling at him, but Cam hesitated, unsure if this was his assignation or the current trendy opening line for a pickup.

The young man saw his uncertainty; his brown eyes narrowing, he stepped into the void with a determined air, taking Cam by the elbow and guiding him toward an empty booth. "No need to worry, Mr. Wilson, just a spot of conversation between two level-headed men over a coffee, and if you're very lucky, a croissant as well."

CHAPTER FORTY

*"There is no way, unless you have unusual self-control, of disguising
the expression on your face when you first meet a dwarf."*
— C. J. Koch, *The Year of Living Dangerously*

10:30 AM

Nora watched the introductions carefully, her eye on May Rogan. Was it at all possible May was the kind of woman who could hire a hit man? She certainly showed no affection toward Val, and Val reciprocated her coldness. May was polite toward Janet but couldn't quite control the aura of aristocracy she projected like an expensive perfume. By contrast, her daughter Louisa was still as charming and frank as Nora remembered. The girl hugged Val and Nora and shook hands with Simon. When introduced to Janet, she said, "I'm very sorry for your loss," in a manner that was dignified and graceful beyond her years.

After they read the menus and placed their orders, Nora started the conversation off with a story about the smooth pickup of the Volvo that morning. Then she sat back and admired the colleges' coats of arms displayed around the room. The old-world air of the Randolph reminded her of New York's Plaza Hotel, she thought, as Val stiffly thanked her stepmother for procuring Jeff Nichols.

"Darling, I simply called Harvey and he took care of everything," May said imperiously.

"Harvey was our father's partner," Val explained. "I'm actually surprised you and Lou came up." She smiled pointedly at her sister. "But I'm always happy to see you."

Louisa's eyes lit up while May struggled visibly to control her displeasure. As their coffee and tea arrived, an awkward silence fell across the table. Val caught Nora's eye and rolled hers in May's direction. The message was clear: "Help me get some conversation going with the bitch."

"I thought you'd be interested to know I've turned up something useful in the search for Bryn's killer, May." Nora described her conversation with Althea Isaacs while she watched May's reaction. "So there's a chance of finding the real killer now."

May sniffed, but Val was excited. "I'm so fortunate to have such caring friends, aren't I?"

"Absolutely." Louisa grinned at her sister. "Where did Bryn live?"

"On Magdalen Road, in a lovely Georgian building," Val explained.

May sipped her tea politely. Nora wondered just how far Val's stepmother would be prepared to go to upset Val. She showed little reaction to the news that Val might be off the hook, but then, maybe implicating Val had never been a part of May's plan. Val had color in her face for the first time since Bryn's murder, her excitement at the possibility of finding the murderer palpable.

"Today I'm going to talk to Miles Belcher, Bryn's boss, to see if he can add anything we don't already know," Nora added.

May nodded, but it was obvious she thought little of Nora's amateur efforts. She certainly showed no sign of worry that Nora might trace the murder back to her. Maybe May was no more than what she appeared to be—a selfish stepmother who had difficulty accepting her stepdaughter.

Their meals were served, toast and scones buttered, omelets eaten. Conversation again ground to a halt. Val lightly kicked Nora under the table.

"So—," Nora said, mentally casting around for another topic.

"Mae is a lovely name. And you have the same blonde hair as Mae West. I always enjoyed her old movies, she just exuded sensuousness." Nora realized this was not the compliment she intended when May answered frostily.

"It's M-A-Y, as in merry month of—. My birthday is the first of May." May unsuccessfully tried to withhold a glare of annoyance.

"Of course," Nora agreed, biting her lip to keep from grimacing. Was there no way to figure out this exasperating woman? This was going to be a challenging brunch. She couldn't even look at Val or Simon.

"When will the funeral be?" May asked, to everyone's surprise.

"You're going to the funeral?" Val asked. "I'm not sure I want you there."

Lou's face fell, but it was obvious Val's remark was directed at May.

Nora held her breath, fearing the argument she had been dreading all morning was about to break out between Val and May. But to her surprise, May answered graciously. "Of course. We both came here to support you."

How clever of May to roll Lou into that one, Nora saw. Now Val was stuck with her. Beside Val, Janet squirmed in her seat. And how awful for her, Nora thought. It's *her* daughter's funeral they're arguing over. But Janet rose to the occasion.

"I'm planning the funeral for Sunday, May, and of course you and Louisa are invited to say goodbye to Bryn." Janet deftly closed the subject. "Those paintings are by Sir Osbert Lancaster, May," Janet said. "They were commissioned for Meerbohm's *Zuleika Dobson*, quite the satire on Oxford life. Are you familiar with it?"

"Oh, you've been here before then?" May frowned, clearly surprised the country woman would know the city's most elite hotel.

"My, yes," Janet smiled. "My parents would babysit so my

friends and I could have an occasional weekend in Oxford. Tony Blair used to drink here when he was at Oxford, you know, but we'd come to the bar hoping for a glimpse of Colin Dexter, or at least John Thaw if he was in town playing Morse. We all thought he was terribly sexy. Thaw, I mean, not Tony Blair. It's too early now, but if you stop by later there will be a delightful trio playing at lunch—a trumpet, saxophone, and of all things, a banjo." Janet smiled prettily.

Nora watched May force a thin smile on her face. Janet had bested May Rogan. Val caught Nora's eye this time, each woman thinking this brunch was definitely not going according to May Rogan's plan.

Nora pointed to a poster indicating that parking facilities at the Randolph would cease the following month. "We got here just in time," she said, pointing out the poster to Simon, as they waited for the Volvo to be brought around. "What did you think of Val's family?" In the bright sunlight Simon's blue eyes looked bleached out. Nora watched him formulate his answer.

"I thought Louisa was very charming and her mother . . . less so," he finished diplomatically. "Now that the ice is broken, I wonder how that crew will get on in there."

"It was interesting that May with a Y invited Val and Janet up to her rooms to discuss the funeral plans," Nora said. "Although I don't know if that was to be helpful or nosey."

"Are you kidding?" Simon snorted. "That was all about showing off her suite at the Randolph and trying to influence the arrangements to her liking."

"I guess so, but it didn't seem to affect Janet at all."

"That's because Janet sees right through someone like May.

She won't have a problem fending off May's suggestions—it is *her* daughter being buried, after all. I think she went along to protect Val a bit longer."

"Simon. . ." Nora hesitated. "Do you think there's any chance May Rogan is behind all this?"

"You mean Bryn's murder?"

Nora nodded.

Simon took a moment, considering the suggestion. "It hardly seems likely she would insist on attending Bryn's funeral if that were the case."

"I guess so." Nora sighed. Would she ever find the real murderer and clear Val? She looked at Simon as the Volvo wagon in a color the dealer called Nautic Blue was brought around. "You can be quite perceptive at times, Mr. Ramsey."

"Call it ESP," he said as he helped her into the car. As they pulled out after a break in the traffic, he put one hand up to his forehead. "For instance, right now I can feel you're deciding the quickest route to Miles Belcher's studio.

CHAPTER FORTY-ONE

"We didn't know we were an odd family."
— Caroline Bridgwood, *Trespasses*

1:30 PM

May Rogan massaged her left temple as she waited for Louisa to emerge from the dressing room. In the stylish High Street shop across from Carfax Tower, the boutique boasted a full-length beadboard door that provided the customer with complete privacy—no small cubicle with a skimpy, worn drape here. A three-way mirror inside ensured that shoppers would not have to emerge clothed in an unsuitable garment.

The morning had not gone at all according to May's plans; thoughts of that horrid brunch filled her with distaste. The headache that ensued would only be assuaged by a bout of heavy shopping.

First Val had shown up with her friend, the writer Nora Tierney, who'd gotten herself pregnant without a husband—and who had the gall to compare May to Mae West. For some reason the woman kept eyeing her suspiciously throughout the brunch, although May had no idea why. She hardly knew her! Nora had a rather good-looking young man in tow, Simon Something, who was supposed to be an artist of some fame. May knew Val certainly wasn't interested in the chap, but she wondered if he was the father of Nora's child. He hadn't reacted to any of May's usual flirting gambits, so she decided that he, too, was probably gay.

Then to her immense disappointment, Janet Wallace was not quite the country tweedie she had been expecting, and her plans for displaying her own superiority had fizzled.

Things had not improved when she had invited Val and Janet up to her suite to discuss funeral plans. May had suggested a regal High Mass at one of the college's distinguished chapels. Janet made it quite clear "her Bronwyn" was having a simple funeral service in the parish church she'd attended as a child and would be buried alongside her grandparents in the family plot in Chipping Norton.

"Of course, if Val would like to have a memorial service for Bryn here in town, I would love to attend," Janet had said.

May pictured her elegant leather heels sinking into the mud in some quaint country churchyard. Hence, the shopping trip for different shoes for her to wear with her navy suit, perhaps a broader court heel in soft navy kidskin. But first, a dress for Louisa.

May's mood improved rapidly when Louisa appeared, pirouetting in front of her. The lilac silk dress she wore complemented her blonde hair nicely, and May decided the color would enhance her own navy suit as they stood side by side in the graveyard.

"Lovely, darling," she told her daughter with true affection. "Wrap it up!" May's favorite three-word mantra eased part of her headache away.

Louisa loved the scroop of the silk as it rustled about her but was even more pleased that the very first dress she'd tried on would suffice so well, giving her the opportunity to initiate her own plans earlier than she'd hoped. She almost hugged herself with delight as she changed back into her jeans, plotting her opening gambit.

"Now that's done, we can tour the Bodleian Library," Louisa enthused as she rejoined her mother. "And then the Sheldonian Theatre, and a long lovely browse through Blackwell Bookshop . . ."

"More books?" her mother sighed, rubbing her temples. "But shouldn't we look for shoes to go with your dress? And I need shoes, too; my heels will simply not do for the countryside muck."

"I brought my black pumps with the chunky heel; they're almost new, Mum. And besides, it will give us more time for the Bodleian tour. The line is probably quite long by now." Louisa smiled happily as her mother's eyes glazed over. She threw in the clincher. "Unless," she said as though the thought had just occurred to her, "you wanted to look for those shoes and maybe a new scarf for your suit. I could go on and do the tour and the bookshop alone and meet up with you for tea." As her mother hesitated, the shopkeeper unwittingly came to Lou's aid.

"We've just gotten a new scarf shipment from America, Ralph Lauren, and of course we have the Harvey Nichols . . ."

Like waving a carrot in front of a donkey, Louisa thought, feeling a glimmer of shame at manipulating her mother so easily. She closed with the finishing touch. "I know! Let's meet at that place Janet was describing, The Old Parsonage, say around 4?" Janet had described the building and her meal in glowing detail and mentioned how much she looked forward to going there for High Tea at some future date.

May seemed ready to leap at the chance to outdo Janet Wallace when a wave of motherly protection swept over her. "Are you certain it's safe for you to go traipsing all over Oxford by yourself?" May asked doubtfully.

At this perceived slight to her town, the shopkeeper drew herself up to her full height. "All of those destinations are close to each other, and it really is a safe town, Madam."

Louisa was already pulling the strap of her small backpack over one shoulder. "Right then. See you at The Old Parsonage at 4 for tea. And don't worry about me; I've got the map Val gave me." She fluttered the pocket-sized folding street map Val had given her at breakfast. Waving goodbye, the girl added: "Have fun shopping."

Lou paused on the street to consult her map, looking back to be certain her mother's attention was engaged. May and the shop-keeper already had their heads bent over trays holding scarves in a rainbow of colors. The girl slipped away, swallowed up by the throngs on the street. Instead of heading through town toward the Bodleian, she consulted her map and turned left down the High Street, toward the Plain and Magdalen Road.

Davey Haskitt walked back from work, slowly making his way down the Cowley Road. He barely registering the slim blonde girl he was forced to walk around as she studied a map. Christ, he hated going back home without the presence of Bryn Wallace. Living in the basement literally under her had given him a sense of being protected by the enfolding wings of an angel. Those dark brown eyes had looked at him with compassion. Her smile could keep him happy for days. Despite what that detective thought, he hadn't stalked her. He'd never shown up at the studio where she worked, for instance. Just watching her movements coming and going kept his inner turmoil at peace, as though he were a part of her days. He missed her more than he thought possible—it was a physical ache—and he was seri-ously considering looking for another bedsit. But then his tenu-ous connection to Bryn would be broken entirely.

Beside, the high cost of renting and low availability of hous-ing in the area made a move difficult. If he left the neighbor-hood, he might not be able to walk to work, either. But surely other people moved house all the time.

Reaching Magdalen Road, he crossed over toward The Inner

Bookshop and picked up a copy of the local rental listings from the free paper stand out front. Waiting to cross the road, he recognized the short, annoyed man he'd jostled on the sidewalk last week. Short Man stood in front of the shop, talking earnestly to a tall, floppy-haired man who had his back to Davey. He couldn't hear their low conversation as he crossed the road, but it seemed the taller man was trying to get away from the shorter one, without much success.

Even as he let himself into his flat, Davey kept an eye on the two men. The taller man broke away and tried to cross the street, only to be stopped smartly at the kerb by a speeding Mini flashing by, followed by three noisy motorcyclists. Probably a lover's quarrel, he thought, wondering why people were so fond of public displays of anger. Davey would never share his pain and discomfort with the entire world, he decided, as he entered his cool, darkened warren and threw himself across the bed.

CHAPTER FORTY-TWO

*"Once, I remember, in an entirely different world, I interviewed
that East Coast photographer who made a good living taking pictures of people as they jumped."*
— Carolyn See, *Golden Days*

3:30 PM

On the way to their interview with Miles Belcher, Simon was
surprised when Nora insisted they stop at an art store.

"You deserve this," she said. "You've been so patient with me.
And you can pick up supplies to take back to Bowness."

He couldn't argue with that. Anything to delay this interview.
He would enjoy the foray into the real art world for a change,
instead of ordering from a distance over the Internet.

The art shop was redolent with scents of oil paints and tur-
pentine. The aisles were crowded with racks of pigments in
different forms, thick pallets of paper in different weights and
thicknesses, and instruction books from beginner to advanced.
Stretched canvases in different sizes hung from racks on the
walls, their emptiness a blatant demand for bold strokes of color.
Running his hand over the soft brushes, he examined a few and
added them to his basket. "It's so different being able to touch
and see these things," he explained to Nora. "And these," he
said, pointing to a gaudy display of paints, "their hues often get
distorted on the Web. Unless you know the name of a pigment
you've used before, they can be difficult to order."

Nora asked him about the different kinds of media he used
and seemed to soak up his discourse. He pointed out tubes of

oils and fat oil sticks, watercolours, bright logs of pastels, and muted charcoals. "I can see your fingers aching to try some of this stuff out," she said.

Maybe he could convince Nora to take a nap, and he could slip away to make some sketches. He mulled this plan over as he loaded the carton into the back of the wagon. Nora sat in the passenger seat, flipping pages in her notebook. Not yet then, he thought, sliding in beside her.

"Where to now, Sherlock?"

She looked at him fondly. "You really are being gracious today."

"I have to admit the idea of someone else coming to see Bryn after Val had gone home seems to be the only explanation. But don't you think you should impress Inspector Barnes with this notion?"

Nora's answer was ready. "It's only supposition at this point; we don't have any real evidence. And he's already had his shot at Althea Isaacs. Too bad if he didn't listen carefully."

"Oh, so now you're in competition with a detective inspector who does this for a living?" Simon watched the blush creep over her face.

"Absolutely not," she declared. "I just think he can't see the forest for the trees, and I'm very good at picking up twigs. We need to see Bryn's boss next."

Simon started up the Volvo. Nora put her hand on his arm to keep him from putting the car into gear. The touch of her fingers on his bare forearm startled him, causing a ripple of desire to spread through him. He shifted in his seat; he was like a bloody teenager around her.

"Wait a minute," she said. "We won't get parking on Little Clarendon. Let's leave the car here and walk."

"Sounds good to me, but how do you know he'll talk to us?" Simon asked as he opened the door.

"I can't imagine how he could not," Nora serenely answered, leaving Simon with the impression she had a line for Miles Belcher he had yet to hear.

Simon and Nora waited at the bottom of the stairs to the Miles Belcher Studio as a string of men and women, chatting happily, left the office, crimson choir robes thrown over their arms. Following Nora up the staircase, Simon said, "I still don't see how you plan to get this man to talk to you."

She stopped mid-staircase and turned to look at him, which brought them almost level in height. She had never looked lovelier. The air and the brief walk had brought rosiness to her cheeks; her green eyes flickered with amusement in the dim hallway. "Want to bet on that?" she asked archly, putting one hand on her hip.

"I never bet with Yankees, especially ones who obviously have the deck stacked against me. Get going." He shooed her up the last few stairs, and they entered the world of Miles Belcher.

Belcher was easy to spot after Val's description of him. As Simon and Nora looked around the clubby interior, Miles noted their presence with the flicker of a glance, not acknowledging them at first, talking to a younger man as he handed over an order slip. "Show them my card and tell them to put that order on my account—oh, and bring me back a double latte like a good lad, would you? Cinnamon on top."

The young man rolled his eyes at Simon, and as he slipped away, Miles Belcher finally gave them his attention. "Yes, and how can we be of help today?" He smirked and looked at Nora's belly. "A family portrait, perhaps?"

Belcher would say the one thing destined to get Nora annoyed. The man's smile was like treacle. Simon hoped they needn't stay here too long. Nora was not put off easily and gave him a charming smile, holding her hand out in introduction. "My name is Nora Tierney, Mr. Belcher, and this is my assistant, Simon. I'm an editor at *People and Places* magazine. My superior, Harold Jenkins, is interested in doing an article on you and your studio and the tragedy you have recently suffered."

Simon couldn't believe Nora was pretending to still work at the magazine and had added him so smoothly to her deception. He still didn't see how this would get Belcher's confidence. Apparently Belcher didn't, either.

"I don't think murder should be capitalized on, do you, Miss, er—" He swept his bangs off his forehead.

"Tierney," Nora answered, continuing as though Belcher had indicated interest. "We're interested in the angle of a popular and important Oxford photographer, someone who has the ear of academics and influential people, losing his assistant at the height of his busy career, and how the sudden loss affects him."

Oh, Nora was smart, Simon thought, going right to Belcher's vanity by slanting the imagined article his way, making him the center of attention. Belcher hesitated; Nora quickly continued. "Mr. Jenkins is an Exeter alumnus, and he noticed in the paper they're looking for a new college photographer. He's been an admirer of yours for some time and is hoping you get that contract. This article might help that happen."

Belcher was hooked. "Jenkins is an Exeter grad?"

Nora nodded solemnly. "Yes, and he's always complaining about the stiff portraits the college produces for its board. 'Now if we only had Miles Belcher doing the shots, they would be perfect,' he has commented on more than one occasion. I'm not going to lie to you, Mr. Belcher—" she said glibly.

No, not too much. Simon studied a stuffed pheasant Belcher kept under glass as Nora continued to fabricate.

"—it would be a great coup for the magazine to have an exclusive article from you on this tragedy, and it would also give you wonderful exposure." She pushed her glasses up her nose. "And then at his next college meeting, Mr. Jenkins would be certain to use his, well, I hesitate to use the word 'influence,' but a well-placed whisper in the right ear—you know how these things are done in academic circles."

That should settle it, Simon decided, watching Belcher's head nod as Nora spoke, wondering if Old Jenks ever went to any college meetings, Exeter included.

"Of course, under those circumstances I might reconsider," Belcher said with a smarmy smile. "Would you like to come into my office?"

Would she ever, Simon thought, shaking his head at Nora as they trooped down the hallway single file. In front of him, Nora reached a hand behind her back and waggled her fingers at him.

Nora was relieved Miles Belcher had responded to her story and not bothered to verify her credentials. After complimenting Miles on the view from his office, she handed Simon her notebook, who accepted it with a sly look. He refused her offer of a pen and withdrew a pencil from his pocket, making a show of preparing to take notes. Nora had the feeling there would be several sketches of either Miles or the stunning scene outside his window when they were ready to take their leave.

It was simpler than she thought to get the man to talk about himself, but then Nora had found most people were easy tellers of their own tales once you showed an interest. The photographer was at the top of this list, preening like a spread peacock as he described what he termed "the early years."

They finally reached the present. She wanted to address Bryn's tragic death and how he had been left scrambling for a new assistant. This was where Nora knew she had to be delicate in her questioning, maintaining the focus on Miles while trying to elicit the information she sought, even as the interview wound down.

"And how have you managed to handle your huge success alone without becoming stressed out?" she asked. "Have you ever considered taking in a partner?"

Horror ran across Miles' face at the contemplation of sharing. "I really couldn't do that, could I, and still maintain the high level I'm known for? I decided to take on an assistant I could mentor instead, and Bryn Wallace was doing an excellent job at that."

Because she was bright, interested, and you could order her around while paying her peanuts, you old toady, Nora thought. Aloud she said: "Miss Wallace was eager to learn at the foot of the master, as it were?"

"Oh, quite. She really wanted to see how I worked. A great asset and help to me, I admit. And the clients liked Bryn, so that was all right."

Nora put on her most poignant expression. "It must have come as a terrible shock to hear she had been murdered."

Miles raised one hand in front of his face as if to block out the thought, shaking his head dramatically and dropping the hand. "It was a nightmare," he said hoarsely.

Nora believed the woman's death had moved him. She leaned in closer to the desk, adopting a more intimate tone. "I imagine you've had to be interviewed by the murder squad and everything," she said sympathetically, ignoring Simon's small cough.

"They call themselves violent crimes units these days and all sorts of titles, but it still boils down to sniffing around people's lives. Very distasteful work I should think." Miles pursed his lips in a moue of distaste.

"It couldn't have been a pleasant experience," Nora commiserated. "Have they any idea who might have wanted to kill her?" She heard a scratching sound and knew that Simon, carefully positioned so Miles couldn't see his pad, was happily sketching.

Miles leaned in, too. "My dear, it sounds as if they are totally in a fog. It was apparently a bright criminal, no clues left at the scene from what I've heard. Although there must be suspects from her life to consider."

"Who would that be, Mr. Belcher?" Nora asked.

He shook one finger at her as though he could not reveal his information.

"Strictly off the record, of course," Nora hastened to add. Simon obediently stopped moving his pencil momentarily.

"Oh, I couldn't implicate someone. That would be heinous. But she did live in a rather suspect part of town, all sorts of loonies around her. She had a string of former boyfriends I would think would have to be considered as well. But that's for the police to divine, not me." He sat back primly.

"Of course not," Nora soothed, then turned her head to one side as though a new thought had come to her. "I remember hearing she used to date that model, Cameron Wilson. He has a reputation as a ladies' man, doesn't he?" This was a shot in the dark for Nora, but it had the desired effect.

"Cam Wilson?" Miles dismissed him with a snort. "Good-looking lad. Fancies himself a bit too much, but most of them do. The only reputation he's getting is for a snow lover, and it's going to cost him his career if he isn't careful." He closed one nostril with his index finger and sniffed delicately up the other.

Cocaine, Nora understood, nodding sagely. "Was Bryn Wallace also a . . . partaker?"

"Not that I ever saw, but who knows what goes on behind closed doors?" Miles' shrug was wide open to suggestion. He really is a smarmy bastard, Nora decided, trying to figure out a way she could introduce a new name without raising his suspicions. Miles consulted his watch and Nora knew her time was short.

"This is definitely off the record," she cautioned Simon, who closed the notebook promptly. "Actually, Mr. Belcher, I heard a rumor Bryn was seeing a married man, someone named Wheeler?"

Miles' face blanched, but he recovered quickly, sitting upright in his chair. "That's absurd! Dr. Wheeler is a highly respected don at Exeter—I shot his daughter's wedding recently. I can't imagine how that rumor got started. Where did you hear that?"

"Just a name dropped, nothing important I'm sure. You know how people love to gossip." Nora stood hastily before his questions continued. "We really can't take up more of your time. You've been so generous. I appreciate the interview. Very stimulating."

As Miles Belcher escorted them back to the door he asked, "Any idea when the article will come out?"

Nora shooed Simon down the stairs and paused at the top, ready to follow. "I never know with these editors, but you'll be the first to know."

CHAPTER FORTY-THREE

"It wasn't the kind of homicide they're used to seeing around here."
—James Howard Kunstler, *Blood Solstice*

3:45 PM

Declan sat in his office doing paperwork, the mountain of memos and reports slowly decreasing as the afternoon wore on.

"How's it going?" Watkins stuck his head in the door.

"Bits and pieces, still. How's Janet Wallace?"

"Back in Chippy until the inquest, courtesy of Val Rogan. She'll call if she needs me before then." Watkins eased himself into the room. "Still shopping the Rogan woman for it?"

Declan pointed to the chair, glad for the interruption. "I keep running things around in my head. It stands to reason she's the killer—she was there at the right time, she argued with the victim, the weapon was close at hand—"

"Motive, means and opportunity," Watkins ticked off. "Not be the first time a lover's quarrel got out of hand. What about Wheeler? See him for a lover?"

Declan sighed. "I looked at that scenario, too. But the man was old enough to be her father, as he succinctly pointed out himself. And there's that hint of blackmail." His desk phone rang, and as he answered it, Declan had the irrational hope it was the duty sergeant telling him Nora Tierney had come to report on her findings.

"Barnes . . . Hallo, McNish, thanks for getting back to me . . . nothing, huh? He was a teenaged father who abruptly left his new baby and girlfriend twenty-eight years ago and hasn't been seen since . . . The Sally Army? I hadn't thought of that. Thanks, I'll give it a shot."

Declan replaced the phone. "That was a London contact. There's no trace of an Allen Wesley ever being in London. No work record, no addresses, and no government papers filed, not even a parking ticket."

"Guess Wesley didn't take off for the bright lights of the big city," Watkins said.

The seed of a hunch took germination in Declan's mind but he had to think carefully about how to follow it up. He was putting on his jacket to talk to Ted Wheeler with Watkins along for weight, when DS McAfee whirled into the room at a run.

"Sir! There's been another murder on Magdalen Road!"

As he pulled up to Magdalen Road once again, Declan was disturbed there was a second murder to worry about before he'd even solved the first. He hoped the two weren't connected, and the site was incidental. Then he saw Davey Haskitt sitting in a squad car at the edge of a small gathering and gave up such hopes. Surely this was no coincidence.

A cordon of constables kept the general public well away from the basement entrance to Bryn Wallace's building, while several patrol cars formed a ring at each end of the street awaiting the crime van's arrival. Declan hurried with Watkins and McAfee over to the uniform waiting for them.

"Looked at first like it could be an accident, a fall, but there's two witnesses say it was deliberate. A teen got hysterical, and the lad from the other day called us." The policeman gestured to the car where Davey Haskitt waited, then led them along a walkway between the building and the neighboring one, avoiding the area in front of the building that still needed to be searched for forensic evidence.

By leaning over the side railing they could make out a crumpled body lying at grotesque angles at the bottom of the stairs, right on Davey Haskitt's faded "Welcome" mat. A puddle of dark blood had spread out from beneath the skull; the open eyes stared blankly up at them in shocked surprise.

The officer consulted his notes. "A young teen, name of Louisa Rogan, London address, saw him being pushed over the railing."

Declan groaned at the name "Rogan" as he looked down at the twisted body. It was McAfee who breathed out the conclusion he'd reached.

"Lor, it's the pedo, Tommy Clay!"

Declan sent McAfee to tighten the perimeter of the scene, then approached the patrol car where Davey Haskitt sat, sprawled against the back of the seat, watching events unfold before him. Although his face was sallow, he displayed an air of indifference tinged with annoyance. "Involved in yet another murder, Davey?" Declan asked, leaning on the door.

"Bloody wanker fell right past my window, fer Christ's sake, then that girl wouldn't stop screamin'. Given me one hell of a headache, I tell ya."

Declan nodded briskly. "The sergeant told me you phoned it in."

"Had to, didn' I? Needed help with the bloody child, thought she was gonna vomit all over me." He pointed to the other squad car, where Declan had sent Watkins to see to Louisa, who was seated inside.

"What exactly did you see? It could be very important, so take your time."

"No time ta take. I was lyin' on my divan, come in from work a second afore, and these two blighters decide to stop on the pavement right in front o' my window." He looked properly put out at being disturbed.

"I'm sure it was annoying, Davey. So their arguing got your attention?"

"Didn' hear no arguin'. Just the opposite. Voices too low to hear anythin'. All I could see looking out were their legs. Then sudden-like the short one turned to leave and that's when he came sailin' over the railin' to my stairs and landed, plop! In front o' my basement door like a bleedin' sack o' pitaters. Right ugly mess, too."

Declan was making notes. "Go on."

Davey puffed up with bravado undermined by the lack of color in his face. "By then the kid's meowing like a kitty with its tail caught in a door. I got up and took a look."

"Where was she exactly when you went out?" Declan asked.

"Ya mean after I stepped over the stiff? On the top step, bawlin' and retchin'. I'm tellin' ya, I thought it was goin' ta be all over my shoes. I had to use her bloody cell to call you plods."

Declan nodded encouragingly. "You're doing fine, Davey. Did you get a look at the other person?"

"Naw, alls I saw's legs in jeans and then the punter took off. Well he would, wouldn' he?"

Declan straightened up. This was not as helpful as he'd hoped. One other thought occurred to him. He stuck his head back down to Davey's level. "Did you recognize the man who fell?"

"'Course. I seen him walkin' round here all the time with his bulgin' muscles, like someone should care. Bumped inta him last week on accident and thought he's gonna tear me head off, bloody sod. Musta had some temper—was that pervert down the block, they say liked to show his willie to little tots."

"Thank you, Davey. The sergeant will be along shortly to take a formal statement. Just stay here and relax."

Davey snorted. "Relax in the back of a bloody plod car? Even *I'm* not that stupid."

CHAPTER FORTY-FOUR

*"The Whistler's fourth victim was his youngest, Valerie Mitchell,
aged fifteen years, eight months and four days, and she died because
she missed the 9:40 bus from Easthaven to Cobb's Marsh."*
— P. D. James, *Device and Desires*

4:05 PM

As she hurried toward the Banbury Road and The Old Parsonage,
it seemed to May Rogan that the afternoon had flown by as she
foraged delightfully in new and interesting shops. She could not
resist a few small purchases, such as a simply lovely scarf in muted
tones of royal blue, lilac and gold. She would drape it dramatically
over one shoulder of her navy suit, anchoring it enticingly with
her good sapphire pin. She assured herself it was not too loud for
a funeral. She could hardly be expected to care about the dead
woman, after all, and was only attending for Val's benefit.

Navy court shoes had been a challenge to find in August. She
had finally triumphed in a tiny shop just outside the Covered
Market, where the thrill of her victorious pursuit had relieved
her headache and thrust her into her current cheerful mood.

Perhaps she would call Val and see if she wanted to eat dinner
with them when she returned from Chipping Norton. Louisa
would certainly be in favor of the idea. May pictured the rest of
her day: a short rest after tea, followed by a nice sherry. A late
meal would be in order for all three of them, a grand gesture on
her part. They might try that modern Indian place, described as
"classy," on Turl Street that she had seen advertised in the book-
let in her room. It would definitely be at a place of her choosing
if she were picking up the tab.

May rummaged in her leather purse for her cell phone and dialed Val's flat. She was annoyed when Val's machine picked up, but she was careful to leave a gracious message. Lately she had noticed Louisa examining her from an appraising distance, causing her to mull over her own behavior. It was disconcerting, to say the least. Perhaps this dinner would help to eliminate that type of scrutiny. Louisa and Val would enjoy being together, and May'd be there to ensure Val would not negatively influence her stepsister. May decided she was being very modern to foster this kind of meeting.

She reached The Old Parsonage and its walled garden. Admiring the draping wisteria, she chose an empty, round table outside. Settling into a white wrought-iron chair, she stacked her parcels on the next seat. Her eyes roved over the patrons as she scanned the other tables, looking for any sight of Louisa. The garden was filled predominantly with groups of women. May dismissed the Laura Ashley skirts and blue-jeaned tourists. One group of three women who laughed too loudly wore blue visors printed across the brow with "Wycked Wyves of Oxford" in gold. Cheeky Americans on a pub crawl, May decided. She checked her watch again. Just after 4. She slipped her shoes off while she waited for her usually prompt daughter, knowing Louisa would happily live inside a bookshop if she could.

May wiggled her toes and considered the attraction of books for some people. She couldn't see it herself. Reading was much too boring and cerebral a pursuit. There was so much more to be gained from the healthy constitutional walks she preferred— window-shopping, Louisa called it. Of course May knew it was important to have read the latest books to remain *au courant*, but she skimmed the reviews for critical information to hold up her end of the conversation at social gatherings. A waiter appeared at her elbow, interrupting her train of thought with a discreet clearing of his throat.

"Tea for one, Madam?" he asked solicitously.

May looked around the garden area again. "No, I'm meeting my daughter here. But bring me a menu and pot of Darjeeling while I wait, please."

May was starting to fret. 4:40 and still no sign of Louisa. Worse, she wasn't answering her cell. This was not like her at all, even given the stop at Blackwell; Louisa had taxi money if she had gotten too tired or laden down with books to walk the short distance. May wished Val were at home to go looking for Louisa, but she had no idea if Val was back to Oxford by now. The only other people she vaguely knew in town were that couple from breakfast, Val's friends, and she had no way of contacting them, either.

The remnants of her tea were cold, reflecting the chill that passed over her despite the warm, sunny day along with a sense of foreboding that dissipated slightly when the waiter appeared at her elbow. "Would you be May Rogan, by any chance, Ma'am?"

May nodded. A message from Louisa at last; she had been worrying for nothing.

"There's a call inside for you," the waiter continued. "A detective from St. Aldate's wishes a word."

CHAPTER FORTY-FIVE

"'Who told Thad she was dead?' Rena asked. 'Thad killed her,'
Eva said. 'He already knew.'"
— Reynolds Price, *The Surface of Earth*

4:45 PM

Val went down the stairs into the co-operative to find Lottie
bent over the register, closing up the till. The other artists had
gone. Quiet reigned, but Val knew that when it was busy, the
place hummed with voices and activity. It gave Val a feeling of
accomplishment, remembering this was her brainchild, now fully grown. With Lottie's help, she had sorted through the maze
of applications and grants to set up the co-operative almost three
years ago, and now they were looking to expand.

The music was turned down low, but Bette Midler belting out
"Boogie Woogie Bugle Boy" had Lottie's foot in motion. Some
part of Lottie was always in motion, Val mused.

"And how does our garden grow, Mother Hen?" she asked
Lottie, who looked up and rushed around the counter as quickly
as her bulk would allow to hug Val ferociously.

"I heard footsteps and was just about to tell you to come back
tomorrow," Lottie said, finally releasing her tight hold. She
stepped back and cast a critical eye on Val. "You're the best business partner and friend. How are you, really? You're much too
pale and have lost weight. Damn you for that."

Val shrugged. "I'm coping. I took Janet home today, and we
spent time talking about Bryn, walking about the village where
she grew up. It felt good to do that even if it was upsetting at times.

I heard lovely stories from her childhood, little anecdotes about funny things she said or did. Janet was a wonderful mother."

Lottie nodded sympathetically. "You poor thing, you've been to hell and back. You don't deserve this one bit, not one moment."

"You don't know the half of it," Val answered, filling Lottie in on the long hours of interrogation at the police station, and the longer night spent in custody. "It isn't a nice feeling being a murder suspect."

"I can only imagine. It gave me the creeps when they stopped by here." Lottie's concern was written in her deep frown. "This had to be a random act of violence, no?"

"I keep telling them it must be something like that, but I was with her just before—you know, just before, and we were overheard arguing. A silly spat, but it looks suspicious to the powers that be." Val raked her hand through her short hair.

"That's absurd. Come and have a piece of shortbread, and I'll tell you about the commission's report on the expansion. You need to focus on your future right now." She guided Val behind the counter.

Val took a deep breath and let it out. She could always count on Lottie to make her feel better.

When she let herself into her flat, Val was immediately assailed by the silence. She had enjoyed Janet's stay these last tumultuous days. Her presence had kept this quiet at bay, this unnatural absence of movement, noise, and life that pointed to the next hours, days, and months that Val would be alone.

She looked around the familiar flat through new eyes. The cluster of wooden and porcelain boxes scattered on a low table next to the couch did not look charming today and held only the sting of loss. Bryn used to leave Val notes in those boxes after they'd spent the night at her flat, always choosing a different one so Val had to hunt for it. The notes were delightful scribbles or lines of poetry she would keep in her pocket for the rest of the day, reaching in at times to caress the paper fondly, a reminder that she was half of a couple, part of a whole. There were times she'd looked at a wall hanging she was working on without inspiration, but after re-reading that day's note, an idea would occur to her, and her creative juices would restart.

Val avoided the table now and flung herself on her couch, slipping off her shoes, feeling a keen sense of disconnection she assumed would be her constant companion from now on. Her eyes roamed the room, observing the stamp Bryn had left on it. Books from Bryn sat on the shelves. A glass bowl filled with stones gathered on their walks occupied the center of the table. Framed photographs that Bryn had taken, some of the two of them, were hung in prominent positions on the walls. She wondered if she would be expected to pack these things away in an attempt to forget her partner or leave them on display as badges of her pain. Neither option sounded appealing.

Val slid off the sofa to stand in front of one of the pictures. She was reluctant to touch it or hold it and instead stood gazing into it, searching for a hidden message from Bryn as to how she was to continue her life without her.

It was one of the few color shots Bryn had done, of a young girl about three years old dressed in the kind of party dress with smocking that mothers of little girls adore. The child's shiny black shoes and white tights contrasted with the pale pinks and purples of the dress. She stood at the very edge of Balliol's quad, one foot delicately resting on the banned lush green grass that only dons were allowed to walk on, ready to launch her body onto that perfectly trimmed carpet. Her head was cocked to one side, looking about for witnesses or informants to her planned indiscretion, the delight of the act immediately to follow already apparent on her open face. This anticipation brought a glow to her whole countenance, leaving no doubt that one second after the shutter had clicked, the girl had thrown herself onto the grass and run around in frenetic circles, dancing and leaping in forbidden freedom.

The photograph spoke of optimism and innocence but even more to the unbridled joy at being alive at just this moment in just this place. Bryn had titled it *Carpe diem*. For Val, this act of grasping and snatching life required an effort of amassing strength and emotion she felt she no longer possessed.

Val shifted her eyes from the photograph, turning her back on it with a shudder. She noticed the message light on her answering machine blinking insistently, the number three lit up in red, demanding her attention. She sighed deeply and shuffled over to the gadget. From now on, responsibilities and work would be her only motivation for getting out of bed in the mornings.

She hit the play button and the tape rewound. First was May's voice: "Valentine, it would be so nice if you joined me and Louisa at dinner tonight. Call me at the Randolph when you return from the countryside." Val was not surprised May didn't mention Janet Wallace and caught the casual way May dropped "the Randolph" into the message with a certain air of propriety, as though she owned the place.

Next was Simon's clear voice, asking if she had plans for the evening. "We saw Belcher. Give us a call when you get back from taking Janet home. Cheers." Val now had two offers for her evening, but she wasn't certain she felt up to anyone's company. She hoped the third message was not another invitation, but instead it was May's voice again, agitated and shrill, almost breathless:

"Val! Are you there? Louisa's in trouble, the police are taking me to her, right at Bryn's apartment. There's been another murder—please come!"

Chapter Forty-Six

"Nearly all of the seven dwarfs of pregnancy have shown up by now:
Sleepy, Queasy, Spacey, Weepy, Gassy and Moody.
The only one who hasn't checked in is Happy."
— Sarah Bird, *The Mommy Club*

4:50 PM

Nora walked with Simon around the corner from the Belcher Studio, and they sat in Browns enjoying tea. Simon added a plate of toasted crumpets, which he buttered, slathered with honey, and ate with typical relish. There was nothing wolfish about the way he ate; it was more his spirit of enjoyment that Nora found amusing.

"I've never seen anyone who can shovel it in like you and not gain a pound," she said enviously, cleaning her glasses on her linen napkin.

"Genes," he mumbled through sticky crumbs, wiping his fingers on a napkin.

Nora thought of Kate, also long and lean. "Were both your parents tall and thin?"

Simon nodded as he washed down the last bite of crumpet with the rest of his tea. "Mom was no slouch, but Dad was taller than me. I'll show you some pictures when we get back to Ramsey Lodge."

"I'd like that," Nora said, shifting in her seat with the beginning of a slight backache. "What did you think of our interview? I'm dying to see your sketches."

Simon put up both hands in protest. "Not our interview, definitely yours. I was merely the observer, not the one with the huge pair of bollocks."

"Assistant," she corrected, looking around to see if anyone had heard him. "But still, didn't you find him astonishing?"

"I found him incredibly self-centered and melodramatic, which reminded me of May Rogan, and rather an old nanny in some ways. The sketches were mostly of the street outside."

"Yes, he was all of those things, Simon, but we did find out who Wheeler is."

Simon set his cup down hard on its saucer. "We are not going to bother an Oxford don with your questions today. Besides . . ." He consulted his watch. "You should get a nap in before we check with Val and decide what to do with her tonight."

Nora shook her head at his insistence. "You are really rather sweet, Mr. Ramsey, and I love you for thinking about not leaving Val alone."

After they paid the check and returned to the Volvo, Simon slid behind the wheel, and for once Nora didn't question him. She looked tired, and a nap seemed in good order. In fact, if he didn't get them home soon, she might fall asleep in the car. She was trying to keep her eyes open when something roused her.

"Simon, do you think Bryn Wallace used cocaine?"

"I don't know, Nora, but Val would."

"Yes, Val would know," Nora said. "I'll have to figure out how to ask her directly without upsetting her."

They pulled up in front of Nora's flat, and Simon shut off the car. A small gasp escaped Nora. "What is it?" Simon asked.

She looked at him fully, engaging his eyes and taking his hand, which she placed on her stomach. "I felt the baby move, Simon. A tiny thump, a real kick."

He kept his hand where she had put it. He could feel the warmth radiating from it, willing the child inside to announce her presence again. And then he felt it, a flicker of definite movement that made Simon catch his breath.

"There! Did you feel it?" Nora asked. Her face radiated pure joy.

Simon's heart flipped over with longing for this to be his child, their child. "Yes, Nora, I felt her. Strong little gal, isn't she?"

"There you go, calling him 'her' again," Nora teased.

Simon leaned closer to Nora in the car. "Nora, thank you for letting me be a part of this. I don't want you to do this alone. Maybe, just maybe, I can keep my eye on you—and the girl." He laughed at her chagrin, rubbed her belly affectionately, and kissed her on the forehead, wishing wholeheartedly it could be more.

Nora dozed on the brass bed in her bedroom. It had been months since she'd slept in her old room, and it didn't feel familiar or comfortable anymore. This flat wasn't her home. Where was her home?

Home used to be Connecticut, and in some ways always would be, at least in her memory, the place where her family had been intact before her father's death. Nora was acutely aware she was fortunate to have had the stable upbringing she'd experienced.

Her mother had always been caring but never Nora's confidant, too filled with nervous energy for the sweet mother-daughter chats Nora longed for. Amelia Tierney Scott was currently enjoying an unexpected second marriage after nine years of widowhood. Nora was grateful her mother had not parked on her doorstep after learning of her daughter's pregnancy, although Amelia had insisted on receiving monthly photographs.

The Scotts loved to travel, and the grandmother-to-be had already informed Nora she planned to arrive with Roger for the birth of her first grandchild. Nora was certain the sights in the Lake District would keep them occupied as she bonded with her infant. It would all work out, she thought with a sigh. The birth was still too many months away for her to obsess about it now.

Instead she had Bryn Wallace's murder to preoccupy her, which made her think of Declan Barnes. Nora had mixed feelings about the inspector. She'd seen there was goodness in him and respected him for doing his job, but she couldn't forgive him for the way he'd treated Val. So why was she wasting precious energy daydreaming about the handsome, well-dressed detective? Nora sighed and rolled over. Her raging hormones must be in full gear. Any woman with good eyesight would be attracted to Barnes, and she was just in overdrive.

She was annoyed for feeling intrigued by Declan, almost drawn to him, when in Simon she had the best mate possible, one she even knew she was compatible with sexually. As she relied more and more on Simon, the chemistry between them grew. Simon was thoughtful and considerate, maybe a bit possessive, but no one was perfect.

At times like this she had trouble sorting out what was real and what was illusion. She would have liked to have her father's opinion. He had been the voice of reason, always willing to listen, to point out the pros and cons of a situation, never making decisions for her but helping her to see clearly the way to the right path.

Wide awake now, Nora sat up and stretched. She pictured her father hovering over her shoulder, and she silently asked him his opinion about the two men to whom she felt attracted. Five seconds later she smiled ruefully when Simon knocked gently on the door.

Chapter Forty-Seven

"I was never so amazed in my life as when the Sniffer drew his concealed weapon from its case and struck me to the ground, stone dead."
— Robertson Davies, *Murther and Walking Spirits*

5:15 PM

Watkins stood up as Declan approached the panda car where Louisa Rogan sat, a stricken look on her pale face. Declan followed his sergeant a few feet away from the car to confer.

"You're not going to believe this, guv," Watkins said. "The screamer is Val Rogan's stepsister."

Declan looked at the blonde head he could see peeping up from the back seat. "What the hell was she doing here? No, don't tell me—she was going to solve Bryn Wallace's murder to clear her sister." His irritation rose as Watkins nodded. "What the hell is it with all of these women messing about in my case?"

"The girl, Louisa, was supposed to meet her mum for tea at 4. I told McAfee to call the mother and pick her up, since she's a minor."

"Good thinking, Watkins. Just gone 5," Declan said after consulting his watch. "The mother must be frantic by now. All right, let's see what we've got."

Declan made his way back to the front of the apartment building and leaned over the railing; Charlie Borden was already working. He wouldn't have chosen pathology, even if he had gone into medicine the way his mother had hoped. He remembered the disappointment on her face when he had announced his intention to join the police force. His mother had struggled to mask her feelings, murmuring, "Very nice, dear, I'm sure." Eventually she had taken it in her stride. When he would show up for dinner in his uniform, her smile lit up the neighborhood. He missed her, even though she had been gone for six years. Still, he was glad she was not around to see the evil he encountered every day as a detective.

Declan straightened up as Charlie finished dictating and put his machine away. "Can't get me home early one night, Dec?" Charlie asked. "I was all set to watch a rerun of *Ground Force* this evening." The pathologist repacked his bag. "Good thing I set the DVR."

"Didn't know you liked those poncey shows, Charlie. What's happened to you?"

"Too much death and not enough sex, if you must know. The wife's off visiting her mum for the next few days." Charlie walked up to the steps. "This looks like an accident on the face of it, except two witnesses say he was pushed. I understand the victim had form for exhibiting himself to minors. Any chance an angry parent was getting back at him?"

Declan rubbed the back of his neck where he could feel tension taking hold. "Anything's possible. His name's Tommy Clay. One witness says Clay and another man stood here talking when the other bloke gave Clay a shove and took off. Whether he meant to kill Clay or just get away from him is anyone's guess."

Charlie nodded. "Doesn't sound like self-defense, though, no open fighting, no defensive marks on his hands. I'll see what turns up when I get him on the table, but right now it looks like the fall to the concrete caused massive skull fractures. There would have been intracranial hemorrhaging. I'll get him in tomorrow."

"Text me with the time. Thanks, Charlie."

Borden waved and set off. Declan turned back to the body, watching the flash of the SOCO's camera. Seeing the grotesque position Clay's body had taken after its fall, he was struck more strongly than ever by the notion that Bryn Wallace's body had been arranged.

So many intertwining paths. Surely there was a connection between the two murders. Declan knew from experience that links often were not seen at first or even at second glance. Watkins joined him.

"The mother's arrived, Dec."

"Now maybe we can get some answers. Come with me, Watkins."

As they approached the panda car holding Louisa Rogan, Declan saw the mother squeeze in beside the girl and try to soothe her. Louisa had the wide-eyed, hollow look of someone in shock. She had stopped crying and was sniffling into a tissue. "Mrs. Rogan, is it?"

The mother patted the girl's hand and got out of the car. "Are you the person in charge of this fiasco?" she challenged, the ire plain on her attractive face.

"Detective Inspector Barnes. This is Detective Sergeant Watkins. How is your daughter holding up?" His concern momentarily softened the mother's look.

"She's had a tremendous shock. I can't see why it was necessary to leave her sitting in the back of a police car being gaped at as though she were a common criminal."

"I quite agree, Mrs. Rogan, but as your daughter is a minor, we required your presence to move Louisa to better quarters. Perhaps you would accompany your daughter to the station, where it will be more comfortable and we can get her some tea?" He thought he had snuffed that one nicely when a familiar voice rang out loudly from the barricade.

"What do you think you're doing to my sister, Barnes?"

Declan looked over to see Val Rogan impatiently trying to cross the police line. He motioned for the constable to let her in, and she ran over to the car. "I was just asking your stepmother to allow us to question Louisa at the station, where she can be more relaxed."

Val's golden eyes blazed at him. "I'd hardly call your station relaxing."

"Your sister is a material witness to a murder, Miss Rogan, and like it or not, she needs to be questioned and her statement taken. If you'd like to accompany her and see that I don't mistreat her, please do so." Declan was becoming impatient with the entire Rogan family. He turned and stalked off to the MGB.

In his mirror he watched Mrs. Rogan slide into the panda beside Louisa while Val ran back to her own car. He negotiated the crowd of onlookers and police vans and turned for St. Aldate's, the other two vehicles close behind.

Chapter Forty-Eight

"Interviews always make me nervous."
— Auberon Waugh, *Consider the Lilies*

5:50 PM

It was Val's idea to call Jeff Nichols, who responded gracefully and agreed to be "a presence," as he called it, when Louisa was questioned. They waited for him in the stuffy hallway at St. Aldate's, sitting on the station's hard wooden benches. Val noticed that Lou, who had avoided her mother's questions by pretending to doze against May's shoulder, had in fact fallen into a light slumber. Trauma was exhausting, Val knew.

The heat of the last few days accentuated the sour mix of aromas in the station that Val remembered clearly. May wrinkled her nose in distaste. "I still can't believe she went there, of all places." Recrimination directed at Val was evident in May's tone.

"You aren't trying to blame this on me? We never discussed it—you might remember I only saw her in your presence today." Val was indignant. "Maybe she was curious, maybe she was . . . I don't know, trying to escape you for a few hours. It's not uncommon for teens to want to be alone at times, May."

"I'm not concerned about Louisa spending time without me, Valentine. It's what she gets up to without my supervision that worries me. She's fifteen. You can't understand because you're not a parent."

Val considered this. "That's probably true," she acknowledged. "I've seen Bryn through Janet's eyes these last few days, and the tie between them is enormous."

That Val would agree with her seemed to be the last thing May expected. She was startled into speechlessness, and the two women sat lost in their own thoughts until Val spoke up. "May, I had nothing to do with Lou going to Bryn's flat today. I didn't suggest it or even hint at it. I don't see what gain there could be, and I would never put Lou in any kind of jeopardy. I love her."

The words "and not you" hung unspoken between them. Years of resentment sprang up in Val's mind as they stared each other down.

Then May looked down at Louisa and unexpectedly shrugged the tension away. She gently swept Louisa's hair off her face as the girl dozed and said, "Do you remember your mother at all, Valentine?"

Val had been expecting to be corrected for using Lou instead of Louisa. "I don't know—I mean I have some vivid memories I pull up from somewhere, almost like snapshots of frozen moments. I guess what I remember best is her smell. It was the sweet scent of the almond soap she used, or maybe it was her shampoo, mixed with her perfume, a spicy, flowery scent. She always wore the scent L'Interdit and told me the story over and over, how Givenchy created it for Audrey Hepburn—" Val choked at the recollection and fell silent, concentrating on the swirled pattern on the tiled floor.

The sound of ringing telephones and murmured voices in the background filled the space around them. Suddenly May blurted, "I've always thought you rather looked like Audrey Hepburn."

"Louisa Evelyn Rogan," the girl dictated clearly into the tape, bolstered by the presence of Jeff Nichols sitting beside her and her mother and sister sitting behind her. She listened to the inspector who had given Val such a hard time as he dictated for the tape's benefit: "Also in the room are DS Douglas McAfee; Miss Rogan's solicitor, Jeffery Nichols; her mother, May Rogan; and her sister, Valentine Rogan." Everyone in the room shuffled and settled back in their chairs. Louisa was reminded of the lull before the curtain rose on a new play.

"Miss Rogan, please start with this morning and describe your activities for us," Inspector Barnes said.

She told him about the day's brunch, instinctively understanding he was covering this useless bit to get her to relax. Nora had said he was quite intelligent, even if he had gotten off on the wrong track with Val, and she agreed. He wasn't traditionally handsome, like a movie star, but he was easy to look at and carried himself like someone important. He would also be a strict father, she judged, wondering if he had any children.

"When did you decide you wanted to go to Magdalen Road?"

"I knew when I came here I wanted to help Val. It was when I was trying on the new dress my mother bought me that I figured out how. I didn't want to spend my whole day going from shop to shop. I wanted to be out there trying to prove to you that Val could never have killed Bryn." She said this with increasing assurance, then dropped back to a lower tone. "I thought if I could just look about the place, maybe talk to people who knew her or had seen someone else that night . . . it was a place to start."

"And how did you convince your mother this was a reasonable thing for you to do?" Declan asked.

May gave a minor start; Val cleared her throat. The detective's stern glance in their direction stilled them both.

"I told her I was going to tour the Bodleian Library and then spend hours at Blackwell. I wanted to do that, too, but this seemed more important—at the time."

Declan nodded as if he understood, making eye contact with Louisa. "Did you set off on foot?"

"Yes, Val had given me a map to find my way around town, and I walked down the High Street, taking my time, and over the bridge, picking out things on the map as I went along." Her tone became wistful. "The Botanic Gardens looked nice, and I almost stopped there—now I wish I had."

"Did you stop anywhere before reaching Magdalen Road?" Declan prompted.

"I went into a grocery on the way to buy a bottle of water. The walk was longer than it looked on the map, and I got warm. And I stood for a bit on the bridge, just looking down the Cherwell." The girl's voice grew pensive. "There were people punting, and I watched them for a few minutes. It seemed like fun, and I thought I would ask Val to take me before I have to go home." She shrugged. "And then I came down Magdalen Road and found Bryn's building. I was surprised at how pretty it was and just looked at it a bit from next door."

"And after that?"

"I went inside the lobby and read the names on the mailboxes. There was a bench, and I sat for a moment, waiting for someone to come into the building so I could follow them into the secure part." Louisa spoke faster as her anxiety rose. "Bryn's name is still on her mailbox," she added.

"Why don't you take a sip of tea, Louisa?" Declan pointed to her cup.

Jeff Nichols patted her arm and spoke reassuringly. "You're doing just fine. All we want is to get to what you saw. Take a few deep breaths and try to think of it as a movie. Describe the scene to us."

Louisa nodded. "I was standing in the middle of the lobby trying to decide what to do next, looking out at people and the cafe across the road. A woman walked a dog past the building. Then these two men crossed the road and came by the building.

And then they stopped in front of it, sort of to the left, my left," she explained.

"So if I were standing outside the building on the sidewalk looking at you inside the lobby, they would be on my right," the detective clarified.

"Yes. They stood there a few moments talking, and then the shorter one turned to leave, and the taller one pushed him roughly and ran away. The short man fell over the railing to the basement stairs, and I couldn't see him anymore." Louisa swallowed hard. "I had my cell phone and I thought, 'I have to call 999,' as I ran out the door, but when I got to the stoop and looked down . . ." Her face crumpled with the memory of the horror she'd seen. She covered her face with both hands.

May coughed and shifted in her seat. Declan pushed on.

"Excellent, you're really doing well, Louisa. Forget the body and try to pull your mind back to the other man, the taller one. Can you describe him?"

The girl looked at her hands before answering. "He was definitely taller than the other man, but the lobby is up a flight of steps from the street, so I only saw the top of his head. He had on a baseball cap with the brim curled in on each side, the way some do them, you know?" She made a folding gesture with her hands.

"Yes, I know what you're talking about," Declan said. "How about color? Any logo on it? Or printing?"

Louisa scrunched up her face and was suddenly eager. "Yes, there was an elaborate design, sort of like entwined initials, in silver embroidery. The cap was maroon, or burgundy, in that family."

Declan hunched forward. "Could you make out the initials, Louisa? Close your eyes and think back very hard."

Louisa did as she was told, and everyone in the room waited for her response.

"I think a K and maybe an M or a W?" She was less certain

and clearly agitated now. "I'm sorry. I just had a glance at it; I didn't know it would become so important."

Her mother couldn't stop herself from interjecting, "Of course you didn't, darling."

"DI Barnes, perhaps a good night's sleep would improve Louisa's memory, don't you agree?" Nichols spoke with quiet authority.

"Just what I was about to suggest," Declan said graciously, terminating the interview.

CHAPTER FORTY-NINE

"'The sex instinct,' repeated Mrs. Talliaferro in her careful cockney,
'. . . is quite strong in me.'"
— William Faulkner, *Mosquitoes*

7 PM

Simon put the phone down. "That was Val. She's still at the station with Louisa and May. She told us to go ahead and have dinner without her."

They threw together a cold salad, Nora cutting up cucumbers as Simon opened a can of tuna. "I can't believe there's been another murder, and right on Bryn's doorstep, Simon. They have to be connected somehow," Nora said, pushing tuna and cucumbers around her plate with a lack of enthusiasm.

Simon brushed the hair off his forehead. "I know it seems *too* coincidental, but what connection could there be? We haven't stumbled across anything linking Bryn with this Clay person." Even Simon's appetite had lost its edge tonight.

"Poor Val, to be back inside that station so soon. This whole thing must be like sleepwalking through a nightmare for her."

"I suspect it felt that way even before today's events, dar— Nora." Simon caught the endearment and kept his eyes on his plate.

Nora blushed. "Yes, of course you're right. You're always right, Simon; you have such good sense. Maybe you'll be the one to solve these murders."

He looked up to see if she was making fun of him, but Nora appeared sincere. "I prefer to leave that to the professionals, despite your opinion of them." He decided a change of subject would do them both good. "Would you like to see the sketches I made at Belcher's today?"

"Of course," she answered. "Let me use the loo while you're getting them."

Simon rose to clear the plates and retrieve his pad. He left it on the table and started a pot of herbal tea to get them through the evening. When he heard Nora resume her seat, he glanced over and saw her leafing through the tablet.

"Simon! This one of the scene out the window is amazing— are you going to paint it?" She flipped the page. "And look at Miles here, all waving arms. I can almost hear his whiny voice." She gave a fake shudder and flipped to the next page. The subject was done in profile with only a few lines to suggest features and wavy hair.

Simon was certain Nora would recognize the firm expression and determined lift of the chin to be her own. He sat down while the tea steeped.

"The glasses are a dead giveaway," she said, pushing hers back up her nose.

"I wasn't trying to hide that it was you," he said. "What do you think?"

Nora sat back, considering. "I think I have been very selfish, dragging you all over Oxford to do my bidding, checking out cars and people, helping me pack and sort my life and Val's. Tomorrow is a day for Simon, the artist. Here is your assignment: You are to take off in my car with your art bag and not look back until dinner, when I will expect to be retrieved for a proper meal."

Simon was already shaking his head. "And what will you do all day?"

"See those books?" She pointed to the shelves running around the room. "They all have to be sorted into piles, some to give away, some to store, and a few to take. That will probably take me all day. I can sit here and sift through them slowly. And I'll be available for Val if she needs to talk."

Simon's resolve was weakening.

"I won't move any heavy boxes. I'll just pack cartons and leave them for you to stack up when you get home."

It was a very tempting offer. "If you think you really wouldn't overdo it—"

"I'll be slow and relaxed all day, and you'll have a pad full of drawings to paint when we get back to Bowness." Nora was already pulling a book off the shelf. "Here's a place you might want to drive to, quite nearby, excellent views . . ."

Simon watched her shiny, auburn curls move as she pointed out attractions for him to explore, unable to shake the feeling that Nora was steering him out of the way.

Nora and Simon sat on the sofa, reading in quiet companionship as the evening wore on. Val had called and updated them on Louisa's interview. The pages of Nora's mystery blurred after that as her mind went round and round the murders, trying different theories on for size. Could this Oxford don be involved? What about Cam Wilson? She felt weary and finally put her book down, picking up one of her pillows. Propping her head against it on the sofa arm, she placed her feet expectantly across Simon's lap. A smile broke across his face. He closed his book.

"Would Madam be interested in the Ramsey Special this evening?" he asked, holding one foot by the heel.

"You have such wonderful ideas," she said with relish, but to her surprise he pushed her feet off and stood up. Her consternation changed to comprehension when he returned from the bathroom with a bottle of skin cream. She was glad she had shaved her legs that morning, curling her feet back onto his lap as the rosemary scent reached her. The cold lotion gradually warmed in his hands as he massaged Nora's feet and legs, relaxing her tired calf muscles by reaching under her skirt, stopping at her knees. She liked the feel of his strong hands, too firm to tickle, touching her skin, his long fingers insinuating themselves between and under her toes in a way that seemed sensual and intimate.

Nora relaxed her legs slightly, wanting him to slide his hands higher, feeling the heat build between her thighs. She closed her eyes to the sweet rush of desire that filled her, a sensation she hadn't allowed herself to experience deeply in months. The memory of their only coupling swam over her, the recollection still powerful. Nora willed Simon to comprehend her hunger as she became more aroused, hoping he would somehow have the insight to know she was giving him permission, not knowing how to convey her need when she had kept him at arm's length. He was working on the leg farthest away from him, and as Nora relaxed the closer one into his lap, she felt his erection. Surely if she began to massage him with her foot . . .

At that moment Simon seemed aware he was unable to conceal his hardness and dropped her leg. "All done!" he said brightly, uncomfortably breaking the moment.

Nora curled onto her side, stretching her arms and yawning, checking her watch to cover her embarrassment. "Almost 10 and I'm exhausted. Thanks."

Simon stood at his cue. "I'll just take this with me. Have a good rest."

Grabbing his book, he hurried into her bedroom, quietly shutting the door behind him.

Nora thumped her pillow in frustration. Was that just a physical reaction? Didn't he desire her anymore? Or was he simply doing what she had clearly told him she wanted—leaving her to sort out her life without the added distraction of a relationship?

She turned onto her back, wide-awake now as she questioned her logic against the tumult of emotions this man was capable of stirring up in her. Could she expect him to take any alliance between them seriously when she was pregnant with another man's child? But that man was dead and would never be a father to this baby, she argued with herself. She remembered the longing she'd felt to share her pregnancy with someone when Simon had placed his hands on her and felt the baby move. Could he come to love the child, perhaps even to see it as his own if he were there from its beginning? Was she crazy to imagine or hope this was possible?

From the bedroom she heard a groan; then all was silent. Nora wrapped her arms around the growing baby, contemplating the best decision for the future of her child. She wasn't about to pretend she could sleep.

CHAPTER FIFTY

"The bodies were discovered at 8:45 on the morning of Wednesday 18 September by Miss Emily Wharton, a sixty-five-year old spinster of the parish of St. Matthew's in Paddington, London, and Darren Wilkes, aged ten, or no particular parish as far as he knew or cared."
— P. D. James, *A Taste for Death*

Tuesday

9:30 AM

Declan just couldn't see it. No matter which scenario he envisioned, he couldn't find a connection between the murders of Bryn Wallace and Tommy Clay. He sat at his desk and stared at the lists he'd scribbled. The only two things the victims had in common were that they lived on the same street, and their deaths were apparently provoked by acts of anger.

But the methods were so different; could they really be the same person? Declan didn't want to think he had two murderers running around Oxford. Why would Bryn Wallace's killer want to silence Tommy Clay? Had Clay seen something he shouldn't have? Perhaps Clay had ferreted out information about the murderer. He picked up his intercom and buzzed Watkins in the murder room, supervising the logging of information on Tommy Clay's murder.

"McAfee heading up the house-to-house? . . . Good. Any joy from those photos the team is showing around? . . . Figures. Charlie's doing the Clay post; want to tag along?"

Hanging up, Declan pushed his notes aside and sifted through the files on his other cases. They had arrested two teens for the computer thefts, and that looked like a solid case. He initialed a few reports and put the folder for employee evaluations aside for the fourth time that week. They would have to wait.

Declan drained his coffee mug, and his eyes lit on the chair Nora Tierney had recently occupied. He pictured the woman with her arms held out in front of her for handcuffs, humor in her eyes, and felt a twinge of something he was reluctant to name.

The postmortem of Tommy Clay revealed few surprises, except for the magnitude of the man's personal equipment.

"Goodness, he was built like a donkey—no wonder he couldn't stop from waving that thing around," Watkins said, with what almost sounded like respect.

Declan was not impressed. "He didn't use it wisely," he said grimly, yanking off his surgical mask.

Charlie Borden stripped off his gloves. "As I thought. In very good shape other than the effects of the fall. Skull fracture rupturing the basilar artery is the immediate cause of death. Multiple other fractures consistent with the fall. Concrete is very unforgiving to the eggshell of our heads, gentlemen."

"Thanks, Charlie."

The two detectives stuffed their paper suits in a wastebin. "Any idea who you're looking for?" the pathologist asked.

"We're going to interview the girl again, see if she remembers any more details. She got a better look at him than the Haskitt boy did, but she was standing in the lobby above him and only saw the top of his head. Not even hair color—he had a baseball cap on."

Charlie grimaced in sympathy. "Like there's only a few thousand of them around, and women wearing them, too. Good luck hunting."

"We need more than luck to solve this one, Charlie," Declan answered, picking up on something Charlie had just said. "Watkins, we have to ask the Rogan girl if there's any chance the killer was a woman."

"You're not thinking Val Rogan? She was in Chippy all day, wasn't she?"

"But we don't know exactly when she arrived back in Oxford or what her actions were." He saw the reluctant look on his sergeant's face. "I'm grasping at straws, aren't I?" he said miserably. They walked out into the bright sunlight and clean air.

"More like a whole haystack, if you don't mind me saying so, guv."

Chapter Fifty-One

*"In the opinion of the late Queen Elizabeth, Captain John Smith
was the most accomplished and versatile liar in England."*
— Noel B. Gerson, *Daughter of Eve*

9:45 AM

Perhaps it was the result of being an only child, Nora thought.
She had become so accustomed to creating other worlds and
imaginary playmates that massaging reality felt permissible. She
pondered her lack of guilt as she sent Simon out for the day.
He carried his backpack stuffed with art materials and fresh
sandwiches, including three hard-boiled eggs she had made
that morning while reviewing her plan. In the grand scheme of
things, she judged, waving from the window as Simon disappeared, surely a small white lie could be overlooked. A small
falsehood that led to a greater achievement was often a necessity.
Historians would back her on that. Or philosophers, or someone.
Satisfied the Volvo was on its way, Nora closed the window.

She had the day to herself. Even Val was occupied, accompanying Louisa to her second interview.

"I need to be there, Yankee," Val had told Nora on the phone.
"I can sort out Barnes if he starts to get too tough on Lou. She's
an innocent bystander in all of this, and I'm not about to let him
harass her. And before that I have to stop at the co-op and see
Lottie."

Nora faced the room, ready to enact the next stage of her
plan. Last night she had gone through the books, quietly making stacks and piles all over the room, gambling Simon wouldn't

emerge from her bedroom. If he had, she was prepared to use her insomnia as an excuse. She'd worked quickly, not allowing time to flip through her favorites or linger over choices, consigning each book to a pile: take, store, give away. She could not bring herself to toss a book, any book; the local Oxfam shop would take any the community library couldn't use.

There were some built-in shelves in her rooms at Ramsey Lodge, but she couldn't take an abundance of books and so was judicious about her "take" pile, determined it should be the smallest. She also needed to leave room for the books she would need for the baby, and Nora smiled at the thought of introducing her child to her old favorites and the new ones they would explore together.

There was one bad moment when a pile of storage books fell over, but their landing on the rug blunted the noise to a soft thud, and Simon had not appeared. When Nora's heart rate slowed, she began re-shelving the books, grouping them according to their final destination. She had collapsed into a deep sleep on her sofa a few hours later.

Today it was a simple matter to fill a labeled carton and move on. Nora worked steadily and checked her watch when she was done. Less than two hours with only one break, she noted with satisfaction. The shelves stood empty, and she resisted the impulse to dust and wipe them down. She could do that when she got home. As she washed her hands she wondered if Ted Wheeler lunched at Exeter.

Nora got a taxi to Exeter, glad to sit back for the brief trip to the college. She was aware more and more now of the baby's movements, an internal floating sensation she was learning to distinguish. It seemed that when she was quiet the baby was more active, but perhaps that was because she was concentrating on his movements then, and her awareness was heightened.

She pictured him moving his arms as though he were waving a wand and had a sudden recollection from when she was six, when she had been allowed to touch her aunt's swollen belly, turgid with eight months' gestation. A foot pushed her aunt's skin outward in a hard lump. Nora had pushed it back, and it had responded to her touch magically, kicking out again and again as though they were playing a game together.

After that, pregnancy had taken on the aura of a paranormal process, imbued with an element of wonder that all of her understanding of biology could not explain. Perhaps if she knew more she would feel less fragile, more in control. For once she saw Simon's need to be in control from a different side, as a way to diminish fear. Maybe that was why he was able to be so calm in the face of upheaval and fluster. As the taxi pulled up in front of Exeter, Nora tossed around the idea of calling the sonographer and confirming the sex of her child.

A student leaving the college graciously held the heavy wooden door for her as she stepped over the high threshold. Inside, the porter sat behind his desk, surrounded by pigeonholes for mail. An older gentleman who looked dour, he smiled genially enough as she approached. Nora boldly smiled back as she projected what she hoped would be read as familiarity. The ruse she had decided on came easily to her lips.

"Hello, nice to see you again. Is my Uncle Ted in? I've got some exciting news for him," she said, placing her hand over her belly and thrusting it out. "I've just found out the sex—it's a girl!"

The porter smiled at her delight and came out from behind his glass partition, head cocked to one side as he tried to place her.

Nora thrust out her hand. "Ted Wheeler's niece, Nora," she

said warmly. "I'm not surprised you don't remember me. I wasn't showing when I was down for the wedding." Don't let him ask me any details, she prayed, knowing only that Wheeler's daughter had been married in the summer.

"Very nice, miss, congratulations. I'm sure Dr. Wheeler is looking forward to some little grand-bairns of his own one of these days." The man's Scottish brogue had been softened by years in Oxford. He consulted a log on a hook above the desk. "Let's see, your uncle should be—here, wait a minute—" The porter slapped his forehead in consternation. "Ach, I'd plum forgot—he's off to London today, showing his students how to research at the British Museum. I'm afraid you've wasted your trip here."

All my plans down the drain, Nora thought, but instead smiled extravagantly at the man. "No problem, I'm in town for a few days. When would be a good time to see him?" And how am I going to get away from Simon two days in a row?

"That's all right, then, he'll be in college all tomorrow. You can catch him just after 4:00 in his rooms when his tutoring's done."

Nora noted the name engraved on the man's badge. "Thank you so much, Wilson. Now don't spoil my surprise and tell him I'm coming. Is he still in his old rooms?"

"Yes, ma'am, just across the quad and up C staircase. And I won't even mention you were here."

CHAPTER FIFTY-TWO

"It is odd, how one's idea can change."
— Mary Roberts Rinehart, *The Wall*

2 PM

Lottie was leaning on the co-op desk opening the paper, a thick, black headline proclaiming: "SECOND MAGDALEN ROAD MURDER." Although she hadn't yet turned on the music, her pen beat a tattoo on the counter in its stead. She smelled Val Rogan's grassy perfume before she saw her, and her mood lifted immediately.

"Let's see that, Lottie love," Val asked.

"Anything for you." Lottie smiled broadly and handed over the paper. "Half my bacon buttie?"

"No, thanks." Val glanced quickly at the paper. "I'm scanning for Lou's name. She could be in jeopardy if her identity were known."

Lottie sucked in a breath when Val described how Lou had come to be at the site of the murder. "I hope you don't feel responsible for this situation, Val. Yes, Lou went to Magdalen Road to help you, but the fact it misfired badly is not your fault."

Val sighed and handed the paper back to Lottie. "Thanks. I know, but I can't help but feel responsible. At least there's no mention of Lou by name."

"This can't be a coincidence—two murders at the same address? Just what was Bryn up to, Val?" Lottie tapped a pen on the counter top.

"I don't know, Lottie. It's too unreal to contemplate." Val came around the counter. "Let's look over the Board proposal before the other artists fill this place up and we can't hear ourselves think."

"Yes, let's," said Lottie, pulling out an envelope and patting the chair beside her.

CHAPTER FIFTY-THREE

"I've always been a liar—it runs in my family."
— Sarah Baylis, *Utrillo's Mother*

6:30 PM

Simon arrived at dusk to find Nora looking glum as she washed the last of the shelves. He was impressed with her industry. Cartons overflowing with books stood in rows around the room and spilled into the hallway. "Did you have a good day?"

Wisps of hair escaped Nora's ponytail and clung to her damp face. "All done here." She stood, arching her back. She looked tired and out of sorts.

He stifled the desire to embrace her. Instead he picked up her bucket and carried it into the kitchen, dumping the soapy water down the sink and rinsing it out. "I had a wonderful day, although I felt a little guilty I wasn't here helping you. You must have worked all day."

"It didn't take as long as it looks," she said. "Besides, you've been wrapped up in my friends and their problems; you deserved some time to yourself. How did your day go?" She washed her hands and put the kettle on for tea.

Simon took out a pair of mugs they'd left unpacked. "I spent the entire day at Blenheim Palace—what an ostentatious building, so god-awful it's kind of wonderful. I've got pages of drawings and a few watercolours. I'll show them to you later if you'd like. I didn't have time to get into the saloon for those Laguerre figures."

Nora seemed to brighten at this news. "Then you must go back tomorrow. I mean, our time here is growing short and you want to get those in." She poured the tea, and they took their mugs to the table.

Simon blew on his to cool it. "I don't know. Maybe I should leave something for our next trip here. We'll be back in January to see Nigel Rumley."

"No!" Nora half-shouted. He startled at the urgency in her voice. "I mean—no, you deserve to get it all in on this trip. It's going to be a long winter at Ramsey Lodge, and I won't be responsible for you not having interesting work to do besides my fairies." She fidgeted in her seat.

"We'll see," Simon answered, wondering what Nora had up her sleeve. "Are we seeing Val tonight?"

"No, she's bonding with her wicked stepmother and her sis, although I detect a slight thaw in the arctic there. Val called to say Barnes had another go at Louisa today with little result."

"He gets around, doesn't he?" Simon said.

"I get the impression you don't care for the inspector." Nora scrutinized him over her steaming mug.

"Let's just say I'm cautious of someone who dresses that well, looks that good, and can change his personality at will."

"That sums him up," Nora said. "Another person might say it's what makes him a good detective."

"Another person has every right to his or her own opinion."

Nora laughed heartily. "Why Simon Ramsey, I almost think you're jealous!"

Nora chewed an antacid for the heartburn that plagued her after the Greek meal they'd finally decided on for dinner. "I'm longing for one of Cook's home-made meals," she said.

"I'm sure too many takeaways add to your heartburn," Simon

said, tying up the garbage bag. "I'll take this down to the bins so we're not smelling it all night."

Nora nodded from the sofa, reaching down for her pad. She looked at the notes she'd made. She couldn't make any real progress until she'd spoken to Ted Wheeler. She *had* to convince Simon to go out again tomorrow.

When he returned Nora was heading for a shower. "Simon, it's getting so crowded in here with all of these boxes, isn't it?"

"Yes," he said, looking around. "I'm going to tape the rest up. Maybe I can get some of them over to the storage unit tomorrow."

"That would be wonderful," Nora enthused. "When I get out of the shower I'll finish clearing out the closet so you can take those boxes, too." If she gave him directions to the storage center that got him lost it would buy her a few hours.

CHAPTER FIFTY-FOUR

"To know is not enough. One must try to understand, too."
— André Brink, *A Chain of Voices*

7:30 PM

Before leaving the station for the night, Declan called McAfee into his office. "Watkins will remind Janet Wallace she has to return Thursday for the inquest. Would you assign someone to go down the witness list and remind the others?"

McAfee nodded and left Declan's office looking gloomy. This, Declan knew, was the inevitable result of too many unsolved crimes hanging about, especially murders. Long hours, little sleep, and not enough evidence flowing in created an air of frustration. He had to keep his team focused and believing they could solve these murders. Tomorrow morning at his briefing he'd give them all a pep talk. Although, he thought dourly as he stuffed files in his briefcase, he had no idea what he could say to increase their morale.

The evening was lovely, the lowering sun creating shadows and bringing out the much photographed golden glow of Oxford's buildings. This was Declan's favorite time of day, when he reminded himself how fortunate he was to live in such a glorious place, crammed with history and tradition. All that awaited him was a lonely evening reviewing case files, so he walked up the street and paused to look into the window of the Alice in Wonderland shop, where the inspirational little girl was said to have bought her barley sugar candy. He drew the fragrant air of a nearby rose garden into his lungs deeply, trying to empty his mind of all thoughts of murder, stabbings, skull fractures, and red-haired pregnant women.

Nora Tierney. Declan had to acknowledge he looked forward to seeing her again. He imagined she would accompany Val Rogan and Janet Wallace to the inquest. He couldn't figure out why he was so intrigued by the woman. She was pregnant and moving out of Oxford, making a relationship distinctly unlikely. Yet she exuded an appealing vibrancy and an interest in life marked by her own streak of originality.

His stomach growled at the same time his thinking cleared. Unlike the other women he knew, Nora Tierney would understand his deep need to find the answer to the mysteries he encountered every day. Deciding to quiet his stomach with a stop at the kebob van on St. Giles, Declan returned to the station, lowering his tall frame into the MGB. *Dec, old boy, you've been alone far too long.*

Lottie entered The Blue Virgin, nodding to a few acquaintances. A little company would serve her well tonight. These past few days had been rough, covering all of Val's hours, worrying about the toll Bryn's death was taking on her partner. She hoped things would settle back to normal soon. Taking a seat at the bar, she complimented the bartender on her new eyebrow ring.

"Thanks, Lottie. I can change the little beads on it to match my outfits. What'll it be?"

Lottie thought hard. "I think a vodka martini with double olives will do." The music changed to a Coldplay song; the porn video was not playing at the moment. Lottie tapped one finger on the bar in time to the music and thought about where she wanted to be at this time next year. If the co-op renovation were approved, she and Val would be working again side by side on that project for a few months. Once that was done, she would suggest a vacation for them, maybe Spain. They hadn't taken serious time off since opening the co-op, and both certainly deserved it.

Her drink arrived. "Here you go, love. Where's Val tonight?"

Lottie didn't feel up to explaining the whole situation. "Val's busy. But she'll be back here soon, I promise." She drank deeply from the glass, the cold vodka cooling her throat and bringing her head to a better place.

Chapter Fifty-Five

*"I may sound cruel and hard-hearted, but in the long run I'm not
sorry any of it happened."*
— Nora Johnson, *The Two of Us*

Wednesday

10 AM

Wednesday's paper had reduced the death of Tommy Clay to a
small article on page three:

"No New Information on Second Magdalen Road
Death." Cam threw the paper down on his kitchen counter and
breathed a huge sigh, not exactly of relief, for that would be a
long time coming, but at least he felt the immediate danger had
passed.

It had been an accident, plain and simple, Cam rationalized.
He had planned on turning himself in until he'd come to his
senses several hours and a few snorts later. How could he convince anyone, let alone the police, that he hadn't killed Clay on
purpose? He'd have to tell them Clay was planning to blackmail
him after seeing him at Bryn's flat on the night of her murder. It
was too powerful a motive for anyone to believe a simple mishap
had taken Clay's life.

No amount of arguing could make the bloody man understand that while he had gone to see Bryn Wallace at the height
of a particularly good high, he'd lost his nerve at the door to
her building. He'd been standing outside when that Rogan dyke
came out of Bryn's flat; he'd ducked down the side alley before
she could see him. Afterwards he'd gone into the lobby but had

hesitated in a moment of clarity and checked his watch. When he'd seen the time, he'd wondered if Bryn were even awake. He'd left soon after, but not soon enough. Tommy Clay had seen him enter the lobby and was prepared to go to the authorities with his information unless Cam bought his silence.

"You could buy yourself a little peace of mind, Mr. Wilson," Clay said over coffee that day. "I know a few people at the local station—Detective Inspector Barnes was actually over my place just the other day. It was easy enough for me to find you—he'd have no trouble at all."

Cam looked the man up and down in revulsion, wondering what the slimy bastard and the high-level detective could have in common. He tried to quell the rising panic. After a moment, he said, "I haven't any disposable income."

"Oh, I don't know about that, old chum. If you were to cut your blow in half, I'd be happy with the money you'd save per week to start." Clay tapped the side of his nose.

Cam blinked twice rapidly. He'd indeed gotten flying high from his dwindling reserve stash just to attend this meeting. His mouth hung open without a quick retort.

"Don't play innocent with me, you cheeky bastard—you're high right now," Clay said with a sneer. "I know a cokehead when I see one."

Cam's cocaine paranoia took off like a shot. Clay must be undercover drug squad; that would explain him being chummy with Barnes. "I take offense to those remarks," he told Clay.

Clay seemed to think this comment humorous, grinning from ear to ear without remorse.

"And I noticed you used the phrase 'to start'—I'd be a fool to get involved with you. The payments would only get higher and higher." Cam broke out in a sweat, apprehension turning the coffee bitter in his stomach, his pulse picking up speed. He felt trapped and disoriented, confusion clouding his reasoning. The conversations around him suddenly became loud and distorted, the fruity perfume of the waitress overpowering.

Cam stood up and so did Clay. They left the cafe, ostensibly to continue the discussion at Clay's flat. When they crossed the street, Clay stopped in front of Bryn's building.

"Yes, it was just about here I saw you that night, Mr. Wilson," Clay said.

The roar in Cam's head was unbearable. His heart beat so fast, it felt like it would tear right out of his chest. He hated Tommy Clay and what this little man was trying to do to him. He could lose it all because of the grinning fool standing in front of him.

Clay seemed to grow wider, larger, to loom over him, threatening to choke the air out of him. In desperation Cam pushed the demon away, giving the man a mighty shove. The rail caught Clay in the small of his back and flipped him neatly over. By the time he hit the concrete bottom, Cam was halfway down Magdalen Road.

A convulsive spasm ran through Cam, fluttering the newspaper in his hand. He considered a quick snort to calm himself down, but first he had to read this article and confirm that his identity was unknown. That seemed to hold true as he scanned the piece, but his fury grew as he read the snippets of information the reporter had dug up to end the article:

Sources confirm Mr. Clay has form for indecent exposure to minors and was on probation.

Cameron dropped the paper and slid down onto his Le Corbusier lounger. This was who he had let get to him—a man who'd hinted he was an undercover cop, someone closely acquainted with the local plod—when in truth he was a kiddie flasher. Bloody hell!

CHAPTER FIFTY-SIX

"A Frenchman named Chamfort, who should have known better,
once said that chance was a nickname for Providence."
— Eric Ambler, *The Mask of Dimitrios*

Nora closed the door after Simon and Val left on their third and last trip to her storage unit. Last night she had thought she'd be able to get away to see Wheeler. But when Val called early that morning to see if Simon needed help, there was no way she could gracefully refuse.

Lottie's unexpected arrival a minute later interrupted Nora's thoughts on the sticky problem of interviewing Ted Wheeler without Simon tagging along. Lottie hugged Nora with delight, crushing the shopping bag she carried and chattering about the size of Nora's growing belly.

"I'm glad to see you, too, Lottie. Come in, although I warn you, it's pretty bleak in here with all the packing going on." Nora led her to the living room, which was empty now except for a pair of pine chairs pulled up to the counter and a wing chair from Connecticut. Several boxes labeled TAKE were stacked in one corner; the area rug stood rolled and bundled in another. Their voices echoed in the nearly vacant room.

"You just missed Val. She and Simon took the last load of furniture and boxes to the storage center. Lottie, you can't believe how strange it feels watching my things carted away," Nora said.

They sat at the counter, and Lottie withdrew two tins, one a large square embossed in gold, the smaller one a circle with a basket of fruit stamped on it, both recycled from previous use. "One to eat now," Lottie tapped the smaller one, "and one to take back to Bowness. Val told me how much your Simon likes my shortbread. I'm looking forward to meeting him." Today Lottie wore her black hair twisted up on top of her head, anchored with a clip covered in a bunch of plastic cherries, the wiry ends splaying out wildly. Pink flamingo earrings danced from her lobes. In deference to the warm day, she'd rolled up the sleeves of her madras cotton shift, a bright plaid of aqua, pink, red, and yellow that fell from her shoulders and obscured her full figure.

"If you can handle tea out of slightly chipped mugs, we'll surprise him when he and Val get back."

Lottie said wistfully, "It must be nice to have someone like that in your corner."

"How's the extension application coming with the Planning Board?"

"There's a meeting this afternoon. I'm tracking down Val to go over the presentation. We've made it past the first part." Lottie tapped a bright red fingernail on the counter. "Simon's idea for the new layout will be a big help."

Nora had a sudden thought. She examined it with interest, like a child investigating a shiny coin found on the sidewalk. "Who sits on this board, Lottie?"

"The usual townies, anxious to preserve the integrity of the building, several patrons of the arts, and a few gallery owners. The final decision to let us have a long-term lease is determined by majority vote, but it won't be worth our while to do the renovations without knowing we can stay there." Lottie's knee jiggled to some unheard music.

Nora's coin turned over and spun around. "Gallery owners . . . anyone from Hanson's?"

"The big guy himself. Fancies he's a preservationist, you

know." The flamingo earrings nodded and swayed.

"Did you know," Nora said casually, "Simon had a very successful show at Hanson's over a year ago? Hanson still has a few of his landscapes and is always anxious for more. He did some sketches yesterday for paintings to work on this fall and winter." She shifted on her stool. "Most of those will go to Hanson's."

"That's wonderful!" Lottie gushed, her knee hammering with excitement. "Maybe it would be a good influence on the board if we mentioned Simon's association with the project?"

The coin dropped right into Nora's pocket. "I think it would be better if Simon went to the board meeting with you and Val in person, don't you?"

Nora was thrilled to see Simon and Val when they returned. "It's a good thing you came back now or the shortbread would be all gone."

"This must be the infamous Lottie, maker of the finest shortbread in the UK," Simon said genially, pumping the woman's hand.

Lottie blushed heavily, red staining her neck and round cheeks. They stood around the counter, munching away. Nora puzzled over bringing up the board meeting without appearing too obvious while Val filled Lottie in on Lou's second interview. The only new piece of information the girl recalled was that the dog being walked past Bryn's building was a Schnauzer.

"Val, do you need me to pick up Janet for tomorrow's inquest?" Nora asked. "Lottie said you have an important board meeting this afternoon."

"Thanks, Nora, but I should be out of that by 6. Those old toadies wouldn't miss their gins, and Janet's not expecting me until later."

Come on, Lottie, put some of that excess energy to good use. Nora held her breath.

"Val," Lottie said suddenly, "what do you think of Simon assisting us in today's presentation? After all, the new floor chart for the renovation was his idea, and I think his presence would help to sway old Hanson, since his pieces sell from there."

Bless you, Lottie. Nora was perfectly willing for Lottie to take credit for the idea.

"Hanson's on the board?" Simon asked.

Keep quiet, and let it all play out. Nora twisted her paper napkin into a tube, then unrolled it and started folding it into an airplane as the discussion took place around her.

"Do you know him?" Val asked.

"Know him? My big show there was well attended, if I do say so myself. He calls me his golden boy because he sells my pieces pretty regularly."

"Would you come with us? Please, Simon?" Val begged.

"We need all the help we can get," Lottie added.

"Well—" Simon glanced at Nora, who decided it was time to speak up.

"I'd love to have a few hours to shop," she said pensively.

"May rubbing off on you, Yankee?" Val said with a smile, turning to Simon. "You can't seriously want to be dragged around shops for baby goods when you could be fighting for artistic freedom."

Simon put up his hands in surrender. "All right, sounds good to me. But you'd better let me see the whole proposal so I don't make a damn fool of myself."

Nora sat back feeling victorious. Maybe it was another white lie, but again, it was only a small one, and she could always look into one or two shops on her way to visit Ted Wheeler.

Chapter Fifty-Seven

"Love weaves its own tapestry, spins its own golden thread, with its own sweet breath breathes into being its mysteries—bucolic, lusty, gentle as the eyes of daisies or thick with pain."
—John Hawkes, *The Blood Oranges*

McAfee put the latest forensic report in front of Declan Barnes with a flourish.

"Remember you told me to get DNA samples from everyone connected with the Wallace murder, sir?"

Declan looked up from the memo he was reading. The brass higher up had been patient, too patient. The longer these murders stayed unsolved, the less secure the populace would be (and the less secure Declan's position would be, if he were reading between the lines correctly). "What's turned up then, McAfee?" Based on his huge grin, the constable clearly felt his gold star was shining once again.

"Some hairs on the body didn't match Val Rogan, but did match—" McAfee said, unable to resist pausing dramatically, "—Davey Haskitt."

Declan interlocked his fingers behind his head. "The bakery boy. Hmmm. Of course, he did find the body, so that might explain it."

McAfee persisted. "But didn't he tell us he walked in, saw she was dead, and left immediately for the neighbor's to get help? Even if he stood over her for a bit, his hair would have been on the surface of her shirt or jeans."

It would be difficult not to let the constable have his fun. "And where were these hairs found?"

"Inside her shirt, sir," McAfee finished triumphantly.

Declan put both hands on the arms of his chair. "Feel like taking a walk up to the Covered Market, McAfee? Let's go see what Davey Haskitt has to say about this."

McAfee practically bounced beside Declan as they strode up St. Aldate's. Bright sun brought out the crowds in droves, and they wove their way through them to the bakery. Davey Haskitt sat in pride of place in the window today, carefully painting the rubber-mouthed expression on a fondant Mad Hatter. The detectives watched silently from the corridor, waiting to be noticed.

Davey stiffened when he saw them, then looked down and finished his work. When he completed the tiny likeness, he set it carefully aside. They heard him speak to the woman behind the counter. "Going out back for a fag." She nodded, waiting on a customer in the line. Davey motioned to them with a toss of his head.

Declan led McAfee down the inner corridor and out onto Market Street where Davey waited for them, lounging against the back of the building and lighting his cigarette.

"Hullo, Davey. Nice work in there." Declan hoped to provoke a spirit of cooperation.

Davey tightened the elastic band holding his lank ponytail. "You here again 'bout that wanker croaked at my door? Still have bloody patches, ya know. Turns me stomach."

"Try bleach," McAfee offered.

"We need to run over things one more time," Declan said. "Not about that event, but about Bryn Wallace."

Davey stood up straighter, puffing furiously. "I told you all I know 'bout that," he said peevishly.

"Are you certain you haven't left out a tiny detail or two?" Declan asked.

"Like what?" Davey picked at a scab on his forearm.

"Like the fact that several of your hairs were found inside the victim's shirt."

Davey flicked his stub into the road with a practiced gesture. He shrugged his shoulders. "So maybe I touched her, you know, just to see if she were breathing or not."

"Reasonable, except that still wouldn't explain contact inside her shirt." Declan caught McAfee's eye.

"Why don't you accompany us to the station to help us get to the bottom of this, sir?" McAfee asked professionally, unable to resist jiggling the handcuffs in his jacket pocket.

"Look here, I didn't fondle her, if that's what you plods think. She was . . . she was . . ." Davey sputtered and sat down heavily on the upturned crate that served him on his breaks.

"She was what, Davey?" Declan resisted the impulse to lay his hand on the lad's shoulder.

The boy hung his head, his words coming out in thick gasps between sobs as he tried to swallow. "She were all tangled up, lyin' there, lookin' all broke . . . I thought she'd fallen, but the blood . . . she was cold, too . . . I fixed her like the angel she was, ready to dance off to heaven. I wanted to keep her pretty. Some blokes mighta tried to change a lezzie's ideas, but not me. She was fine as she was. Her necklace was up round her eyes, like someone'd tried to yank it off and it stuck there. So's after I'd—fixed her up, I tucked it back inside her shirt, next ta her heart." He looked up at them with genuine distress. "But I could never hurt her—"

"Because?" Declan prodded.

"Because . . . I loved her."

THE BLUE VIRGIN

Chapter Fifty-Eight

"In the matter of Jezebel's Daughter, my recollections begin with the
deaths of two foreign gentlemen, in two different countries,
on the same day of the same year."
— Wilkie Collins, *Jezebel's Daughter*

4 PM

En route to the board meeting Simon and Val insisted on dropping Nora in the town centre for her shopping expedition. Rather
than argue, Nora let them leave her on the corner of Beaumont
and St. Giles. She waved goodbye after wishing them luck and
promised to take a taxi back to the flat the minute she got tired.

Nora couldn't imagine being tired anytime soon. She was en-
ergized by the hunt, and waited impatiently for a crowded bus
careening around the corner as she crossed the road past the
Martyrs' Memorial. She had the irksome sensation that Cran-
mer, despite his immobility, was giving her a disparaging look as
he held tightly to his bible, inscribed "Maye 1541." Nora smirked,
wondering if May Rogan would fancy knowing there was a third
way to spell her name.

Walking down the block across from Balliol and Trinity,
Nora paused to linger in front of two shops. Now she could
truthfully say she had been shopping. It wasn't her fault if nothing appealed to her and she'd gotten bored and moved on. She
could explain her closeness to Exeter spurred her to do something useful. Sometimes pregnancy had its virtues, she thought
smugly, only twigged slightly by the knowledge Simon wouldn't
be thrilled to learn she saw Wheeler on her own. She was dis-

concerted by what an accomplished liar she had become. No, shrewdly inquisitive. That sounded much better.

Wilson was on duty, and when Nora stepped over the sill, the porter smiled with recognition and waved her on. Before he could stop her to chat, she hurried through the archway into the quad, winding her way around the green rectangle of forbidden grass and past the 17th-century dining hall. Glancing up at the open windows, she spied a section of the collar-beam ceiling and the top edges of the venerable oil portraits that looked out over the long rows of wooden benches and tables inside.

Stairwell C was clearly marked on the outside door, embedded in the ivy-encrusted east wall. She entered, climbing up stone steps smoothed and sloped by thousands of footsteps to the first landing, where she stopped to peruse the cards on the two doors opposite each other. "E. A. Vance, MA, PhD" was typed on one; the other was handwritten, noting "M. Smith-Glass, Lecturer" occupied those rooms.

She climbed up another flight and, winded, was happy to stop at the second landing, happier to see "T. Wheeler, MA, PhD" written in strong copperplate on the door facing her. She slowed her breathing, rehearsing her story for Dr. Wheeler, as close to the truth as she dared.

Nora took a deep breath and knocked firmly on the door. She waited a few moments and, not hearing movement inside, knocked again. The stairwell door below opened and shut; rapid footsteps started up. Nora was suddenly skittish about being found outside Wheeler's door. She hammered the door again, this time calling out: "Dr. Wheeler?"

The footsteps continued to approach, and Nora saw they belonged to a thin man with large, bony hands and a bald spot on his crown. "I'm Dr. Wheeler—how can I help you?" he said as he completed the last turn of the stairs.

Nora swallowed. "My name is Nora Tierney, and I'm a friend of Bryn Wallace's. I wondered if I might speak with you about her for just a minute for a story I'm writing." She flashed him what she thought her most engaging smile, but the don did not appear pleased. In fact, he seemed disturbed.

"I'm not certain I knew Miss Wallace well enough to comment," he answered stiffly, shifting an armload of books he carried to his other side.

"It would start with her leaving the world of fashion to work on the other side of the camera," Nora said earnestly. "I was told by Miles Belcher you were very pleased with the work he did on your daughter's wedding." She could see by the stubborn set to his jaw that Wheeler wasn't going to cooperate. Mentioning Miles hadn't seemed to carry any weight at all. Nora hurried to persuade him in any fashion she could.

"It would be a very flattering article, if you're concerned, Dr. Wheeler. My best friend is Val Rogan, Bryn's partner. I would never write anything to dishonor Bryn's memory. The point would be about unexplainable and profound sudden loss." Nora saw this had been a better tack to take.

"Who did you say you were writing for?"

His searching look had Nora clinging closer to the facts. "I've just left *People and Places*, and I'm trying to break into freelance. I wanted to start with a profile of someone I knew and admired." As she said this, Nora realized this was truly an option open to her. She added quickly: "I wouldn't stay for more than a few minutes."

Wheeler tapped his pockets for his key. "Just ten minutes then. Where are my blasted . . . oh, I gave them to Vance while I added to my notes on *Rebecca*." He turned the handle, which opened easily, and gestured for her to proceed into his rooms. "Do you know Du Maurier, Miss Tierney?"

"One of my personal favorites. I know Hitchcock had to promise her to keep the heroine unnamed before she would agree to let him film it." Hoping this nugget from Simon's eternal trivia would endear her to Wheeler, Nora entered the room, tripping over the outstretched arm of a man who lay facedown on the rug.

"Edward!" Wheeler knelt down quickly next to the man and felt for a pulse. His face ashen, he looked up at Nora in disbelief as he pronounced, "He's dead!"

CHAPTER FIFTY-NINE

*"Arthur, who had a masterly way with meetings, was gathering this
one together for a conclusion."*
— Robertson Davies, *The Lyre of Orpheus*

5:15 PM

Simon was pleased he'd decided to accompany Val and Lottie
to the Planning Board meeting. Hanson, the gallery owner, had
been happily surprised to see him, indicating to the other members
that the association of "one from my fine artists' stable" with
the project had clearly elevated its status, in his opinion.

Their pitch had gone well, and Simon described the floor plan
and traffic flow he had devised for the renovation. As Lottie detailed
the types of artisans who would benefit from the co-operative
and how their presence would enrich Oxford, her snappy performance
and outgoing personality gained everyone's attention.
Val finished up by explaining the actual construction process they
intended. All original architectural features would be left intact
and highlighted with painted detailing. A plaque explaining the
history of the building would be installed by the till.

The board appeared impressed and thanked them for the presentation,
indicating a final decision would be made by the following
Monday.

"Simon, thank you so much!" Lottie bubbled over. "Did you
see Hanson wink as we left, Val? I think it's in the bag."

"Yes, Simon, many thanks to you. Having a man as part of
our presentation was a true advantage. It took away any look of
us being militant male haters. And not just any man," she hastened
to assure him.

"I think it would've gone just as well without me, but I'm glad you think it helped," Simon said graciously as they piled into the Volvo. "It didn't take nearly as long as I'd expected."

"Let's celebrate," Lottie said. "Drinks and food on The Artists' Co-operative!"

"Yes, let's, Simon, before I have to go get Janet," Val agreed. "We can swing by and pick up Nora."

But when they stopped at the flat, Nora was still out. They left her a note telling her they would be back in an hour and sped away to grab pub food at The Bear and raise a few glasses to toast their outing.

CHAPTER SIXTY

"Just before noon, there was a little bang and, weeping,
the man fell dead."
— Fanny Howe, *In the Middle of Nowhere*

5:30 PM

The last thing on Nora's mind was food. She sat on the top step
of Ted Wheeler's landing, waiting for the police.

"We shouldn't disturb things," she told him gently. She had
just finished backing him out of the room and used her cell
phone to call the Oxford police. Nora wanted to ask the don
polite questions about the dead man but didn't know how to
do that without sounding intrusive. She felt empty of purpose
or meaningful conversation. That would come soon enough,
she knew, when the crew from St. Aldate's arrived. She looked
at Wheeler, concerned by his pale face, and saw his hands had
started to shake.

Wheeler had insisted on standing watch near his colleague
and leaned on the windowsill, gazing out over the lush, green
quad as though he were searching it for answers. "I don't understand . . . it can't be," he mumbled. He looked at his hands and
thrust them into his pockets.

Nora rose to breathe in the fresh air at the window. They
stood there side by side, not speaking, hearing the sirens before
they saw the flashing blue lights bouncing off the outer walls.

There was movement near the porter's lodge, and soon Wilson was leading two men toward them through the gathering
crowd. Even at this time of heightened tensions, they avoided
the grass quadrangle.

Nora thought one of the men looked familiar. As they came into view up the stairs, she recognized Sergeant Watkins, accompanied by a uniformed constable.

When he pegged her and recognition set in, Watkins shook his head in disbelief, greeting her with a grim scowl. "Wait till the guv hears this."

CHAPTER SIXTY-ONE

"Death leapt upon the Rev. Charles Cardinal, Rector of St. Dreots
in South Glebshire, at the moment that he bent down towards the
second long drawer of his washing-stand . . ."
— Hugh Walpole, *The Captives*

6:15 PM

Declan had spent a tedious hour with Davey Haskitt, finally
leaving him in the interrogation room under the watchful eye
of a constable to change his formal statement on finding Bryn
Wallace. The detective made a note to let Charlie Borden know
he had confirmation that the body had been arranged.

Davey's statement about the necklace Bryn wore suggested
the murderer had tried to take it off but had stopped when it
caught on Bryn's hair. Declan had the Luckenbooth charm and
its legend researched. It was a traditional betrothal gift, and he
was not surprised when he went back over Janet Wallace's statement to learn it had been a gift from Val Rogan.

If Davey had interfered with the body only, Declan still was
left with the task of finding Bryn's murderer. The report on Val
Rogan's blouse had shown that the brown dots were nothing
but fabric dye. At the moment he had no evidence to arrest her,
although he wouldn't be calling her up today and telling her
that. And there was still Tommy Clay's murderer to pursue. His
instincts told him there were two separate killers in Oxford, and
he had to decide when to inform the Super.

Declan felt as if he were in a vortex, picking up speed as the
details of the two murders on his desk continued to change and

build. Some kind of end point was tantalizingly just out of reach. Kneading the back of his neck, he tried to ease the tension headache that had been brewing all afternoon.

After a quick knock, the door opened and a constable entered with a message he held out to the detective. "Guv, if you think you have a headache now . . ."

Chapter Sixty-Two

"'You look familiar,' said the interviewer as he flexed a rubber band between his thumb and forefinger."
— Cindy Packard, *The Mother Load*

6:30 PM

Nora sat in the faculty lounge at Exeter, gloomily sipping her tea, knowing she was going to be found out by both Declan Barnes and Simon Ramsey in the same day. She did not relish the rebukes that would undoubtedly come from both of them, even if they were richly deserved. She certainly wouldn't win any awards for Impending Single Mother of the Year. What did her actions say about her judgment? When she'd tripped over the body in Wheeler's room, she'd grabbed the desk as she pitched forward to keep from landing on her stomach. She could have hurt the baby! She laid her hand on her belly; the baby responded, waving its fragile arm or leg. Nora cried softly into her tea.

It was all too much. Losing Bryn, worrying about Val and then Louisa as the deaths continued. And now this . . . Nora's tears flowed in abundance. She took off her glasses.

The female constable saw her distress and came over with a box of tissues. She sat next to Nora and sympathetically patted her back. "There now, you have a good cry and get it all out. Not a nice thing to stumble over a body, is it?"

"No, not at all," Nora sobbed. The woman didn't know the half of it. She made an effort to control herself, wiping her face and blowing her nose noisily. "Thank you," she said, looking across the room to see how Ted Wheeler was holding up.

Watkins had cleared the faculty lounge, leaving it empty except for a slew of mismatched tables and chairs, strewn with today's newspapers. When he'd left the two of them there, he'd given them strict instructions not to talk to each other, so Wheeler had taken a seat on the far side of the room.

The don looked wretched, his face blanched up to his bald pate. His head was hanging down, his eyes flickering from under hooded brows, darting around the room as he clenched and unclenched his hands. He muttered to himself, bewildered. She wasn't surprised; he'd known the dead man and would be in shock. But she sensed something furtive in his behavior. Her contemplation was interrupted by the door opening and Declan Barnes entering.

Here we go. Nora slid down in her seat, hoping Declan would notice Wheeler first. But he had obviously been told of her presence and scanned the room until his eyes fell on her. His face was suffused with fury. He glanced over at the don, who sat up stiffly at Declan's entrance.

"Detective Inspector Barnes, as you both have occasion to know," he said formally. "I'll be with you in a moment, Dr. Wheeler." Declan took long strides until he stood in front of Nora. She looked up at him, remaining in her seat, hoping the blotchiness of her face from crying might soften his temper.

"I don't even want to know how you got in here, but I do know why. I thought I made myself quite clear to you about getting involved in police business. There should be laws about people like you interfering—as a matter of fact, there are. Do you know I could have you arrested for Breach of Peace, if nothing else?" He was not shouting; his low, terse voice was even more intimidating.

Nora had the good sense to remain quiet and nod in capitulation.

"You will wait here," he said, brooking no argument. Declan turned to the don, withdrawing his notebook. Pulling out a chair, he sat across from Wheeler with his back to Nora.

"I understand the dead man is your colleague, Dr. Edward Vance?"

Wheeler nodded, croaking out of dry lips: "Mid-nineteenth-century classics."

"And do you have any idea how he got into your rooms?"

Another nod, another croak. "Gave him the key myself." The woman constable brought Declan a cup of tea and gently took Wheeler's to refill it.

"When was that, sir?" Declan asked.

On her side of the room, Nora closed her eyes in exhaustion. Declan had been enraged sixty seconds ago and now dropped into his professional detective persona. He knew he was dealing with a fragile witness and needed information before the man fell apart. One part of Nora marveled at his self-control, while another pondered the identity of a man who was able to change his disposition to suit the moment. How would you ever know the real Declan? Could a woman get used to his chameleon style? And then she realized she was exactly like him: charming one minute, a con woman the next. She opened her eyes.

Ted Wheeler took a long sip of the fresh tea before answering. "I saw him on my way to the Bodleian, after my tutoring session. He had left a book home and wanted to check a quotation in one of mine."

"So you loaned him your key to get this book?"

"Yes, he was to leave it on top of my desk with the door unlocked so I could get in."

"Was the book Dickens' *David Copperfield?*"

"How did you know?"

"It was found open on your desk, as though he had been leafing through it when he was stabbed."

Wheeler nodded in comprehension. "Stabbed—I thought it might be something like that. At first I thought he'd had a heart attack, but when I knelt down to check his pulse, I saw . . . the puddle underneath."

Nora was devoutly grateful she'd avoided these details and would carry into her nightmares only a sketchy image of the man lying at her feet.

"Do you usually go the library in the afternoon, Dr. Wheeler?" Barnes asked.

"It varies, but normally I'm in my rooms at that time of day." There was a pause, then he uttered the same thought that had just occurred to Nora on the other side of the room. "Do you suppose—I mean, we're about the same height, from behind—" He stammered, unable to deliver the question.

Declan had no such confusion and confirmed Nora's thought. "I'd say it's a definite possibility you were the intended victim, Dr. Wheeler. And we need to know why."

Declan questioned Ted Wheeler for ten more minutes. The don insisted he knew no reason why anyone would want to murder either himself or Edward Vance. Wheeler's wife had arrived and was waiting outside, and Nora watched him hurry out of the building, accompanied by the constable, leaving Nora and Declan momentarily alone.

She tried to gauge his mood as he approached her. Before she could adequately assess it, she found herself blurting out: "He's lying, you know."

Declan sat down in the chair next to her, not bothering to hide his exasperation. "And you are obviously a great judge of liars."

"It's obvious he was frightened, beyond the shock of finding a dead man in his rooms. When we found Vance, he kept muttering that he 'didn't understand it, it couldn't be.'"

"It couldn't be what?"

"You're the detective," she told him tartly. "I can only help you so far."

After a long pause, he shook his head in weary resignation. "You really are something else, Nora Tierney. You don't let up for a minute, do you? I should have you thrown in a cell right now . . ." His voice trailed off, and Nora met his probing eyes. He seemed to be searching her face for something.

She held his gaze steadfastly until he stood up. "But instead I'm taking you home."

Despite everything, Nora found herself enjoying the ride in the MGB, wishing she lived even farther out of town to prolong her return. They didn't speak once the car started. It was too noisy, and she didn't know what she could say that wouldn't make matters worse.

As Declan pulled the MGB up in front of her building, she hoped the presentation had run long, or Simon was still out with Lottie. But when they walked around back, she saw lights on in her flat. Reluctantly she led the detective upstairs. Simon heard her key in the lock and came out of the bedroom, talking before he saw them.

"I was just starting to think of searching the streets for you. Laden down with shopping bags are you?" He stopped when he saw Nora was not alone.

"Not quite, I'm afraid, Mr. Ramsey." The detective was blunt. "Our Miss Tierney has been out assisting the police once again."

Nora stood there, staring at a spot on the rug, as Declan explained the situation.

"I see," Simon said.

"I'm glad *you* do because I'm tipped if *I* do," Declan answered.

Nora's face burned. For one moment the two men's eyes met, and she thought she saw a flash of understanding pass between them.

They sat down, and Nora gave Declan a brief statement of her actions that afternoon. Simon winced when he heard how she'd found the dead man and literally tripped over the body.

Closing his notebook with a snap, Declan stood. "I'll see you both at the inquest tomorrow."

"Thank you for bringing Nora home," Simon said as he showed the detective out.

Nora stayed in her chair, mute, as Simon closed the door, then returned to stare at her. What could she possibly say or do now?

"Have you eaten?" he finally asked tersely.

She shook her head. He left her sitting there and went into the kitchen. Suddenly she remembered they'd taken the sofa to storage. Great—tonight was the one night they were supposed to sleep together in her bed. A minute later the microwave dinged, and she heard him jerk the door open. He grabbed a knife and fork and set a steaming plate in front of her.

"Eat this," he instructed coldly. "I'm taking a shower." He stomped off to the bathroom, just managing not to slam the door.

CHAPTER SIXTY-THREE

"Nobody could sleep."
— Norman Mailer, *The Naked and the Dead*

Thursday

4 AM

Nora tossed and turned on her side of the bed in what should have been a night of comfort. She endured Simon's coldness as a just sentence, regarding his rigid back throughout the night as her due. She'd been prepared for anger, annoyance, and disappointment. It had taken her until now to figure out he probably felt all of those things in spades but didn't feel he had the right to express them. What a restrained creature he could be, a cliché for British reserve, but Nora had come to see this as charming. Still, he was kind and thoughtful and always treated her with respect. She had done more than just let him down. She hadn't taken into account the fact that he might feel betrayed.

Nora knew she hadn't handled the situation in the best manner and needed to express that to Simon. She also knew she couldn't apologize to him or to Declan Barnes for trying to figure out who had killed Bryn Wallace. Perhaps her method needed improvement, but her motives did not, although righteousness was a cold bed companion tonight.

She felt a surge of loneliness surrounding her like a dark cloud. Simon didn't stir. Nora thought back to the days in Bowness just before she'd found out she was pregnant, when she'd hoped for more of a relationship with Simon. Weeks of attraction and a growing chemistry between them finally came to a head the night her recurring nightmare brought Simon in to her bedroom.

She had cried out as she relived the night of her father's drowning, in a distorted nightmare that had plagued her through the years. Nora had tried to scream but couldn't take a breath.

"Nora—wake up!"

Nora swam out of the darkness, realizing she could fill her lungs with sweet, cool air.

"It's Simon. It's all right, just a bad dream." He rubbed her back through the thin cotton of her nightdress, soothing the rigidity out of her taut spine until her shuddering stopped. Finally awake, aware he could feel the warmth of her bare skin, Nora pushed away from him. Simon allowed his hands to fall casually.

"I'm sorry. I hope I didn't wake anyone else," she said.

"No need to be sorry. I haven't seen anyone else storming this end of the lodge." He sat back on the edge of the bed as she got out of it. "Want to talk about it?"

Simon was in Nora's way as she tried to tuck in the sheets her thrashing had dislodged. She pulled one corner hard, and he got up and lifted the comforter off the floor. "Get back in bed," he ordered.

"I just want to tuck this in right."

"In case you haven't noticed, Nora, your lips are blue, and your teeth are chattering."

"And in case *you* haven't noticed, you are not my father!" Her words shot through the still room. Nora sucked in the sides of her cheeks to still the huge sob gathering in her chest, but hot, salty droplets were already running over her top lip and into her mouth. She looked down at her toes; they felt like individual icicles applied to her feet.

Simon waited patiently as Nora climbed into bed. He piled up the pillows and drew the comforter up and over her shoulders, then sat next to her. She sank back into the nest of down pillows and in a hollow voice described the terror of her dream and the reasons that it haunted her, the night she wished above all others she could take back.

"I learned then that we are who we are by the choices we make," she ended, weary from confession. "I'm really very tired now." She was wrung out, firmly shutting her eyes to indicate dismissal.

Instead the bed creaked as Simon leaned closer until his breath poured down her neck. He whispered into her right ear. "I have two things to say. One, it was not your fault. An accident is something that is not supposed to happen. And two . . ."

His voice stopped, commanding her attention, the warm breath still near her face. She opened her eyes to find his face inches from hers. He touched the tip of his index finger to the tiny scar that chickenpox had left at the corner of her mouth in the second grade. ". . . this is the first place I'm going to kiss you."

His eyes searched hers, and she saw the question in them she had avoided answering before this. He leaned forward and kissed her gently on the scar. "I want you to see I am a man of my word." His breath on her neck stirred her hair as he planted small kisses there.

Nora's core felt warm and liquid as her neglected body responded to him. She tried to suppress a moan that gathered deep in her throat.

"So lovely—I want to draw you," Simon murmured, kissing her lightly at first, then with more insistence. "I want you, Nora."

"We shouldn't," she whispered, telling herself to push away. Instead she helped him pull her nightgown up over her head. He slipped out of his robe and under the covers, bringing his warmth and sturdiness. The shock of his nakedness had her arching toward him. His lips and tongue caressed a lazy trail from her neck, lingering over her breasts, then continuing down her stomach to her apex. She turned off the conventional part of her personality with a quiver of resignation, aborting thoughts of impetuous behavior, and gave herself up to the pleasure they created together.

Nora shook herself out of the memory, listening to Simon's regular breathing, trying to distinguish if he slept or not. Carefully, with excruciating slowness, she fit herself along his back, curving into him, grateful for the warmth and solid comfort he gave her. She snaked her arm under the comforter and over his waist, closing her eyes against the dark cloud and settling down for her first real sleep of the night. There was a slight movement then from Simon; Nora thought he was going to push her away and held herself tightly in check.

But Simon simply moved his arm down, covering hers and the hand that lay against his chest.

Val sat at her window, blowing smoke from her spliff out into the night. From her bedroom Janet gave a gentle snore. Bryn's mother had gone to bed shortly after they'd arrived back at the flat, leaving Val to doze on and off fitfully. Huddled against the window frame in the cool night air, Val swore that one of these days she would give this crap up for good.

Bryn would never touch the stuff. She had liked coke too much the few times she had tried it and was terrified of becoming addicted, confiding to Val that the easy access to drugs was another reason she'd left modeling. Bryn also always limited herself to two glasses of wine, afraid of any excess. But Val smoked grass the way others had a glass of wine—on occasion for relaxation—and Bryn had never hassled her about it. Oh, hell, Val thought, drawing deeply, we all have our vices.

Val searched the fingers of moonlight that reached through the leafy trees. She couldn't shake the feeling someone had been in her flat. At first glance, nothing was missing; it was more a shift in a pile of papers, the lingering sensation of a foreign presence. She hadn't mentioned it to Janet. She was probably imagining things.

Where did that leave her? Only confused and tired, she decided, leaving the window for her sofa, plumping up her pillow to get a few hours of rest before the trauma of the inquest.

Ted Wheeler got up as the first rays of dawn slid into his bedroom. He crept out of bed trying not to disturb Jess. His wife had been appropriately sympathetic all evening after what she called "the tragedy" of finding Edward Vance murdered in his room. To her anguished husband, it sounded as though she thought it was rude of Edward to have gotten himself killed in Ted's domain. Ted had avoided telling her it was possible he himself had been the intended victim. The thought had never occurred to her, and he was just as glad it hadn't.

Tying his robe against the early morning chill, Ted put the kettle on and sat at the same table where Kath used to do her homework and where they often played Scrabble. He put his head in his hands, wishing he could catapult them all back to those simpler halcyon days.

When he and that Tierney woman had found Edward's body, he'd tried to convince himself it was something innocent, a heart attack or an accident. But Declan Barnes had known murder when he saw it and had concluded Ted was the intended victim. It had happened in his room, and it was his usual time to be there. Ted shivered despite the warm robe, wondering how he could stop this craziness without destroying everything he'd worked to attain. There had to be something he could do.

He tried to steel himself to take action of some kind. If the truth came out, Jess would stand by him, but he hated the thought of her pain and embarrassment. He toyed with the idea of going to Barnes, but his suspicions alone were worthless. Indeed, he might put himself in an even more dangerous position.

But what could be graver than living a life in which every shadow represented terror, in which he was never safe, not even in his own province? Ted straightened up, resolving what shape that action should take.

CHAPTER SIXTY-FOUR

"Now that we are cool, he said, and regret that we hurt each other,
I am not sorry that it happened."
— W. H. Hudson, *Green Mansions*

Simon finished dressing in Nora's bedroom. They had fifteen minutes until they had to leave for the inquest, and he couldn't let this awkward silence continue. He tossed around various opening lines, struggling to clarify what he needed to say to Nora. Opening the door, he heard her in the hall talking on the phone.

"Later today then. Please use my mobile number, thank you." She turned as she sensed his presence, firing out an apology. "Simon, I'm so sorry I handled things poorly and hurt you in the process. You didn't deserve that; you've been nothing but wonderful to me."

Simon was surprised but inclined his head in acceptance of her statement. He walked toward her, wanting to take her in his arms and hold her, but instead he simply took her hand and guided her to the counter. She sat upright on a stool, seemingly prepared to take her medicine like a good girl. He'd never seen her so contrite. He was not the type to yell or scold, but Nora had to understand he was not a pushover. It was the only way to restore the honesty between them.

"Nora, I respect you for wanting to clear Val, I really do. I thought you knew that I was willing to help you by going with you to see Miles Belcher and by not insisting I accompany you to see Althea Issacs."

Nora nodded in agreement, dropping her head almost meekly. Simon continued.

"So I find it difficult to understand your need to go further without me. I've thought perhaps you had to pursue this alone, to feel you'd helped Val yourself. Maybe you have a need to make it right without my help, and if you do, then I shouldn't stand in your way."

Nora remained silent but looked up to meet his eyes.

He ran his hand through his hair as he continued his soliloquy. "But I can't wrap my mind around you putting yourself in danger. You seem determined to put yourself and your baby in jeopardy, and I can't stand by and watch you do that without comment. I love you both too much."

She had been following him intently, and he watched her eyes widen as she digested this statement. He hurried to continue.

"I'm not saying that for you to say it back to me—I'm well aware that unfortunately you find yourself in a completely different place right now—but I'm hopeful that might change if you can see what *I* see about how we are together. In the meantime, I promise not to let my feelings interfere with our collaboration. But you must promise me something in return. You must not put yourself or your child in danger."

He didn't wait for an answer, pulling her to him in the embrace he had been aching to give her since last night. He could feel the bulge of the baby pressing into him, her breasts just skimming his chest. She embraced him back, her head curled into his neck. It was a moment of sweetness he hoped would not be their last.

"You think on all of that, and we'll talk more on our way back to Ramsey Lodge," he told her, his lips in her hair. Releasing her, he pointed to his watch. "Come on, Sherlock. Dr. Watson says it's time to go."

CHAPTER SIXTY-FIVE

"The gentlemen of the jury retired to consider their verdict."
— Wilkie Collins, *The Evil Genius*

10 AM

Nora was impressed by the courthouse, a lovely castellated building. Val told them that around the corner was St. George's Tower, a small stone keep built in 1074 above the chapel of St. George. That chapel had established the first learning center in Oxford. The sense of history in this town filled Nora with awe; she had lived here for seven years and was still learning things about it.

As they made their way inside, Nora was surprised to see two television vans parked outside, their tall antennae snaking up into the clear morning air.

"That's how little news there is here, Yankee," Val said. "Too bad they won't let them inside. Much more dramatic when I'm carted away."

Nora smirked at her friend as they found seats. "Reminds me of *Witness for the Prosecution*," she said. Although a bit shabby and now used only for inquests, the building retained many features of the classic English courtroom. Stairs led down to the gaol cells from a square, elevated prisoners' dock facing the judge's bench. There were hard wooden benches for the witnesses and visitors, the better to keep one awake, Nora thought. She hoped Val would hold up in the tiny witness box. Awaiting the start of the inquest, Nora sat wedged between Simon and Val on a bench, with Janet on Val's other side. "Where's the wicked step-mum today?" Nora asked Val.

"I insisted May take Lou away from Oxford for a few days until the funeral, to let her recover from her own ordeal," Val said. "For once she didn't give me an argument. They boarded a bus this morning to Stratford for a play and an overnighter."

"Complete with the usual shopping tours," Nora said.

"What else?" Val said.

"Now don't you two be too hard on May," Janet interjected. They turned to her in surprise. "She's protective of her daughter. I can understand that. And shopping is her hobby, just as I get pleasure from a concert."

"Oh, Janet, you are too understanding," Val laughed, but she hugged Janet warmly.

"All rise for Her Majesty's Coroner, the Honourable Mr. Gardiner."

At the bailiff's command, the assemblage rose to its feet. The coroner entered the room from the right, behind the judge's bench, stepping up and taking the elevated judge's seat situated under a canopy. The man portrayed the same air of brisk seriousness as his father had when he had held the very same position.

"Detective Inspector Barnes," the bailiff called. The shuffling and whispering stopped as Declan approached the witness stand, easing his large frame into the box, ignoring the narrow bench and standing upright.

He gave his rank and described the events following his notification of the death of Bronwyn Wallace, with the subsequent Scene of Crime Operation. Today he wore a well-cut grey suit with a subdued burgundy tie. This, Nora decided, must be his official witness kit. He was a handsome man who, even on the witness stand with his most official professional countenance, exuded dynamic vitality.

Beside her Simon stirred. Nora looked out of the corner of her eye at the man sitting calmly by her side. She remembered his warm breath in her hair as he had held her against him, the hard edge of his collarbone against her face, the dizzying fact that he'd announced he loved her and the baby. He was right when he said she needed time to think. His pronouncement and the call she'd made this morning when Simon came out of the bedroom caused a knot of anxiety to rise in her chest. Too many things to consider. Reaching into her bag, she pulled out her notebook and a pen, making a list of chores left to accomplish before Bryn's funeral Sunday. If all went according to plan, she and Simon would leave for Ramsey Lodge on Monday. She stopped to listen to Mr. Gardiner clarify a few minor points, then Declan was dismissed and replaced by Charlie Borden in his role as medical examiner.

Nora glanced over to Janet, who was stoically following the pathologist's testimony. When he described Bryn's stab wounds, Janet winced and looked away. Nora distracted herself by turning to a clean page in her notebook.

If she were going to leave Oxford on Monday, it had to be with the assurance that Val was no longer a prime suspect in Bryn's murder. Nora wrote BRYN in the center of the page, then drew arrows from the name, listing all the people she knew who'd had contact with Bryn Wallace during the last few days of her life. Davey Haskitt was followed by Miles Belcher. Nora knew Bryn had been at the co-op and added Lottie Weber; then Ted Wheeler because of the note he'd written her. She considered these: Yes, love for Bryn and jealousy at being cast aside for Val could have been a motive for the three men. Could Lottie have been jealous, too, of the time Val dedicated to Bryn? Passion might have played a role in any of these relationships, and Nora knew passion often erupted into anger. But she had trouble imagining a woman being capable of such a violent act.

In an outer circle, she wrote: Cam Wilson, Unknown Belcher

clients, Althea Isaacs, Tommy Clay, and Unknown in the Modeling World. She perused these. Too far-fetched for blind Althea to pull this murder off. The Unknowns were an entire region she could never hope to investigate. Of course, Tommy Clay might have been Bryn's killer, but that didn't explain his own death or the murder of Edward Vance. Or, should it really have been Ted Wheeler?

As the pathologist was dismissed, Nora put her notebook away, waiting to see who would be called next. Her hands grew clammy; beside her, Val stiffened. Mr. Gardiner consulted some papers lying in front of him, and Nora felt the charged atmosphere in the courtroom. Reporters readied tape recorders, and bystanders sat up alertly.

"In British law, a verdict of homicide can be determined to be either a lawful or unlawful killing. It is my duty to conserve the resources of the court and the Criminal Prosecution Service. Part of this is to prevent a double investigation of the same event where there is the possibility there will be legal proceedings against an individual or individuals. In this case there is the distinct probability and . . ." Mr. Gardiner paused and directed his look to Janet. ". . . the strong hope this will occur. Therefore I am adjourning this inquest to allow for further investigation and gathering of evidence before I make that determination. Since the independent pathologist has already made his examination in the event of a defense motion, the remains are to be released to the family." He stood and the bailiff shouted: "All rise!" In the flurry of movement and escaping reporters, Nora realized they were done for the day.

"Of course, this was the expected outcome of today's inquest . . ." droned one reporter to his cameraman, recording a sound bite for the noon news, live and direct from the courthouse steps. Nora's group quickly walked the short distance to the coffee shop at the Museum of Modern Art.

"That actually was easier than I'd thought," Val said, glancing at Janet, who remained quiet but appeared in control. They all ordered coffee. As they waited, Nora took out her notebook, asking Janet about the few days she'd spent at home.

"I had so many kind notes and letters and visitors from my neighborhood and church. The vicar was very kind and helpful, of course. My cousins from Coventry will come down for the funeral, and I made all of the arrangements for Sunday."

"And she decided to sort through Bryn's things without waiting for my help," Val admonished.

"There wasn't much," Janet protested. "I found a lovely ivory purse that Bryn had hardly used. I thought I might use it in the spring, if you don't find that too ghoulish," she asked of the table.

"Not at all, it's a lovely tribute," Nora reassured her.

"Bryn wouldn't have wanted it to go to Oxfam if you liked it, Janet," Simon threw in.

"I hope you cleaned it out. Bryn could really pack stuff in those tiny things," Val said as their coffees were placed in front of them.

They stirred as Janet answered. "Actually, there wasn't much at all, just some hard candy, a few pence, and three ticket stubs from the movie *Notting Hill*."

"We really loved that one," Val said, "especially the funny bits and the lovely plaque on the garden bench in the end. And that flatmate was such a scream!"

"Who else went with you, Val?" Nora asked, taking out her notebook and adding "disconnect headboard" to her chore list.

"Lottie. We went together one night after work, Bryn's treat. And that reminds me," Val directed her question to Nora. "Did Simon tell you about possibly going out on a canal boat ride with Lottie tomorrow?"

"No, but that sounds lovely. We'll pop around the co-op later and tell Lottie to set it up."

"Maybe May will let Lou come with us. Safety in numbers." Val sipped her coffee. "The co-op's closing at noon for inventory, but Lottie will be there until 5 or so."

Outside the coffee shop window Miles Belcher disengaged himself from a reporter.

Janet clutched Val's arm. "Miles Belcher—I never liked that man, and I only met him once. He's lecherous."

"That's part of his act, Janet," Val said. "He's as hetero as Simon—it makes some models feel comfortable to think he's gay and not a threat. He's just flamboyant." Nora flipped a page in her notebook. "Not another list, Yankee!" Val grabbed the notebook from Nora, who lunged for it.

"Just things left to do," Nora insisted, holding her hand out.

"Not so fast, dear pal." Val held the notebook out of Nora's reach. "You know our Nora is a bit compulsive with her lists, Janet. We have to keep her honest. Let's see . . . Davey, Miles, Lottie, Ted Wheeler." She glanced at Nora. "Some to-do list here." Her eyebrows rose in question.

"Oh, that's just Nora's list of people she's investigating," Simon chimed in heartily. "She's been going at it without me, and it seems to have backfired on her." He proceeded to fill Val and Janet in on Nora's unexpected find last evening.

"Another death!" Janet said with dismay.

"Ted Wheeler, huh?" Val mused. "I wonder how he got mixed

up in this." With a flourish, Val ripped out the page and handed Nora her notebook. "You, dear friend, have enough on your plate without going out on dangerous assignments." Val stuffed the page into the pocket of her jacket. "I will not have you crusading all over Oxford tracking down dangerous criminals on my behalf. Jeff Nichols assured me as of today I have nothing to worry about. The 'bloody' spots on my shirt were fabric dye." She pointed at Nora's belly. "You worry about the wee one."

Nora bit her lip.

Simon laughed out loud. "We seem to have ganged up on her in this department, Val. I don't think I've ever seen Nora speechless!"

Nora shook her head at their teasing. Only Janet didn't laugh.

Instead, she put her hand on Val's arm. "I need a favor, dear." Janet had a steely look.

"Anything, Janet," Val replied, exchanging a look with Nora.

"Take me to see DI Barnes."

CHAPTER SIXTY-SIX

*"When Lady Ann Sercomb married George Smiley towards the end
of the war she described him to her astonished Mayfair friends as
breathtakingly ordinary."*
— John le Carré, *Call for the Dead*

11:15 AM

Declan stood in the murder room reviewing notes from last
night's crime scene. Three large white boards ringed the room,
one for each of the recent murder victims. His nostrils flared
from the stink of whiteboard marker as he scanned each board
for something that would leap out and link the murders. He was
certain the same person had not committed all three—the meth-
odologies were too different—but they shared an aspect of rage
or passion. The window of opportunity for catching the murderers was constricting, leaving Declan frustrated and discouraged,
exactly the kind of attitude he hoped to avoid in his team.

He had tried to understand Bryn Wallace, absorbing the aura
in her flat, exploring the details that had defined her life. He
had talked at length to her mother, her partner, her boss. Other
team members had talked to people on the fringes of her life.
He was still working with few hard facts. The definitive evidence included Val Rogan's argument with Bryn shortly before
her death, Cameron Wilson's and Ted Wheeler's notes, Tommy
Clay's death, and a probable attempt to kill Wheeler. Edward
Vance's background checks had not revealed any reason for him
to be murdered. Declan decided to sift through the statements
given by Wheeler's colleagues and had just lifted the folder when
Watkins appeared in the doorway.

"Guv!" Watkins was uncharacteristically excited. "The Magic Cafe's got two employees putting Cameron Wilson on Magdalen Road with Tommy Clay just before he was murdered!"

"Hal-lo! Now we're going somewhere," Declan answered, his mood on the rise. "Let's visit Mr. Wilson at home, shall we?"

They were headed down the staircase when McAfee met them halfway up.

"Sir—Val Rogan's downstairs with Janet Wallace, insisting on seeing you. She says it's important."

Declan hesitated, then continued down. As he approached the lobby, he saw Janet Wallace pacing.

She turned to him with an anguished appeal. "I need to speak with you."

Declan analyzed the entreating look on her face and turned to Watkins. "Take McAfee and pick up Wilson; bring him in for questioning." As they left, he turned to the two women. "Come upstairs to my office."

After they were seated Declan asked, "What's this all about then?"

"I can't go home not knowing who took my daughter's life." Janet was straightforward. "I feel like Bryn's father is somehow mixed up in this."

Declan stifled an audible sigh. This was not what he had hoped for; it would do nothing to help him solve either Bryn's murder or the others. "In addition to computer searches, I had a London colleague assist me in trying to locate any history on the man. He seems to have vanished after leaving Chipping Norton." He sat back in his chair. "You didn't find anything in Bryn's papers, correct?"

"Nothing." Janet looked crestfallen.

"You told me her father didn't have any relatives in your area," Declan said.

"No, Allen wasn't from Chippy. He came for a summer job

before starting University. We met at the pub."

"But he was from London?" Declan asked.

"He was always vague . . . 'Down South,' he would say, spoke of Greenwich and London, but no family to speak of."

"Do you know which University he was to go to?"

"He told me Birmingham, and after he left it was one of the first places I checked, but he wasn't enrolled there." Janet shifted in her seat. Val patted her arm.

Following a sudden impulse, Declan leafed through the murder book on his desk and brought out one of the photographs of Ted Wheeler. "Is there any chance this could be Allen Wesley?"

Janet scrutinized the picture. Val leaned over her shoulder to look. "I don't know. He's the same height, but Allen was thinner, almost gaunt. And he had such a full head of hair—" Janet looked up. "I just don't know. It's been twenty-eight years since I saw him, and we were both so young."

Glumly, Janet handed the photo back.

"I'm sorry not to be of more help," Declan said kindly. "I expect you were relieved not to have to testify today, Miss Rogan?"

"I hope to be able to testify when you catch Bryn's murderer." Val was firm in her response.

"Nora has some ideas," Janet said with a pointed rise in her chin.

"And what would those be?"

"She has a list," Janet answered. "Show him, dear," she instructed Val, who withdrew Nora's crumpled page from her pocket, smoothing it out.

"It's not really a list, Janet, just some circles around Bryn's name," Val explained, handing the paper over to Declan.

Declan scanned the sheet, noting Ted Wheeler's name was underlined. Across the top of the page Nora had jotted *Notting Hill*. He frowned. "What's this reference to Notting Hill?"

"Not the place, the movie," Val explained. "We went to see it together."

"Who do you mean?" Declan's internal alarm sounded. His frown deepened as he shifted papers on his desk, searching for a file.

"Bryn and me and Lottie Weber," she answered. "We all loved it."

Declan rubbed his chin thoughtfully. "I see." Thinking back to the night Bryn Wallace was murdered, the detective's pulse quickened. He stood to indicate the interview was over. "I'm sorry not to have been more helpful."

Janet rose, taking his offered hand. She appeared to have lost her spirit. "Please excuse me for taking up your valuable time."

"I understand totally, Mrs. Wallace. This has been a difficult time."

Janet nodded and left the office with Val, who met Declan's eyes with a hard glare he read as her personal challenge: Find the real murderer.

"I hope I'm about to do that, Val Rogan," Declan whispered to the closed door. Watkins and McAfee would be back soon enough, and he was already warming to the task of breaking Cam Wilson.

CHAPTER SIXTY-SEVEN

"'You want to hear a good confession, Mac?' Chatworth leaned
against the armrest breathing a stream of friendly booze."
— Wilfrid Sheed, *Transatlantic Blues*

11:20 AM

"What do you supposed that was all about?" Nora asked Simon
after Janet hurried Val away.

"Couldn't say, but I expect we'll hear soon enough." Simon
finished his crumpet. "What should we do now—did Val leave
your to-do list?"

Nora evenly lined up the sugar packets in their ceramic holder
as she considered how to reply. Since his morning declaration, Simon had been in an expansive mood, one she hesitated to destroy.

"Simon, what would you say if I wanted to talk to just one last
person? You can come with me. That way I couldn't be in any
possible danger—do you think you could handle that?" She kept
her eyes on the tablecloth. "It would be just this one person before we leave Oxford, to see if I can tie up loose ends. After that I
promise to leave the detecting to Declan Barnes and Company."
Nora turned to him with an earnest expression, holding up her
hand in a pledge. "Cross my heart and hope to die." At Simon's
pronounced wince, she added, "Sorry, unfortunate American
oath, but you get the idea."

"Who do you want to speak to?" Simon queried.

Nora knew he was hooked. "Ted Wheeler."

Simon parked the station wagon on Broad Street, directly across from the main Blackwell bookshop.

"Just what is our approach to be?" Simon asked Nora as she debated over bringing her bag. Then she remembered the call she anticipated and slung the quilted bag over her shoulder.

"Our approach? Close to the truth, I suppose. We're getting ready to leave Oxford, just wanted to see him again before we did."

"But why would we want to see him again?" Simon asked. "Anyway, why *are* we seeing him again?"

"I told you." Nora was patient. "He was in one of my circles."

"Yes, you did tell me, but I thought that was only the first part. When do we get to the part that makes sense?" Simon guided her across Turl Street and around several bicycles stacked against the wall by Exeter's entrance. "How do we know he's here?"

"You can wait on the street if you're going to have that negative attitude, Mr. Ramsey," Nora said.

"I believe we have an agreement regarding that, Miss Tierney," he responded, holding the door open for her.

"Let me do the talking," she whispered to him as the porter looked up. "Just me, Wilson, recovered from yesterday. This is my husband. We've come to see how my uncle is holding up."

The man assumed a sorrowful expression and came out from behind his desk.

Simon hissed, "Uncle? *Husband?*"

"So sad," Wilson said, shaking hands. "Your uncle is quiet today, to be expected I should think. You'll find him in the Fellows' Garden." He waved them through and turned to answer a question from a group of tourists crowding the doorsill.

Simon followed Nora around the quad. "I won't pretend

to have a problem posing as your husband, but how did Ted Wheeler suddenly become your uncle?"

Nora blushed deeply. Simon shook his head. "*That's* how you got in here yesterday." "You never cease to amaze me, Nora Tierney."

"That sounds like a good thing to me."

They turned off the quadrangle past the library and into the Fellows' Garden. Variegated hostas drooping bulbous, pale lavender blooms lined the pathway next to the library's mullioned windows. A craggy rock garden spilled vinca vine and mosses, and shiny green shrubs lined the opposite wall. But dominating the space was the ancient chestnut at the garden's far end, arching long, kinked branches over the stone wall and reaching across the road.

At first Nora thought the garden was empty. Then she saw the don seated on a bench at the tree's base. His attention was directed at a small leather-bound volume he held in his narrow hands. As they approached, Wheeler noticed them and stood, closing the book after marking his place with a red ribbon attached to the spine. Nora murmured, "He doesn't know the uncle bit." She held her hand out, introducing Simon.

"We wanted to come by and see how you were feeling today. You had a terrible shock yesterday," Nora said, adding, "Just for the record, I've decided not to do that article on Bryn Wallace."

"I think that's best all around. It couldn't have been too nice for you either, Miss Tierney. Please sit down." He made room for them on the bench. "Edward's wife asked me to find an appropriate verse for his funeral. I was just looking at some Yeats he admired . . ." His voice trailed off, and Nora studied the don's face.

Wheeler looked tired, his skin blanched, dark circles rimming his eyes. She decided to stick to honesty for a change. "Dr. Wheeler, I'm trying to find an explanation for someone wanting to kill both you and Bryn Wallace. The only connection I see is that she worked for Miles Belcher, and you used him for your daughter's wedding. Do you think there's a connection?"

There was a long pause. Nora heard a bird in the upper branches chirping.

"I'm afraid there is, Miss Tierney. You see—" Wheeler faltered. He swallowed hard, then looked up into the branches as though he would find guidance there.

Nora sat up straighter, watching the man struggle, anticipating a confession. Her fingers crept beside her to find Simon, who grasped her hand, both of them feeling the emotional charge of the moment.

"Do either of you know the history of this tree?" As they shook their heads he continued. "It's known as Bishop Heber's chestnut, and each year the boat club watches it bloom with great attention and a considerable number of wagers. Legend says if the foliage of these branches succeeds in touching Brasenose College opposite, Exeter will beat its neighbor in the Bumping Races."

There must be a point to this. Nora waited patiently, jumping when Wheeler's voice rose.

"It's about tradition! Traditions handed down through the years, a way of doing things that time cannot erode. As much as these rituals are scoffed at, there are many who envy being a part of it, some who would do anything to belong—" He broke off, considering her. "I've already decided to go to the police. I might as well tell you."

Simon tightened his hold on Nora's fingers. A passing prattle from a group of students on their way to the Bodleian Library came from the lane behind them. Nora hoped the don would not be distracted.

Wheeler licked his lips and spoke quickly. "Belcher knew I headed the college's search committee for a photographer, and he wanted a hold over me to get Exeter's contract. He was desperate to be a bigger part of all of this." Wheeler's widespread arms indicated his surroundings. "Bryn flattered me the first time we met. The plan was for her to seduce me, get me in a compromising position and snap! Something Belcher could use as bait. 'Exeter Don Caught With Pants Down' was the kind of headline that would end my career. He'd promised her a good bonus. Instead, she had the compassion and grace to warn me about him. Her moment of morality would have cost her that job—Belcher wouldn't have kept her after that."

"We had no idea," Nora breathed.

"Here is this lovely girl warning me about this appalling scheme. She actually told me she was off men, had a female partner from The Artists' Co-operative. On top of that, she started to cry and asked me if I was her father—I was properly gob smacked!"

"Her father?" Simon interjected. "Why would she think that?"

"I'm tall and slender like him and the right age. At my daughter's wedding she noticed this—" He held up his left hand and they saw the pinkie finger had a bow to it. "I broke this finger the summer I worked in Chipping Norton. Janet must have told Bryn about it. Of course, I had no idea Janet had named our daughter Bronwyn. Janet loved Welsh names." Wheeler hung his head.

"You're Allen Wesley?" Nora was stunned. "Did you tell Bryn that?"

Wheeler had gone paler than ever. "My first reaction was humiliation. I couldn't own up to it just then—I had built an entire life without her or her mother. I didn't know how to react." The don looked away. "So I didn't confirm it. I told her she was mistaken, the finger was a coincidence, and she accepted that and left, disappointed." He looked back at Nora. "I was so naïve." He shook his head. "I should have gone to the police about Belcher right then, that very day. After realizing what Bryn was giving up for me, I decided I had to talk to her and make it right. I called the studio and disguised my voice, but she wasn't there. Then I tried to find her at that co-op, thinking she went there to meet her partner, but she wasn't there either, so I posted a note that night instead. I thought she would contact me and we would sort it all out. It bought me time to figure out how to tell my wife." There was sadness on his face. "I told Jess this morning. After being stunned, she had the good grace to feel sorry that I'd lost my first child without ever really knowing her." The man's beseeching look begged them to understand.

Simon stirred in irritation at Nora's side. "You went to the co-op that same evening?" Nora asked. "Was it closed?"

"Just about. One of the owners was there. She gave me some excellent shortbread. I didn't tell her Bryn was my daughter though."

"Have you seen Miles Belcher since this happened?" Nora asked.

"No. This morning I decided to confront him with what I knew, but then I thought, what if he's a murderer? I decided to go to the police instead, but first I stopped to see Mrs. Vance, and then I found myself here . . ." Wheeler looked sheepish. "Do either of you know the Yiddish word 'schlemiel'? It means a bungler, a chump. But the word origin comes from a famous tale where the hero sells his shadow." He dropped his head in shame. "I sold my shadow, my responsibilities, and my first love to teach at Oxford. I was the son of a dockhand, brought up in Wapping, and when my parents died, I molded myself into someone who could speak well and read the right books. I studied hard and got into university, but that summer in Chippy would have cost me my future. I left Janet and our baby behind to become the person I thought I had to be. It all seemed so important then, but I'm no better than Belcher." He shook his head in dismay. "Kath thinks she's an only child, but I robbed her of her sister."

The don's tale had Nora feeling sorry for him. She couldn't judge this man. He would have to live with his choices and his regret. Simon squeezed her hand and let it go.

"What will you do now?" Simon asked.

"I'll go to the police and speak to my remaining daughter. But first, can you help me? I need to find Janet Wallace."

Chapter Sixty-Eight

"The Ray Charles concert was over though it had been—and still was to be—a strange, bizarre evening."
— Cyrus Colter, *Night Studies*

12 NOON

"Don't even ask me to go near the Belcher studio. We're heading to see Declan Barnes immediately." Simon said, backing out the Volvo to the delight of the woman in the blue Mini waiting for his spot. "Who knows when Wheeler will decide to get around to telling him about Belcher?"

For once Nora didn't argue. "I still feel like I'm missing something here, Simon. Do you think Miles Belcher would kill Bryn because she didn't carry out a plan to get him the college contract? And then kill the man he thought was Wheeler to cover up his attempt at blackmail?"

"Perry Mason would say people have murdered for far less," Simon said, winding his way through the town's convoluted restricted-access roadways.

"Tickets on sale for *Twelfth Night* under the stars," Nora read aloud. "Maybe next time we're here."

"Maybe the next time we're here murder won't get in the way of our visit," Simon said. Traffic slowed to a crawl along the High, the sidewalks overflowing with shoppers. Simon had to stop frequently for pedestrians in zebra crossings and buses with the right of way. Nearing St. Mary's, he slowed to allow a squat yellow Volkswagen Beetle to back out of a parking slot.

"Simon, pull in here. We'll stop to talk to Lottie about the canal boat, and I can use the loo," Nora said, gathering her bag and her cell phone. She didn't add that she wanted to follow just one more hunch.

Simon did as asked. "Not trying to avoid Barnes, are you?" He was pleased at Nora's disconcerted expression.

"Not at all, just trying to use the ladies' and accomplish something at the same time. Barnes is probably at lunch, anyway."

"I'm still interested in why Janet Wallace wanted to see him."

"Me, too. And that's another thing. I don't want to run into her and Val there. We need to give Wheeler time to reach Janet first. I don't know how I'd hide the news that Bryn was his daughter—I'm still a bit shocked about it myself."

"You're being much too kind to Wheeler," Simon said as he guided Nora down the stairs to the co-op.

"One part of me is angry with him for deserting Janet, but another part just feels sorry for all he threw away."

Outside the co-op a handwritten notice read:

Closed Early for Inventory: See Us Tomorrow!

Simon pushed on the door and found it unlocked. The cooperative was empty, the stalls deserted, their interior lights turned off, muting the colorful displays. Some artists had thrown sheets over their wares. The only sign of life was the music, Billy Joel singing "It's a Matter of Trust." As they looked around, Lottie came out of the storeroom under the stairs behind them, consulting a clipboard.

"Hello, you two! What are you doing here?" Lottie held her hair away from her face with a bright orange banana clip that matched her high-top sneakers. She was in heavy work mode, wearing washed-out overalls and a lime-green T; traces of dust and bits of excelsior from the storeroom stuck to her.

"We stopped to talk about the boat trip," Simon said as Nora went directly to the ladies' room. "And a pit stop for Nora. She thought Val might want to ask Louisa to come along."

"Sounds good to me as long as she leaves the wicked step-mother at home," Lottie said, leading him to the till counter. "We're all set for noon with a gourmet lunch on board. Plenty for one more. I saw Val briefly; she stopped in before running Janet home to tell me the inquest was adjourned."

Lottie gave Nora a sympathetic look as she joined them. "Goodness, you look exhausted, Nora. Sit down." She gestured to a chair by the till. Lottie walked behind Nora to turn down the volume on the music.

"I'm mentally tired, Lottie," Nora said, flopping down on the chair, her bag on the floor beside her. "We just had the most incredible interview with Ted Wheeler. He said he stopped by here last week looking for Bryn?"

Lottie was making notations on her log and didn't look up. "He thought she might have come here to meet Val."

"He also said you gave him some of your excellent short-bread," Simon hinted.

"For that you have to give me a hand in the storeroom, tall one," Lottie said with a grin, picking up her clipboard.

"All yours," Simon answered. He followed her out the entry door to the storeroom tucked under the stairs. "What can I do?"

Lottie led him down between rows of metal shelving to the back of the storeroom and pointed to the top shelf. "See that box marked 'Christmas'? I need you to open it and count how many of each kind of ornament we have and note the number on this sheet. You do that, and I'll put the kettle on."

Simon used the small stepladder she pointed out to take the carton down. He blew collected dust off the top and set to work, anticipating his reward.

Nora closed her eyes in Lottie's absence, enjoying the piano music of the next song on the disc, a duet with Ray Charles. She remembered Simon's trivia about Joel naming his daughter Alexa Ray for the influence Charles had on his music. She would have to start thinking of names soon. Maybe something connected to her family. Reaching into her bag, she checked that she hadn't missed a call on her cell phone. Ted Wheeler's revelations were disturbing, and the hunch that Lottie could add more to the picture or know something suddenly seemed absurd. She would be happy to dump this whole mess where it belonged, squarely in Declan Barnes' lap.

"So. Wheeler told you he'd been here?" Lottie's voice startled her.

Nora opened her eyes, yawning, watching Lottie go behind the counter to set the kettle on a small electric hob. She was so tired. It must be time for her nap. Maybe after their stop at the station, she could have Simon drop her off and send him to Blenheim Palace for a while. "He said he'd come here looking for Bryn."

"Oh, yes, he told me all about that slime Belcher's idea and Bryn's refusal to play along." Lottie's movements were brisk.

"Did Wheeler tell you he was Bryn's father?" Nora asked.

Lottie nodded. "It's amazing what confidences tea and shortbread can induce."

"Men are all alike when it comes to their stomachs," Nora said. Lottie's comment struck her. "Lottie, you knew about Wheeler and didn't tell Val?"

Lottie continued as though Nora hadn't spoken. "But Bryn wasn't here to pick up Val. Val had left early to shop for Bryn, for a meal they were going to share together." Lottie said this with a brittle smile, tapping one hand on the counter in time to the music.

"It must have been terrible for Janet and Bryn to be abandoned that way. It's so important to have someone in your corner." Nora cradled her stomach. "I see that more than ever with this baby on the way."

Lottie was reaching for the kettle when her hand stopped in midair. Slowly, she turned and looked at Nora. "It's important to go on living when you've been abandoned," she corrected. "Someone takes your love away, it changes your life forever. It changes who you are."

Nora sat up at the tone of Lottie's voice. Instinctively she reached down and pulled her bag onto her lap, shielding the baby. "Did something like that happen to you, Lottie?"

"I should have gotten used to being left out." Lottie was standing completely still, a faraway look in her eyes. "First it was the movies, then the dinners she stopped inviting me to." She gave Nora a small, sad smile, then turned and dreamily spooned tea into a ball strainer.

The movies—like *Notting Hill*. Yes. Nora felt a surge of despair as it all clicked, and the pieces fell into place. "It must have been awful for you," she said, trying to keep the normalcy in her voice. Her hands tightened on her bag. Where was Simon? She cast a glance at the stairs. "I'm sorry."

"Don't be." Lottie spooned tea into a ball strainer she hung over the lip of a squat ceramic teapot decorated with large gobbets of glazed clay fruit. She saw Nora's searching glance toward the storeroom. "Don't worry about Simon. I have him doing some work in exchange for his shortbread. Quid pro quo, you know." Moving quickly, she poured hot water into the pot and swished it around, dumping it down the utility sink. She filled the teapot and dropped the strainer into the pot. With increasing agitation, Lottie replaced the lid with a heavy clunk. "There we go. Just a moment and we'll all have a lovely spot of tea.

Bryn was lovely, too, wasn't she? So good at so many things. Really, how could I blame Val for being attracted to her? It wasn't Val's fault Bryn was beautiful enough to make Val drop everyone who'd worked beside her, shared her vision, for so many years."

Lottie rambled as she stirred the tea, bringing the pot to the counter and thumping it down so hard Nora expected the pot to crack. The knife Lottie used to cut the shortbread was under the counter, and she pulled it out casually, playing with it in her hands. Nora gulped. *Where was Simon?* "I never realized you were more than close friends with Val—"

"I *wanted* to be more than Val's friend. But years of hard work didn't stack up against Bryn, a beautiful bastard of confused sexuality. That's who Bryn really was—did that gutless Wheeler tell you that?" Lottie pointed the knife at Nora. "Oh, yes, you said he did." Lottie's black pupils were huge, her mouth curved in an unattractive sneer. The disc moved on, and Lottie sang along with Billy Joel asking how much a person can take before the heart starts to break.

Nora eyed the knife, listening with growing trepidation as the meaning of the lyrics sank in. Her heart beat loudly in her ears, and she cast a beseeching glance at the door, willing Simon to appear. Keep her talking. Isn't that what they did in the movies? "Lottie," she said softly, trying to control the tremor in her voice. "Tell me about Bryn. Did you go to see Bryn that night?"

Still the ideal hostess, Lottie nodded and reached under the counter. She brought out her plaid tin, snapping the container roughly on the glass countertop, tapping the knife on the lid. "She didn't deny one bit of Belcher's scheme when I confronted her. I told her she wasn't good enough for my Val. She took my place! She said she didn't even know if she could live in our world." Lottie's voice rose. "She was a fake! And you know what she said to me?"

Nora felt the baby move. White-knuckled, she clutched the

bag against her stomach and swallowed hard. She was in a movie and didn't know her lines. "What, Lottie?" Tears blurred her gaze. She sat glued to the chair.

"She said she was 'really very tired and had a headache' and I should go. She dismissed me! And turned her back to me to put pots away from her bloody dinner! My entire future vanished, all due to her, and she's too bloody tired to talk about it!" Lottie stared ahead, eyes blank, as her fingers tightened on the blade. "Those knives were right there. I didn't even hesitate. I was surprised at how easily it went in—you should have seen those big brown eyes widen when she turned around then!" Lottie was triumphant.

Nora's heart leapt into her throat. She struggled to her feet, but before she could escape, Lottie grabbed her arm, jabbing the knifepoint at her side. Instantly Nora swung her bag to her side, trying to put it between the knife blade and the baby. But Lottie's hold was too tight, and the sharp point pressed beneath her rib, stinging her like a bug bite.

"Why Vance, Lottie? Did you mean for it to be Wheeler?" Nora kept her tone soft and confiding, hoping she sounded understanding, praying Lottie would trust her and stay calm. *Simon, Simon!* Her eyes swept the entry, but she couldn't see past it to the storeroom.

"Wheeler was supposed to be there. I wanted it to look like he committed suicide, then everyone would think he killed Bryn and couldn't live with himself." Lottie cocked her head to one side. "I even had a note typed up. It would clear Val and bring her back to me. I'd already stabbed that man when I saw it wasn't Wheeler." She shrugged. "If it was Wheeler who died, I would've gone to the police and told them the old fusspot had come to see me and hinted at confessing in remorse." Lottie's laugh had a high, tinny sound.

Was that a glimmer of motion at the stairs? *Not now, Simon.* Now it was too dangerous. The knife was too close. Once more Nora felt the baby moving. She tried to concentrate. "Lottie, don't you think—"

"I don't *think*! I just *do*! I keep it all together and cover for Val when she needs me, and make her feel better when she's down, and she loves *me*, my Val. But not enough to choose me over that bitch." Lottie's words bubbled out of her mouth.

"I don't think I want any tea today, Lottie." Nora tried to inch closer to the counter with Lottie still holding her arm tightly. If she could reach the teapot, she could throw the hot liquid on Lottie and get away.

Lottie saw her eye the teapot and pulled Nora farther away from the counter, into the middle of the room. Her powerful fingers gripped Nora's arm like a vise as the pressure of the knife increased, tearing her blouse. Nora felt the cold blade against her skin, scant inches away from the baby, who shifted and kicked. Tears choked her, swelling her throat, blurring her gaze. *Not the baby, please not the baby.*

"If anyone's escaping, it will be me," Lottie said. With her other hand she pushed Nora's bag aside to pat her stomach. "Is Simon Ramsey the father of this brat?"

Simon stepped boldly into the room, striding toward Nora. "Yes, I am, Lottie. Now let Nora go."

"Simon, please, not now," Nora whimpered. He would make Lottie feel threatened, and her only hope was to keep Lottie calm. She felt a sting as the knife pressed harder against her. Nausea rose in her throat, and she broke out in a cold sweat. The baby was too close! She dropped her bag and moved her hands to the opposite side, hoping it would play its kicking game and move toward the radiating heat. Simon froze just a foot away.

Lottie was spinning out of control. "I couldn't part with this talisman." She twisted the knife as she referred to it. "I've become rather fond of it. Bryn Wallace had her Luckenbooth charm, and I have this instrument of her destruction." Lottie's tone turned mocking. "You want to save her, lover boy?" she sneered. "She's another one who doesn't know what she's got."

Suddenly the shrill sound of a cell phone ripped through the air. Lottie turned her head toward the sound. Simon leapt forward and grabbed the knife, wrestling it from her. Lottie turned to him, then back to Nora, a look of confusion in her eyes. She lunged for the knife, making one last hopeless attempt to regain control, then moaned and collapsed at his feet. "I'm tired of pretending," she cried. "I just want it to be over." She huddled on the floor in a fetal position and sobbed. "I just want my Val."

Simon put the knife on the counter out of Lottie's reach. Stunned, Nora reached automatically into her bag for her phone. She had it at her ear as Simon raised the hem of her blouse, checking her side. "Hello?"

"Skin's just broken," Simon said, keeping watch over Lottie. "You were stupendous! Declan would hire you in a minute," he whispered.

"Thank you," Nora said to the caller and to Simon, letting the tension disperse, tears of relief streaming down her face. She shut the phone and laughed, big belly laughs she couldn't contain, arms cradling her baby in the midst of this macabre scene. She looked up at Simon, her face blissful. "I win." She took Simon's hand and placed it over her belly. "It's a boy!"

After Lottie was taken into custody and the knife bagged for evidence, Nora and Simon sat with Declan at the far end of the co-op, giving their statements. Nora explained the day leading up to the scene of Lottie's confession. Declan raised an eyebrow at the news that Ted Wheeler had been Bryn Wallace's father and that Belcher had attempted to blackmail Wheeler—an act to which Bryn had refused to be an accomplice. He in turn described his interview with Janet and Val.

"Your circled list drew my attention to Lottie," he told Nora. "Our murderer had deliberately changed the track on the disc that was playing when we arrived at Bryn's flat. It was the song 'No Matter What,' with the line 'I'll be everyone you need,' Lottie's direct message to Val Rogan. Once I made the *Notting Hill* connection, I knew she had to be involved. I checked her statements and was ready to come here to interview her when Simon rang me."

"A movie about people who don't belong together, falling in love," Nora said. "It fits, in more than one way. I don't know why I didn't see it sooner. Actually it was Lottie herself who alerted me to the fact that she was the murderer."

"How so?" Simon asked.

"I was talking to her about Wheeler abandoning Janet—about how awful it must be to be abandoned by the person you love. Lottie stopped moving." Nora shook her head. "Lottie *never* stood still. That's how I knew something was wrong."

"Don't think that because we got a good result you've escaped my wrath entirely, missy," Declan warned. "If you had trusted me enough to tell me your suspicions about a second visitor right after you spoke with Althea Isaacs, I might have gotten to the bottom of this sooner," he chided her. "And your own life wouldn't have been in personal jeopardy."

"I'd already annoyed you with my snooping," she insisted. "And I didn't know how that would color any information I brought you."

"You always have to have the last word, don't you, Nora Tierney?"

They shared a smile, and for once Nora had the feeling that Declan didn't mind her having the last word.

Chapter Sixty-Nine

"Freddi himself wouldn't have wanted an elaborate funeral or any fuss made over his broken body; but funerals are not for the dead, only for the living."
— Upton Sinclair, *Wide Is the Gate*

Sunday

1:50 PM

Nora stood in the churchyard in Chipping Norton with Simon and Declan, waiting for the start of Bryn Wallace's funeral. The day was sunny and mild, and Watkins had wandered off to read headstones in the ancient graveyard. Nora was pleased to see the two detectives; their attendance was a sign of respect she knew Janet Wallace would appreciate.

"I thought you'd like to know Cameron Wilson has been arrested for the murder of Tommy Clay," Declan said. "Several witnesses saw them in the Magic Cafe just before the incident. We searched his flat and found the blackmail note Clay had sent him, plus a maroon cap from Kelmscott Manor, the one Louisa Rogan remembered. Wilson insists he was trying to get away from Clay and panicked, shoving Clay aside and bolting. He maintains it was Clay's fault he fell over the railing because he was so short. That's ridiculous, because Clay's shorter stature should have prevented him from falling if he hadn't been pushed so hard." Declan's expression told them what he thought of Cam's excuse.

"Will he go to trial?" Simon asked.

"That depends on whether the Crown Prosecution Service cuts

a manslaughter deal with him or not; out of my hands now. Oh, and Ted Wheeler declined to press charges against Miles Belcher, but suffice it to say, Belcher is *not* getting the college contract."

"At least Louisa won't have to testify," Nora said. "May's leaving with her right after the wake. I know Val plans to visit them more often in London. There's been a softening there, good for all of them."

Watkins joined them. "I hope so. Louisa's a nice young lady."

Declan thrust his hand out to Simon. "Good luck on the book project. And thanks for your help at the end there, saving the reckless one."

"You're both welcome at Ramsey Lodge any time," Simon said.

Declan raised an eyebrow. "I love hiking in that area. Who knows? I've plenty of vacation time—I just may take you up on that offer." He turned to Nora. "Best of luck with that little boy of yours. I hope you'll let me know when he makes his appearance and what you decide to name him."

"I will, and thank you for putting up with me," Nora said. She stepped forward to give Declan a heartfelt hug and shake the sergeant's hand. The detectives planned to return to Oxford immediately following the service. Watching Declan walk away, Nora felt a small pang of sadness. Would their paths ever cross again? She found herself hoping so—although she didn't look forward to the turmoil of emotions he was capable of stirring up.

Nora and Simon were alone in a corner of the churchyard. Simon affectionately pushed Nora's glasses up her nose and consulted his watch. "I figured since it had been three whole minutes since you'd last done that, I'd be a nice guy and do it for you."

Nora smirked. "I suppose you think now that you've saved my life I'll be eternally grateful."

"Don't worry, I'll find a way for you to repay me." Simon pulled her close.

Nora didn't resist. "You're far too good to me, Simon Ramsey." She pulled her head back to look up at him. "When Lottie asked if you were the baby's father—"

"And I said I was? Nora, a father is so much more than the cells that created a baby, don't you agree?"

She nodded gravely. "Are you saying you're willing to parent this child without a commitment from me? What kind of fool would make a pact like that?" she teased. Nora put a finger on his lips before he could answer. "The kind of fool who loves me very much." She hugged him warmly. "Just give me some time, but I think we might be able to make a deal. Life often takes great leaps of faith."

"Frost's roads not taken?"

"Or maybe an embracing of the roads one does take, without looking back."

They walked toward the church entry. "I happen to know Kate and Darby and even Ian are waiting anxiously for us."

They walked together slowly, his arm slung over her shoulder. A wave of emotion washed over Nora, and she tried to identify it. And then she had it.

It felt like the evening after a long Thanksgiving Day at her grandmother's. After the turkey dinner, after roasting chestnuts in the fireplace with her cousins while the men watched football, after the women set out pies and cider. There were cold, bright stars in the sky, and she was dressed in her pajamas for the long ride home. Her father tucked a warm blanket around her in the back seat, and the feeling she had now came over her then. It was a comforting mix of pleasure and security, a feeling of rightness, knowing she was going home.

Entering the soaring nave of St. Mary's Church, Nora pointed out the leering devils carved into the peculiar hexagonal porch. "Those are certain to terrorize young children." She and Simon joined the line of mourners filing into the magnificent stone church, the women's heels tapping on its stone floors. Slender supporting pillars with clerestory windows formed an almost continuous band of glass above the nave, giving the church a feeling of great height and lightness. The air smelled of old paper, polished wood, beeswax candles, and a trace of incense. As it had done for thousands of other souls since 1485, St. Mary's watched over the remains of Bronwyn Wallace concealed inside a shiny oak casket. Sunlight filtered through stained-glass windows high over the altar, casting a purple-and-rose beam of light onto the brass plate inscribed with Bryn's birth and death dates. A wreath of tiny pink and white roses trailed a shiny ribbon stapled with the words "Beloved Daughter" in gold foil. Draped over the foot of the coffin was a quilt of satin in brilliant jewel colors edged in narrow cluny lace.

"It's beautiful," Nora whispered to Simon, nodding toward Val's creation. Janet Wallace's nephew escorted them toward the front, removing a ribbon so they could enter the reserved second pew.

May and Louisa Rogan were already seated there. May nodded to them, looking regal in a navy suit decorated with a Monet-inspired silk scarf, caught on one shoulder with a discreet sapphire pin. Louisa looked demure but grown. Nora attributed this more to her recent experiences than to her lovely lilac dress or to the gift Val had given her, a straw hat with a black velvet ribbon and clutch of violets at the back.

The choir was a mixed group of men and women, serious in their task. They must all have watched Bryn grow up, Nora reflected. When they were set, the choirmaster raised one arm, and on the down stroke the resplendent sound of the *Dominus Regit Me* filled the church. Janet Wallace and Val Rogan slipped into their places next to Janet's relatives in the front pew. Val searched for Nora, and their eyes met in sad recognition.

As the choir sang, Nora inspected the laminated card she had been given at the door by one of the ushers, Janet's neighbor chosen for that honor. She scrutinized the stiff rectangle. On one side was a photograph of a glorious sunrise: lavender, pink, and coral streaks spreading across a verdant hill, the orange-gold ridge of the sun sending luminous tendrils over a serene garden with an empty stone bench.

Turning the card over, Nora expected to see a psalm or a prayer but instead found a quotation from Goethe. She recognized Val's input:

The world is so empty if one thinks only of mountains,
rivers and cities, but to know someone who thinks and feels
with us, and who, though distant, is close to us in spirit, this
makes the earth for us an inhabited garden.

Nora felt the pricking of tears at her eyes. She blinked and looked at Janet's straight back beneath the black hat and veiling. Val's dark head was bent to examine her notes.

The baby boy inside Nora shifted and moved. Nora was struck by this new person waiting for his chance at life, while Bryn Wallace's had been cut short by someone she'd thought was a friend. She didn't know this child and already loved him, and Simon seemed to also, simply because he was a part of her. How would Janet come to terms with the loss of her child?

The vicar welcomed them. As they bowed their heads for the opening prayers, Nora saw Davey Haskitt sitting alone in the crowded church to her right. Further behind him, the distinctive head of Declan Barnes, alongside Sergeant Watkins, rose above his neighbors.

Looking over her other shoulder, Nora saw another man taller than his neighbors. Ted Wheeler sat in the very back, sandwiched between an old woman wearing a hat with a long feather, and an even older man with two hearing aids. The don looked miserable. Nora knew that she could never be as gracious as Janet had been. Despite everything, Janet had invited Wheeler to Bryn's funeral. "Janet told me Ted, or Allen, made the choice not to be a part of Bryn's life," Val had said before the service. "She has twenty-eight years of memories with Bryn. He has none, and that is enough punishment."

We never know, Nora reflected, what kind of impact our choices will have. No matter where they come from—a teenaged whim, the hubris of certain entitlement, or the jealousy and anger of unrequited love—the decisions we make affect us in ways unexpected and sometimes unexplainable. Had she made the right choices this time? As she rested her hands on her belly, with the warmth of Simon beside her, she felt hopeful enough to think that yes, she had.

The prayers ended, and Val rose to the lectern, shoulders back. Nora knew Val was fearful of breaking down, but Janet had reassured her that Bryn had not been afraid of showing emotion. Val took her place and smoothed out her notes, looking out over the congregation, clutching the linen handkerchief Janet had pressed on her. She met Nora's gaze, and Nora smiled to bolster her. She took a deep breath, and Nora took one with her.

"Edith Wharton said, 'There are two ways of spreading light: to be the candle or the mirror that reflects it.' Bronwyn Wallace is one of the few people to have been both. She reflected the light of life in the very humanness of her work, and she spread her own light on those of us fortunate enough to share in her love. It is very difficult to think of facing the days ahead without her—" Val's voice slowed, and she paused. "And even harder to find words to express what I think she would want me to say to all of you today.

"My American friend Nora Tierney gave me a collection of poetry by Anne Morrow Lindbergh, wife of the famous aviator, who had to learn to live with the loss of a child abducted and killed. I have chosen one of her poems, *Testament*, for Bryn to speak to us."

Val cleared her throat and paused as if to gather strength, then launched into the poem, relaying Lindbergh's words about a lost child listing the world's beauties to comfort its grieving parent. At the poem's end, Val shuffled her papers to regain her composure.

"Those words were for Janet. I hope they will comfort her in her unimaginable grief." Val made eye contact with Janet and continued. "Bryn and I loved our walks, and our favorite was when we went to Dover. We walked and talked for hours along the beach, watching the tides and the seagulls swooping and diving. It seems fitting that I end with my dedication to Bryn, a poem by Sara Teasdale called *Tides*:

> *Love in my heart was a fresh tide flowing*
> *Where the star-like sea gulls soar;*
> *The sun was keen and the foam was blowing*
> *High on the rocky shore.*

> *But now in the dusk the tide is turning,*
> *Lower the sea gulls soar,*
> *And the waves that rose in resistless yearning*
> *Are broken forevermore.*

A sob caught in Val's voice on the last word. Muffled crying sounded throughout the church as Val made her way back to her pew, the heartrending words lying almost palpably in the air. The choir broke once more into song, and the light of the sun, shining through the chapel, seemed to take on a special intensity. May put her arm around Louisa, and Simon reached out to clasp Nora's hand as she wiped her eyes with a crumpled tissue. Val brushed the tears from her face and took her seat next to Janet. Then the mother who had just lost her daughter reached out to the girl who didn't have a mother, drawing Val to her in a close embrace.

AFTERWORD

Oxford is a jewel of a town encircled by the lush green countryside of the Thames Valley. Not terribly large, its buildings of mellow oolite limestone change color with the light and weather, filling it with the "dreaming spires" described by poet Matthew Arnold. Oxford's magnificently preserved architecture reflects every age from Saxon to the present, including fine examples of Gothic, Jacobean, Palladian, Baroque, and neo-Grecian style, all exhibited somewhere amongst the federation of forty-odd independent colleges constituting the University of Oxford. This mix of "town and gown" is noticed at once when visiting Oxford: The university has its dons, scouts, tutorial system, and those forbidden quads, while the town has its muddle of traffic-choked streets, packed with pedestrians and pubs, shops and meadows.

Oxford has given the world Lewis Carroll, penicillin, the Oxford University Press, and two William Morrises: one of Morris Garage fame, the other the artisan whose textiles and wallpaper designs are still in use. A short list of graduates spread across the spectrum of age and area include: J. R. R. Tolkien, Percy Bysshe Shelley, Robert Browning, C. S. Lewis, W. H. Auden, Evelyn Waugh, Oscar Wilde, Robert Graves, T. S. Eliot, Samuel Johnson, John Wesley, Cardinal Wolsey, Adam Smith, T. E. Lawrence, Roger Bacon, Edmund Halley, John Ruskin, Edward Burne-Jones, Christopher Wren, Professor Stephen Hawking, and Richard Burton. Women of note include Indira Gandhi, Margaret Thatcher, Benazir Bhutto, Dorothy Sayers, Val McDermid, Lady Antonia Fraser, Helen Fielding, and Dame Iris Murdoch. And in the modern age of entertainment: Hugh Grant, Dudley Moore, Nigella Lawson, Rowan Atkinson, and Michael Palin.

With this kind of pedigree, it's easy to see why I took great care to be accurate in describing Oxford's history and the colleges, as well as various locations and sites. The exceptions to this beside my cast of characters are the fictionalized buildings containing my characters' flats, Ramsey Lodge, the undercroft where The Artists' Co-operative resides, and the photo studio of Miles Belcher.

Any errors are completely my own.

Acknowledgments

I offer my sincere thanks to the following people for sharing their expertise, advice, reading, commentary, or support, in no particular order:

In the United Kingdom: Chief Superintendent Jim Trotman, Thames Valley Police; Dr. James Morris, Medical Director, Oxford Radcliffe Hospitals, NHS Trust; P. D. James, London; Dr. Catherine Peters, Somerville College (ret.), Oxford University; Dr. Sandie Byrne, Director, Department for Continuing Education, Oxford University; Susan and Michael Ross, The Old Vicarage, Chipping Norton; Averil and Martin Freeth, Chiswick.

In the United States: Mitchell S. Waters, Curtis Brown, Ltd.; Donna Brodie, Director, The Writers Room; The Oxford Wycked Wyves: K. T. Brill and Dr. Susan Todd; The Oxford Circus: Toni Amato, Alice King Case, Liz Jones, Sam Sartorius; Dr. Clay Warren; Robin Casey; Barbara Davey; Dr. Barbara Ebel; Laura Hamilton; Anne Jacobs; Gretta Keene; Bill Murray; Joan Lautman; Rita Quinton; Sarah Ogden; Gail Schaeffer; Eileen Simmons; Dr. Rachel McCarter; and Kylis Winborne.

This book would not have been written without the workshopping skills and advocacy of the Screw Iowa! Writers Group: Mariana Damon, Nina Romano, Lauren Small and Melissa Westemeier. And to Bridle Path Press, thanks for taking the leap, Lauren.

To Giordana Segneri, heartfelt thanks for your masterful work designing and editing this book into print. You've made me a better writer along the way.

My family and friends in North Carolina and New York have

been stalwart backers, especially The Minnesota Graffs: Jenn and Rob, Ryan, Rachel, Ella, and Kevin, who always make me smile; The New York Graffs: Kimberly and Matthew, who also proofed text for hours; Sean C. Burk, the best thing I've ever produced, for unfailing encouragement; Arthur L. Graff, my rock and sounding board, for helping this to happen in the first place. Finally, I owe an enormous debt of gratitude to my mother, Kathleen M. Travia, for teaching me to read and instilling in me her love of literature.

ABOUT THE AUTHOR

M. K. Graff is the author of poetry, fiction and nonfiction. She wrote throughout a successful nursing career, including feature articles for New York's edition of *Nursing Spectrum*; her background includes working in television and motion pictures on scripts and on set for medical scenes. For seven years Graff conducted interviews and wrote feature articles for *Mystery Review* magazine before studying literature at Oxford University, which inspired the setting for *The Blue Virgin*. She has taught creative writing and memoir and heads the North Carolina Writers Read workshop for adults and young authors. A founding member of the Screw Iowa! Writers Group, Graff is co-author of the group's guide for writers, *The End of the Book: Writing in a Changing World*. She is a member of Sisters in Crime, and her creative nonfiction has most recently appeared in *Southern Women's Review*. *The Blue Virgin* is Graff's first novel.

M. K. Graff in her home library

CPSIA information can be obtained
at www.ICGtesting.com
Printed in the USA
FFOW05n1404080615